P9-AZX-260

the MEANING of birds

Also by Jaye Robin Brown

Georgia Peaches and Other Forbidden Fruit
No Place to Fall
Will's Story: A No Place to Fall Novella

the MEANING of birds

JAYE ROBIN BROWN

HarperTeen is an imprint of HarperCollins Publishers.

Library of Congress Control Number: 2018954199
ISBN 978-0-06-282444-8

Typography by Jessie Gang
19 20 21 22 23 PC/LSCH 10 9 8 7 6 5 4 3 2 1

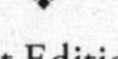

First Edition

To my grandmothers, Edith and Carolyn,
the most beautiful of hummingbirds

1

Now: Three Days After

Hands, hearts, hugs.

I am bombarded at every turn. But I don't know these hands, these hearts, these hugs. They are peripheral, the entire senior class only seen through the corner of my vision. None of them are the hands, hearts, and hugs I want.

"So sorry, Jess."

"Really sucks, Jess."

"How does shit like this happen?"

Best question of the day. How. Does. Shit. Like. This. Happen. And it begins. A collapsing. All of me, falling slowly in on myself.

"Jess, hon." Mom's hand lands featherlight on my

shoulder. The multiton concrete of my body lists toward the familiar touch. A ragged breath escapes, a tear pools in the corner of my eye, then the pool becomes a river, and I can't even try to hold it back, it simply flows. Mom holds me, a steadying pressure that is the only thing keeping me from sinking into the cracks in the ground or flying off into the atmosphere.

Voices murmur. It's a last-minute memorial, hastily put together by Vivi's parents so the students of Grady High School can grieve as a group. But none of them, no one else in this room, can crawl down into the crater in which I now dwell.

"Let's go, hon," Mom whispers in my ear and places a guiding hand on my back. "This is too much for you."

I let myself be led. More hands, hearts, hugs as Mom and my sister, Nina, walk me toward the door of the youth center.

Classmates I barely know speak as I pass.

"Sorry."

"We'll all miss her."

"You were lucky to have love."

Between the thudding ache of my heartbeats, I want nothing more than to yell "Shut up!" They don't know. They can't know. This ache is too raw. Too deep. Too mine.

Outside I gulp at the air. But it doesn't ease the choke. The world, oblivious to my strangulation, spins as usual. Cars drive. Birds fly. The too-hot late September sun presses its rays against me.

"I'm going to run into Whole Foods when I drop Nina off at work. Grab some premades. I know you probably won't eat, but if you decide to, there'll be something," Mom says.

"I can bring home wings, if you want." Nina's tugging her Slim's Hot Chicken apron out from where it's bunched under me on the seat and hugging my neck too hard at the same time.

My mother and sister argue about the type of nutrition a grieving girl needs. I buckle, then unbuckle my seat belt. As Mom shops for roasted vegetables and fizzy water, I trace the clouds with my eyes, wondering, hoping that there is a more. I can't imagine a world where I never see her again. I press Vivi's name on the glass and don't even try to dam the river that rages out of me.

At home, Mom draws me a bath, lights a candle, and pours in some Epsom salts. "This won't take the pain." She holds her hand to her heart. "But it will help with any achiness you feel from crying." She lingers, but what is there to say?

The girl I loved, love, loved is dead. Freakishly. Fast.

All we had was a final hug and an I love you and don't kiss me I don't want to get you sick because I think I may be getting the flu, then a link of pinkies, a lingering smile, and that always, always, always want in my core. And That. Was. It.

I sink, hold my breath, and open my eyes to watch bubbles *pop pop pop* on the glassy surface above me, wondering what it would be like to hold myself here.

To die along with Vivi.

2

THEN: Hidden Talent

Pop. Pop. Pop.

I knew blowing bubbles with gum annoyed my therapist, but she'd been annoying me for three years. Seventh grade. Eighth grade. And now ninth. It only seemed fair. The wrinkle that ran from her left eye down the side of her nose deepened. Success.

Samantha took a deep breath and rolled her pen between her fingers. "Are you ready?"

I shrugged. The truth was, I wasn't ready. Somehow, I'd made it through my first one hundred and eighty days of North Carolina's public-mandated high school instruction without getting into a single fight. But next year, there'd be no more safety of the ninth-grade wing.

No more seclusion from the older kids. It would be all the upper grades walking the halls together. It would be me—queer, overly sensitive, overly prone to fists—against a whole gamut of North Charlotte suburbia kids who were quick to say crap about girls like me. I honestly didn't know how I was going to stay on my hard-earned, not-so-straight-and-narrow path. Especially since there was also going to be no Samantha. I had a love/hate relationship with my therapist.

She pulled a bag out from her desk drawer. "I'm so sorry I'm leaving you like this."

"No, you're not. You can't wait for your honeymoon."

"That's true, but I am sorry I'm leaving my clients, and there's not a thing wrong with me getting married."

No. But there was everything wrong with her moving to Seattle afterward.

"You know I'm only a phone call away. We've talked about this."

"And three hours behind. Our schedules are never going to sync." I knew this because of my relatives in El Paso. I hardly ever got to talk to my grandfather and they were in mountain time zone, only two hours behind us.

She sighed. "Leaving my clients is hard, Jess. Especially you. You've come so far since I first met you as an angry, confused twelve-year-old."

"Yeah, whatever." I twisted in my seat and looked at the little glass birds that decorated the table beside me. Better than letting her see that I was, maybe, getting a little choked up.

"Anyway, this is for you." She pushed the brown paper bag across the table toward me.

I shifted and allowed myself to reach for it. There was no stopping this. She'd met a hunk of burning love. I couldn't really fault her. If given the chance for romance, I'd jump. How many times had I imagined what it would be like to have an actual girlfriend? But it did suck I was losing my therapist, even if it was for love.

I pulled a sketchbook and a pack of pens out of the bag, along with a how-to Zentangle book. "Cool." I flipped the pages and felt certain I'd never be able to replicate any of the designs.

"This is not a present," she said.

"It's not?" I glanced up.

"No." Her face got that bunched-up look when she was really trying to make sure whatever she was saying soaked into my brain. "This is homework."

"Homework?"

"Yes. Over the year, we've worked on a multitude of techniques for you to use in situations when your anger volcano threatens to erupt."

I rolled my eyes. So many sessions spent charting the sequence of my actions that could have prevented my outbursts. I could map the *anger volcano* in my sleep. If I'd shut my mouth here, I could have prevented the other person's reaction. If I'd prevented the other person's reaction, then maybe I wouldn't have shoved them. If I hadn't shoved them, they wouldn't have pushed me back. If they hadn't pushed me, I wouldn't have erupted. Yada, yada, yada.

"Quit rolling those eyes. Show me how much you've learned." She tapped her pen on the table.

"Seriously?"

"Seriously."

"Fine. Clench my fists, spread my fingers, clench my fists, spread my fingers." I demonstrated the technique. "Breathing." I took in a deep breath and let it out in a long, slow exhale. "Walking away while breathing." I stood up and took steps around her office. "Mental singing." I broke into an out-of-tune rendition of "You Are My Sunshine."

Samantha poked her fingers in her ears and started laughing. "Okay, okay, you have learned something. Now this."

I sat back down. "This?"

"Doodling. It won't work in an active situation, but it will help when something happens in class by keeping you engaged, and thus able to stay out of it."

"So, the only way for me to maintain my chill is to have no interactions and no friends."

She groaned. "Jess. That is not what I mean. You have friends."

"Friend. Cheyanne."

"For some people that's all they need. But I'm serious. Get comfortable drawing over the summer. Who knows, maybe you'll discover a hidden talent."

"Not likely." But the fact that this was our last session brought me around to positivity. "Okay, a hidden talent. Got it. Draw to keep focused on staying in my bubble."

"Exactly." She glanced at the clock sitting on her table, then sighed. "You'll be fine, Jess. You've got so much soul. You're incredibly self-aware even in your mistakes. High school is the tiniest blip in your life. I know it doesn't seem like it now, but you're made of strong stuff. You've got all the skills to keep staying out of conflict, to keep your anger at bay. You will survive and you'll do it well."

I wanted to believe her, I really did. But how did you survive without your life raft? When the unexpressed grief over my dad came pushing out of me in middle school, I was a hot mess. Then my mom found Samantha for me.

And now she was leaving.

How was I going to make it without her to talk to every week? I'd told Mom I didn't want, or need, another therapist. But dealing with my stuff alone? Or just on the phone? I hoped Samantha was right about this doodling stuff. Something to keep me chill. Even though something didn't seem nearly as effective as someone.

Someone. Now there was a thought. My brain took off in loops and spirals. If Samantha could meet the love of her life . . . well. There were over fifteen hundred kids roaming the upper halls at Grady. Maybe being out of freshman hall wouldn't be total torture. Maybe there was someone I didn't know about. Someone who might want to hang out with me.

3

Now: One Week, One Day After

The whir of the blender wakes me up. My smoothie-obsessed mother has decided grief is fed with chia seeds, kale, and banana. I'm pretty sure cold pizza works better, but whatever.

I've had a week of excused absences, but Grady High decided that five days is all a life is worth, and they've said I have to return to classes or my absences will give them the power to keep me from passing my classes this semester. Going back to school is the last thing in the world I want, but my mother will disown me if I don't graduate.

Emma Watson looks up at me with her impassive copper-colored eyes. The cat knows everything and nothing at all. She blinks. "Yes, Jess, you can go" is my interpretation. I think she just wants my pillows all to herself again.

A knock on my door. "Jess, Mom says come down for breakfast." Then the creak of my doorknob. My sister has never respected my privacy.

She slides inside my room, then onto the bed with me, and cuddles me like I'm her almost daughter, not her little sister. "Sissy, I'm so sorry. I know how hard this is."

And that's the thing. We all do. Me, my mom, Nina. We did this grief stuff, frontward and backward, nine years ago when Dad got blown up by an IED in Afghanistan. But Nina's pain has dimmed. She doesn't get how I feel like someone took a dulled knife and sawed through my body. All the fester and throb of the old grief acts like a deeply buried splinter brought to the surface. But instead of releasing, it digs in again, a sharp reminder that life sucks and love hurts and it'd be a hell of a lot easier to seal my heart off forever. But I don't tell Nina any of that.

"I'm fine." I wriggle out of her grasp and for once can relate to Emma Watson. "Let me get dressed."

"Are you sure? Do you want me to come to school with you?"

"Nina . . ."

"Fine." She huffs off the bed. "I'm only trying to help."

She leaves and I pull out jeans, a faded black T-shirt,

and out of habit, the pale gray hoodie. A gift from Vivi. I put it back, take it out again, crumple it into a tight ball, and bring it to my nose as if somehow, the essence of Vivi will release from its threads. Paralysis hits me. How will I walk through this day of first bells and morning announcements and class changes and whispers without Vivi by my side?

Bad enough to be one of the few out queer kids at school but now I'm the queer girl with the dead girlfriend.

"I don't think I can go."

Emma Watson barely tilts her head in response.

I pull on the hoodie and wrap my arms around myself. The last day she was at school replays in my mind. The day after's phone call with her mom in my memory. I haven't had the nerve to listen to messages. I can't listen to Vivi's voice yet. I can't be reminded of all the texts and messages I've erased. If only I'd known, I would have saved everything forever.

Another *tap tap* on the door.

"Jess, baby, are you ready?" Mom is nothing but kind. *Holding space*, she said. *I will hold space for your grief.* Mom knows grief.

One deep breath. A choked breath. A breath that stops and locks at the concrete block of my chest and heart. Fuck. "I'm ready." It's a lie.

I step into the hallway of our crappy rental house. Mom takes my hand as if I were eight. My grief surges. Is Mom feeling it, too? Like a vestigial limb? She squeezes in response to my thought. "You're not ready."

I shake my head.

"Baby. It's okay. You're never going to be ready, but the only way forward is forward. It will be hard. It will be crushing at times. But all you have to do is exist in this day. Breathe. Try to eat a little. That's your only job right now. Get through the days. Got it?"

"Get through the days," I repeat.

"Good," she says.

Dad died nine years ago, but I still find Mom crying sometimes.

That's a lot of days.

I take the smoothie she hands me, but also grab a go-mug of coffee. Black with heaping tablespoons of raw sugar, how Vivi taught me. I used to hate coffee before. Before. Before and after. After. My brain races through the demarcations of my life and I want an eraser.

"I'm going to drive you today, how's that?"

"Okay." I don't want to be stuck in the car with Nina and her voracious sad eyes. It's weird. My sister has owned my grief like it's hers. I've heard her talking to the boyfriend du jour on the phone. Dramatizing my situation to make herself more interesting, or needing, or something. It bothers me.

Mom pats my leg as she drives. "Today will be difficult. I'll leave work and come for you if you need me to. Have the office call."

I nod, then as we pass the church cemetery down the road . . . "Did the Bouchards . . ."

Mom's pat turns to a grip. "Yes, when the ashes come back they would like us to come to the lake house. For a ceremony."

I'm lucky. Vivi's parents embraced me. I was like another daughter, they'd said. Someone who sees our girl as perfect as we do. My mom was unsure about the girl-girl thing initially. But after losing Dad, she became a warrior who knew exactly which battles to fight. She did her best to make it no biggie when I told her I was in love with a Vivi not a Victor, even though I knew she was worried about my extended family's reaction and society in general.

But I wasn't worried. People can see when you're happy. Vivi and I had plans mapped out for years into the future. Our relationship was near perfect, hardly any detail left to work out.

But now. So over. There's no working out dead.

Mom pulls the car in front of school. I fight the river raging inside of me. It's time to swim upstream, battle the current as I walk past hands, hearts, hugs, to my locker. Without Vivi.

I'm stitching it together. Holding the parts of me tight as I put one foot in front, repeat. Making my way, not making eye contact. Holding my chin up. Then.

"Sick dyke deserved it anyway."

I galvanize. "What?"

A boy laughs by his locker, a timid girl planted under his arm, and challenges me with a jut of his chin.

The river turns solid. A tsunami of exploding grief leaps out of me and my god it feels good to rage. Samantha's face pops briefly into my mental vision but I blink her away. She left me. Vivi left me. I'm not thinking anymore. I'm forehead to forehead and knee to groin and boot on hand before someone grabs me by the hood and pulls me off the guy, who's left whimpering and confused as to what he'd unleashed with his comment.

In the office, the throb of my collided skull is alive. The most alive I've been in a week. The truth is I'd like to take down the school, brick by brick, if I could. I want to send lava hurtling through the hallways. It's better than caving in to the abyss that threatens to swallow me whole. I will not be grief's bitch.

"Jessica Perez." Vice Principal Williams sounds confused as he rolls the syllables over his tongue. It's not a name he's had to say before. I'd worked for all of high school to keep it that way, doodling my way through when things got sticky.

"That's me." My voice is gruff, tough, a timbre to fell the tallest tree.

"Fighting isn't tolerated at this school. I understand you've had some distress but if this happens again you'll be suspended." With manicured nails, he pulls a glossy black pen from a coat pocket and scrawls onto a pad of pink paper. "A pass, after you stop by Mrs. Swaley's office."

I groan to myself. Swaley is the head tripper. She's not genuine like Samantha. She doesn't really care about helping. She's a smiler and faux friend, worming her way in, trying to get you to talk and spill all the secrets so she can lap them up like milk and purr her way home to her husband and boast about how wonderful it is to be helping young people on the daily. I let the paper glide into the nearest trash can. The tardy is better than Swaley. The reality is, I would give almost anything to punch the shit out of someone, anyone, anything again.

Instead I'm faced with the static of whisper and the heat of stare. All eyes turn as I push down a too-narrow path between rows of desks to get to the back of my English class. Never before have I been so grateful for the somnolent drone of Mr. Alistair's voice and the intense focus it takes for the rest of my classmates to stay awake and end their gawking.

4

THEN: Stork Rhymes with Dork

Nothing to look at here, people, nothing to talk about.

I took a deep breath, stepped onto the bus, and willed away the stares. I planned on making it the next three years without incident.

At least this part of the school day had an established pattern. I sat directly behind the driver in the window seat and curled away from the door. It had been a good strategy last year. Nobody messed around at the front of the bus, so my rides were uneventful. I'd gone from talked about too much in my middle school bully years, to not talked about at all. *You make me happy when skies are gray.*

Tumbling from the bus to the walkway to the crosswalk to the front doors of Grady was different though. In freshman academy, they'd kept us relegated to one wing of the school, one entrance, one locker hall. This year it was open season on sophomores, just as I'd feared.

I walked through the halls keeping my head down, my shoulders rounded, my dad's old camo backpack resting on one side, and my new Sakura pen set that I'd bought—thanks Samantha, and your hidden talent talk—tucked in an outside pocket. A cluster of boys from my old middle school, joined by a few new ones they'd latched onto in freshman academy, tried to incite me as I passed them, "Hey, freakshow, want to fight?" The laughter from the group followed me down the hall as I heard them replaying one of my less stellar moments from seventh grade. I would not react. I would not react. *You are my sunshine, my only sunshine, you make me . . .*

"Can you believe it?"

I looked up. Cheyanne had her sleek black hair up in Princess Leia buns, and was sporting black lipstick to match. She was wearing the jacket she'd told me about when she texted from her San Francisco grandparents' house over the summer—midriff short and made out of fuzzy rainbow-hued pom-pom balls. Underneath she wore a black catsuit and high-topped black Converse. She fit this school about as well as I did, the one main difference being that she was both extremely smart and musically gifted and her killer glare meant that no one ever messed with her. It was exceedingly lucky for me that she'd moved here in seventh grade, even if it was exceedingly unlucky for her to have to come from California to the suburban South. But at least the word queer didn't freak her out. Everybody needs at least one friend and, though she had more than just me, being a band kid and all, at least I had her.

"Believe what?" I watched upperclassmen flow through the halls, keeping an eye out for the couple of other gay kids I peripherally knew.

"Remember how I said I needed to get into honors English because Mom was pissed they put me in the regular one?"

"Yeah."

"They transferred me. It changed my schedule all around and now I'm not in your math class anymore."

This was critical news. This meant I had to go through every day of this semester with a perfect nobody to hang out with.

"It's worse," Cheyanne said.

"Worse?"

"My lunch is switched, too. And I have to get to the orchestra room anyway. Did I tell you? I ditched the violin and am playing the string bass, so Mr. Lunesto wants me to come in for extra practice. Which is stupid because I can play circles around anybody at this school."

Cheyanne's modesty was not one of her strong points.

"Are your parents pissed?" Music was something all the Chen kids were started on early and I'd always gotten the sense Chey's parents considered the violin the most superior of instruments, and therefore the one they required their kids to play. Which of course infuriated Cheyanne because as she put it, "What's more stereotypical than me playing the violin?" It made sense she'd want to rebel. But she'd never quit playing altogether; music flowed through her veins.

"Yeah, they're furious. Best decision I ever made. Now I've got to run. I'll text you after school." Cheyanne waved goodbye and bounced off down the hallway. Kids parted when they saw her coming. The girl was fierce, even if she did just totally screw me with her schedule change.

In math class, uncertainty followed me through the door. Cheyanne would have been third row back, center, so by default I would have been third row, off center. Today though, I had to make seating decisions that could potentially haunt me for the rest of the semester. I chose the comfort of the back corner and a wall. To kill the time until the bell, I started doodling a bird on the corner of my notebook.

It turned out I liked doodling, and spending my summer lost in the instruction book Samantha had given me saved me from a load of boredom. I'd expanded beyond the small square format of the Zentangles into full-page drawings and had managed to fill almost an entire sketchbook.

I was so lost in the therapeutic rhythm and the feel of my ultra-fine pens, that when something bounced against my desk, my hand skittered off the page.

"Crap." A girl stood next to the empty seat in front of me. "I'm so sorry. Did I mess your drawing up? I'm such a klutz."

Before I could answer, she leaned over to look at it. "Huh? Turkey buzzard? You know, they're related to storks. You'd never think it if you looked at the two side by side. Oh god. Stork rhymes with dork. Which I am. Because there's no way you wanted all that trivia. Sorry, I'm ridiculously into birds. It's a sickness."

I'd never seen her before and I definitely would have, dork or not. She had enormous brown eyes framed by thick lashes, a petite nose with a small gold ring in it, a perfectly shaped mouth, and an under layer of purple streaks in her hair. She even had one of those dimples in her chin that some people diss on but I'd always thought were super sexy. She was curvy where I was angular, and Cheyanne-style cool in a vintage floral jumpsuit and worn-in purple Doc Martens.

I slid my hand over my drawing because even though I did enjoy it, it wasn't something I shared with people. "Um, it's just a bird."

The girl slung her tote bag over her chair and flashed a quick grin at me, before sliding into her seat and turning to face my desk. "There's no such thing as just a bird. Once you get to know me, you'll understand that." She smiled then, perfect teeth except for a very charming gap that went exceptionally well with her chin dimple, and, dear God in the heavens, please let this teacher assign our seats today because suddenly getting to know her seemed like the thing that would remedy my entire life.

The math teacher did attendance, then announced to the room, "Okay, people, we're going to do partner work today. Turn to the seat behind you and introduce yourself, then memorize where you are because this is your spot until I say otherwise."

Hello, answered prayer.

The girl turned around again, her bangs slightly obscuring her eyes as she moved, and held out her hand. "I'm Vivi."

Vivi. It sounded like poetry. Vivi and Jess. It sounded strong.

"Um?" She cocked her head.

Right. What even? Smooth move, Jess. Speak. Get your words out. Shake her hand. "Uh. Yeah. I'm, um. I'm Jess."

The girl, Vivi, stared. And I felt something wriggle in my gut.

Oh shit, this is it, she's going to ask for a different partner because of how I look or because I sound like an imbecile. But she didn't. She smiled and nodded and said, "Cool. Nice to meet you."

I kept staring, my eyes locked on Vivi's lips and that cute chin dimple, and my mouth must have been hanging open or something because she cracked up laughing, then turned around to get her math book before turning back with an "I like to get As. Hope you don't have a problem with that."

Nope. No problems here. Sophomore year was looking up already.

5

Now: One Week, One Day After (After School)

I take my earbuds out when I get off the bus. Jay-Z's chorus hangs in my ears. *I got ninety-nine problems but a bitch ain't one.*

I'd take ninety-nine million problems to have Vivi back. Of all the macabre songs to land in my shuffle. If it wasn't so tragic, I'd laugh.

The house is empty. Mom's still at work. Nina probably is, too. The thunder of quiet is deafening.

"Emma Watson," I call. A faded mew answers me from the back of the house. I follow the sound to my room where my cat looks at me from my drawing table. "You think I can have that space?" I point to the bed in a futile attempt to get her to act like a dog and move on command.

She flicks her tail.

"Fine." I dump my stuff onto the floor and scoop her up in my arms. I think briefly about food, but just as fast the thought goes away replaced by a churn made of heartache. Worst diet ever. I hold the cat as long as she will let me, which isn't long enough. When she wriggles free, I turn to the now empty drawing table.

My inks are lined up near the window and I go through the motions, opening colors and carefully placing the caps in the little plastic containers I recycle from the kitchen. I pull out a fresh sheet of Bristol paper and tape it in place at the corners. I insert a clean nib into the end of the plastic pen carriage. Then I sit. Staring at white paper. At nothingness. At snow. I try to dip the pen in ink, but my hand is indecisive.

When nothing comes but pain, I pick up the bottle of black ink and spill a puddle onto the page. I pull the domed circle out from itself with the plastic end of the penholder making a spider, or cracks, but definitely not art. When the penholder doesn't satisfy me, I switch to my fingers, knowing they will stay stained black for days. When that no longer satisfies me, I hold the pricey paper up and tear it into strips. Then I tear those strips into strips. And those strips into squares. Then tinier squares until all I have left is a pile of black stained paper covering my desk. I drop my head into my hands not even caring that my face will end up stained, too.

Art is stupid.

My phone buzzes. Cheyanne wants to FaceTime.

I answer.

"Heard you beat up some backroads boy." Cheyanne's still rocking the fall look she had on at school today. Black tights, short red plaid shorts, massive black sweater, and a wide round-brimmed black felt hat that only she can get away with wearing in the hall without comment from teachers. The resting bitch face is powerful.

"Truth."

"Make you feel better?"

"Like I could do it again."

Cheyanne knew angry Jess, but that Jess has been long dormant. Samantha taught me ways to manage, then the miracle of Vivi happened. Vivi soothed the remaining beast, showed me how to channel my rage into real art instead of doodles. But now? My fingers are firebrand hot. My soul pours out the reminder that art is inextricably linked to emotion and emotion leads to pain. Death can kill more than the person who died. It kills the future you thought you knew. It kills the dreams you were brave enough to have and gilds your stupidity for ever having them in the first place. I actually growl in response to my thoughts.

"Uh. Settle down, tiger. Want to go out tonight? It's teen night at Doolittle's. Levi can get you some vodka. What's all over your face?"

"Ink," I say. Get wasted, dance till I can't move, these are definite things to contemplate, but being around happy people doesn't sound appealing. I offer an alternative. "How about the tracks?"

Cheyanne cocks her head, then shrugs. "Sure, why not. Meet us? After dinner, around seven."

I nod. Levi remains Cheyanne's lapdog. Though I sometimes feel kind of bad for his unrequited crush, I figure it's probably pretty annoying for Chey to be the object of his never-ending pursuit, no matter how subtle. But overall, he's pretty cool as far as dudes go and we both like having him around. At the last second, Cheyanne flashes an uncharacteristic smile and lifts heart hands to her chest. "Love you."

My instinct is to reply with an *I love you, too*, but the river pushes up a wave and instead I give her a thumbs-up and shut down my phone.

6

THEN: A Small Sparrow

I made heart hands to myself. Which was stupid considering I was hidden in the bathroom stall before math class. But I needed a pep talk from somebody. Four weeks of class. Four weeks I'd been an utter dolt and completely nonverbal around Vivi other than a series of blushing grunts and groans.

Today, though, was different. I'd decided to invite Vivi to hang out with me and Cheyanne at the tracks and Stan's Diner on Friday night. It wouldn't be a date because Cheyanne would be there, but maybe I could feel Vivi out a little bit more. By now, she'd have figured out I was into girls, if not by the way I looked, by the school rumor mill. She didn't seem fazed by having me as her partner. She didn't act nervous or put off around me like some girls did. And when I'd stalked her social media accounts, it seemed like she had a diverse group of friends and wasn't someone who'd get stressed out by a girl having a crush on her, even if it wasn't reciprocal.

As our teacher wound down his speech about finite and infinite sequences and assigned too much homework, I worked up my nerve. My hand lifted to reach forward and tap her shoulder, and I was almost there, my finger about to press against her skin when she pivoted around.

I sat back so hard my chair jumped against the floor.

Her eyes widened. "Am I that frightening?"

"No, I was . . ." I lost my nerve.

She reached into her Audubon society tote bag and pulled out a bright Tupperware brimming with some kind of casserole. "My mom sent me to school with this. No way I can eat all of it and it's way too good to waste. Want to join me for lunch?"

My tongue completely seized up and grew so large it wouldn't fit in my mouth, so I nodded and mumbled.

I'd noticed that she usually ate outside, and often alone, but sometimes sat inside with the kids from the International Club when they had their lunchtime meetings. I'd tried to get brave enough to go and sit with her, but my Samantha training usually had me racing away from the chaos of the high school cafeteria to the library with my sketchbook, pens, and pack of cheese crackers.

When the bell rang, she smiled and motioned for me to follow her. I did.

In the cafeteria, she motioned for me to wait by the drink machine. I did. But I also acted like a total creeper, watching her walk across the room, paying way too much attention to how her hips swelled out before sliding back in to round thighs and well-muscled calves. My chest cavity threatened to rip open. I couldn't remember any other crush feeling quite like this.

She plucked two forks from the end of the lunch line and when she got back to me, she stuck them—tines up—in my front pocket, then she grabbed my hand and hauled me to an empty picnic table by the big oak tree outside the cafeteria doors.

She grabbed my hand.

At the table she let go, then plopped down, opened the lid, and reached for the forks in my pocket. Then she patted the bench for me like I was a toddler. "Sit."

I sat.

"Food in our house is a very big deal. My mom is a Cordon Bleu trained chef." She handed me my fork and pushed the container toward me. I lifted a bite and tasted rich layers of potatoes and cream and zucchini.

I managed a guttural groan of goodness.

"She met my dad in France, he's French you know."

Bites of casserole served as a reason for my muteness. But then, somehow, in the way of small miracles, or maybe it was just my heart beating against my vocal cords, I managed a couple of intelligible words. "Do you speak French? I'm horrible at foreign languages." What I don't mention is that my dad was half Mexican and fully fluent in Spanish. I could have been better if I'd tried. Or if I'd had more time with him.

"*Oui, mademoiselle, je parle français.*"

And . . . words gone. This totally cute girl, who'd pulled me, BY THE HAND, to this table and fed me creamy potato goodness, just spoke to me IN French. Hot did not even begin to describe it.

Vivi paused, laughter in her eyes, then leaned closer with a whisper not whisper. "You're really cute when you're nervous, you know."

This was ridiculous. It was time to pull it together.

"I'm not nervous," I squeaked out, my mind circling around the words, *you're really cute*.

She laughed so hard she spit out some of her casserole. "Right," she said once she quit laughing. "Why are you nervous, by the way?"

She was toying with me and I knew it, but I couldn't

tell if she was flirting or messing with me. I looked around. Maybe someone was filming this and it was all a colossal joke to be made viral before the bell rang. Sort of a let's see how nervous we can make the queer girl or, remember how Jess Perez used to be in middle school? Maybe we can do something to make her break her focus. But, we were all alone.

This was it. My moment to branch out. Because even if she wasn't into girls, it would be nice to expand beyond Cheyanne, especially since I never saw her anymore.

"Have you ever been to Stan's?" I looked into Vivi's eyes, then looked away. It had been a year and two really bad attempts at crush confessions since I'd felt this conflicted over a girl.

"You're avoiding my question, but okay. Who's he?"

This made me laugh. "Not a he. A place. Stan's Diner. Pretty much everyone from Grady hangs out there on the weekends after games and stuff." Which I guess was true, but I only went there because it was right behind my house and usually only after school for shakes or on Sundays for breakfast with Mom, but that's what Nina had told me anyway.

"Oh. No, I haven't. We just moved here over the summer from Raleigh."

That explained why Cheyanne hadn't known who I

was talking about when I'd mentioned this cool girl named Vivi who was also into vintage style.

"Do you want to go?"

Vivi threw a piece of potato to a small sparrow pecking around in the dirt near the base of the tree. "Where? Back to Raleigh?"

Ugh. She was not making this easy.

"No, to Stan's."

"Oh." She watched the bird peck at her offering. "I mean, I guess, one day. If that's what people do."

The term *headdesk* came to mind.

Then she glanced up at me and I saw the trickster in her expression.

"Ugh." I said it out loud this time and brought my palm to my forehead.

"Are you asking me on a date?" Vivi drew the sentence out, adding a singsong lilt to her voice.

This was a live or die kind of moment. Would she kill me with rejection or would this be the moment I'd been dreaming of?

She giggled and spared me from answering. "I mean, I kind of got the feeling that maybe you wanted to, and if you did, I would probably say yes."

I sat up a little straighter. "Probably?"

"You have to try first."

I looked around again for the hidden cameras but there was nothing and Vivi sat there, a grin playing on her lips and her eyes waiting. I ran my hand through the long part of my hair and worked up the nerve to spit it out. Finally, I went for it.

"I was wondering, do you want to come hang out with me and my best friend, Cheyanne, who you should really meet, and then, you and me we can go to Stan's and get like milkshakes, or burgers, or whatever you want, and it'd be extra cool if it was a date but it's okay if you don't want it to be either because you know, I get it that you might not be into girls or whatever and I don't want to freak you out, you're just a really good math partner and I like hanging out with you and—"

She cut me off. "Yes."

"Yes?"

"Yes, I'll go with you to meet your friend and to get a milkshake. And yes I like girls. And yes . . ." She finally seemed as flustered as me judging by the way she shifted her hands under her legs, then back out, then back under again. "It can be a date."

I couldn't wipe the grin off my face for the rest of the day.

7

Now: One Week, One Day After (Night)

It wasn't so long ago that the prospect of hanging out with my friends would have been the highlight of my day. But now . . . life feels pointless. I pull on layers anyway, a T-shirt, a flannel, a hoodie. It may only be early October but there's a chill in the night air. Unusual for the Piedmont at this time of year. In my pocket, I stuff my phone, a ten-dollar bill, and my dad's old Case pocketknife.

"I'm going out, Mom."

"Should I worry, Jess?" She stands and walks to me, then runs both hands back from my forehead to the crown of my head. "Your hair's getting kind of long on top. Bieberish. I like it." Then she rubs the buzz cut sides. "And I like these, too."

"So does . . ." I trail off, the unspoken Vivi hanging on my breath. It doesn't feel right to say *did*, the past tense, as if she's gone, but she is, isn't she? I move out from under my mother's hand. "I'm meeting Cheyanne and Levi. At the tracks."

"Not too late. It's a school night. And please, be careful. If you're not home by curfew I'm sending Nina after you."

I grimace. My mother knows the fastest way to annoy me. A quick hug and I'm out the door. Outside the night is cool, the sky lit up by the strip mall that backs up to our street full of tiny brick ranch houses, mostly rentals like ours. I shove my hands into my hoodie's pocket and walk down the sidewalk, glancing occasionally into brightly lit windows to see televisions flickering and families living. At the end of the three-block street, Cheyanne's car is waiting. She sees me and cuts the engine, unlocking her doors and getting out. We clamber over the dead-end's guardrail and walk a well-worn path through the woods. Freedom. Given how strict Cheyanne's parents are, it's something of a minor miracle she manages to sneak out so frequently.

"Where are you tonight?"

"Practicing with the quartet." Cheyanne slings an arm over my shoulder. "My parents are so proud of my civic involvement and my desire to further my musical aspirations."

"How you never get caught at any of your shenanigans is beyond me."

"They care, yet they don't care. And I'm very careful and never do anything stupid like forget my phone or tell my brothers. Besides, my string quartet knows I'm in high school and sometimes I have to call and bail for extra study time. They're very understanding."

"Is that what we're doing tonight? Studying?"

Cheyanne fishes in the pocket of her long tweed coat that makes it look like she walked through the door of some British country manor, and pulls out a bottle of vanilla vodka.

"Whoa, Chen. That's unlike you."

"Having my friend, but more importantly, your girlfriend, up and die from the flu, before flu season, calls for extreme measures."

"It was her asthma. Complicated by a flu-like illness." For some reason, it's important for me to say it out loud, that by verbalizing it, I'll understand.

"Right. The result is sadly the same and requires numbing. Somebody gave this to my dad and it was buried in a liquor cabinet they rarely even open. Believe me, they won't know it's gone." She untwists the cap and hands the bottle to me.

I tip it to my lips and let it scald on the way down. A

cough follows. "That is *nothing* like a vanilla latte."

"Would you prefer we go to Starbucks?" She gives me the classic head tilt and evil bitch stare.

"No. This'll do. Numb might be nice."

"That's the way." Cheyanne nods in approval. "Come on, let's go dangle."

We walk to the railroad bridge. The vodka soaks into my bones and a lovely numbing sets in. Cheyanne leads the way out onto the concrete ledge, just wide enough that the rare train will still set my heart racing even though I know I'm safe. Below us cars drive, their headlights bouncing off graffiti as we sit with our legs hanging in space.

"You brought her here that first day."

"Yep." Vodka gallops down my throat and I know tomorrow's gonna hurt.

"I hated her then." Cheyanne has said this before.

"You could have been my girlfriend. You had the option. I asked that one night in eighth grade." Though it's true I asked, it's not true we would have successfully dated. Though Chey's never labeled herself, my guess is she's aromantic, maybe even asexual. She has no interest in anything other than friend outings and never talks about wanting to hook up with anyone. Take Levi for example. He's been smitten with her since she sat her string bass down next to his but it's been a solid no-go on the romantic front. I'm such a hopeless romantic it's hard for me to understand, but then I guess it's hard for some people to understand girls being attracted to girls.

Cheyanne blows out a huffy breath. It's quickly followed by a whistle coming from the dark on the opposite side of the crossing.

"Your boyfriend's here." I nudge her in the side knowing I'm pushing her buttons and about to get a lecture. A figure emerges onto the tracks.

"How many times do I have to explain that I have no interest in having a boyfriend. Or a girlfriend." I know I irritate her, but I like Levi. And I like Cheyanne. And it's my natural tendency to play matchmaker even when I know I shouldn't. Except . . . the blade of my grief presses in . . . I don't want them to ever feel like I'm feeling now.

"Too many. Sorry for the disrespect."

Cheyanne flicks my thigh to both scold and accept my apology.

Levi bypasses Cheyanne and comes to sit on the other side of me. I lean my head on his shoulder. "Thanks for coming out tonight." I hand him the bottle.

He wraps both arms around me and side hugs before taking my offering. "This is some shit, huh."

"Shit sure enough." I pull out of his arms. "Can we go somewhere else? Tracks are making me sad. Too much Vivi."

"Like where?" Cheyanne takes the bottle from Levi after he swigs, but only to put the cap back on. Part of her never getting caught where she's not supposed to be, is never drinking and driving.

I bounce on the balls of my feet. "Somewhere dark that doesn't check IDs, or, I don't know, let's just walk. Get more booze. Break stuff."

The overpass takes on the slightest vibration.

"Train," Levi says. "Let's go before it gets here. I've got the place." He leads in the direction he came from and we follow, hands out to our sides like we're balancing on a tightrope. We're an unlikely crew, the dyke, the fierce California girl, and the Southern gentleman, but for some reason it works. We follow each other in a line and slide down the wooded slope and step through the busted chain-link fence on the west side of the overpass.

"More vodka for the grieving one," Cheyanne says.

Levi nods. "That would be all of us then." He motions for us to cut through behind a Laundromat and down an alley between a tropical fish store and a used furniture place. We skirt over a block and stop outside of a gas station liquor store where Levi gives a homeless guy in the shadows money for two fifths.

"One for us. One for you," he says.

"You got it, boss." The homeless guy is back out in a flash and hands over one of two paper bags in the shadows next to the building. "Appreciate it, boss."

Levi gives him another five dollars. "Get some food, too."

He's always been a good guy that way.

I think briefly about my mom and how she'd maybe have the tiniest bit of freak-out if she knew we were over here, threading into the sketchier neighborhoods, on a ten-cent school night bender. But the vodka is killing the pain and the motion is keeping me in the now and that's good enough to forget the rest.

"Here." Levi slips behind a dilapidated wooden fence. Junked cars stretch out for several lots. The only sound is traffic. He picks up a rock and hands it to me.

"Won't someone hear us?" Cheyanne asks.

"Folks around here don't budge for gunshots. A little broken glass won't matter."

The weight of rock in my hand is soothing—something about the press of metamorphic layers—and I wonder if I have the strength to crush them. The rage of loss and the fury of alcohol build inside of me and before either Levi or Cheyanne are ready for it, I let the rock sail straight into the back window of a battered minivan. A dog barks somewhere in the night.

I pick up another rock from the ground and throw.

I hold out my hand and Levi hands me another. I throw and throw and throw. Minutes, an hour, time stands still as I lose myself in the crash of hard rock against brittle glass. I only stop when the minivan's rear window is totally shattered.

My arms drop as I stare at the loss of reflection. "I'm hungry now."

Cheyanne holds out the bottle and I shake my head. The breaking glass cleared my mind and I want to keep it that way for a moment.

Without consultation, we turn and head back the way we came. We recross the tracks and head for the bright lights of Stan's Diner.

8

THEN: A Rare Bird

"You invited a *stranger* to the tracks and Stan's? The tracks are our place. Best friend lair. Not some random crush-of-the-day." Cheyanne was riding the bus home with me after school. I'd hoped she'd help my nerves and lacking fashion sense, but instead she was giving me grief.

"She's not a random crush-of-the-day. I like her."

"Oh, come on. What are the chances that the minute you don't have me in class, you'd meet someone *special*?"

The way she said it was super condescending, like I was pathetic without her. The barely beginning of a prickle under my skin was the first tell of a trigger so I took a deep breath in, then out. My hand opened and closed. Cheyanne, however rude in this moment, didn't need me going ballistic on her. She was a true friend, aware that I occasionally lost it, not judging me for it, which made it extra important I maintain my calm in this moment.

But I was super tense and badly wanted to blow. I took an extra deep breath and on the exhale pleaded, "Chey. Do I have to repeat myself? I *like* her, like her."

She rolled her eyes and shifted away from me, mumbling something about how she could have stayed home and practiced her string quartet piece if she'd known she'd be tossed to the side so easily and something else about people always wanting to hook up and how I was like the rest of the cattle.

That's when it hit me. "You're jealous."

She whipped around and one of her braids whacked me in the cheek. "I am not."

"I don't mean in *that* way. You're friendship jealous. You've had me all to yourself for years now. Can I remind you about your band friends, your quartet, your favorite cousin in Mission Hill, and Stacey from the vintage store?"

She crossed her arms and planted her feet against the back of the bus seat in front of her.

I was right. I poked her in the side. "Aw, c'mon, Chey. You're going to like her. She's not like the rest of the cattle." Throwing her words back at her earned me a slight harrumph and a softening of her arms.

"Please," I said. "Give her a chance."

Vivi's parents were scheduled to drop her off at my house around seven. I bounced next to the front door, watching out the window. Nina was home from classes and she and Cheyanne made peanut gallery comments from the couch.

"Oooh, look who has a crush." This from my sister.

"What happens when she finds out you beat up Beau Flaherty in the seventh grade?"

I flipped the bird at Chey over my shoulder. But I did wonder. Beau Flaherty was that kid who always smiled and everyone loved and was president of the student council now and for some reason I can't even remember, I'd made him the target of my outbursts. As a result, I wasn't really the most likable person in school. Right now, Vivi only knew the part of me working with her in math class and the part of me that blushed furiously any time she was around. What would happen when she really knew me? I'd learned to manage my anger issues, and Samantha assured me maturation and distance from triggering events would eventually move me away from anger responses, but how would I be in a girlfriend relationship?

My deep thought time limit expired as a gray SUV

pulled up in front of the house. I stepped out onto the small cement square that served as our stoop and waved. Vivi was dressed to impress in an off-the-shoulder orange shirt, denim shorts, and harlequin-patterned leggings, finished off with kneesocks and her all-the-time Doc Martens.

Cheyanne appeared next to me. "*That's* your type now?"

There was no time to find out what she meant and why the tone, because Vivi waved goodbye to her parents and then practically bounded across the yard. "Oh my gosh, did you see the black-throated blue warbler on your neighbor's tree?"

By now, I was used to Vivi's bird obsession from class, but it was brand-new to Cheyanne, who was already in a mood and prepared for BFF battle. "The what?"

Vivi's usual cheeriness didn't dampen. "The little blue bird. Over there." She pointed and we looked but whatever had been there was gone because her expression of joy faded. "Oh, I guess you missed it." Then she recovered. "But wow! What a sighting. They leave this time of year to fly south and we were in its proximity." She smiled and held out her hand to Chey. "Hi, I'm Vivi. Jess has told me so much about you. I love your Chloé Rouge jacket."

There was a slight tic at the corner of Cheyanne's lip

that told me she was impressed at Vivi's brand dropping but that was all the ground she gave her. "Funny. I only heard about you today."

Vivi's sparkle faded for a split second. Then she laughed. "That is funny!" She nudged me with her elbow, then in a stage whisper to Cheyanne, "Jess gets so tongue-tied around me."

Uh-oh. If Cheyanne had actual claws they'd have just switchbladed out of her fingertips. How the hell did I deal with this? If I took them to the tracks they were liable to throw each other either off the overpass or under the train.

I'm not sure when my sister had joined our threesome on the tiny front stoop but she chose this moment to save me. "Are y'all walking to the tracks? Can I come?"

She was annoying but occasionally golden. Right now was the latter.

"Yes." It came out eager. "Please come." At least with Nina there, we'd have a referee. Plus, Cheyanne thought my big sister was way cooler than she actually was.

On the way, I cast shy glances at Vivi. She watched the dusky treetops as she walked, cocked her head for the sound of birdsong, and moved fluidly, like some kind of primal goddess. The anger I'd felt earlier dissipated in her presence.

Nina kept up a running patter about her first year at community college and Cheyanne filled her in with details about a mutual friend from band. I was glad to have the focus off me and be able to walk next to Vivi.

"I'm glad you came," I said.

She smiled and bumped the back of her hand against the back of mine. "I'm glad you asked me."

I lowered my voice even more. "Sorry Cheyanne's in a mood."

Vivi winked and smiled. "I'll win her over."

Warmth filled me. Cheyanne was the best kind of friend a girl could have but I was geared toward romance and Vivi seemed like the best kind of girlfriend a girl could have. I'd figure out a way to make them like each other.

Unfortunately, it wasn't going to happen tonight.

"You lived in Raleigh?" Cheyanne leaned back against the railroad tracks and thunked her legs over the railing.

"Yep." Vivi laughed. "Loved it. We lived in Glenwood South. Tons of coffee shops. Record stores, artist lofts, even a great vintage store."

Cheyanne pffted. "Please. There's no way it could compare to San Francisco."

Vivi shrugged. "Probably not, but we're both here now, aren't we?"

Cheyanne ignored the comeback and went in for another dig. "I remember Madame Goodman from French III had called your name at the beginning of the year—but somebody said you'd gotten downgraded to Mr. Deworde?"

Vivi lifted a shoulder. "He may not have as good a reputation but I only needed a place to sit while I take my French Literature class online. I placed out of the levels available at Grady."

Nina stifled a laugh and I tried to push my hair back, forgetting that Cheyanne had loaded it up with sculpting wax. This was not going well. Before they could jump into another round of who's better than whom, I stood up. "We better go, I hear a train."

Cheyanne scrunched up her nose and brow and placed a hand on the steel rail of the track. "I don't feel anything."

Nina knew exactly what I was up to, but I guess she was enjoying the show because she sided with Cheyanne, her hand brushing across the metal. "Nope, me either."

Time for another tactic. "Well, I'm starving."

"I could eat," Vivi added.

"I bet you could." It was a stone-cold blow on the part of Cheyanne made obvious by the way her eyes skimmed up, then down, Vivi's figure.

Vivi didn't let it slide. "Are you body shaming me?"

Cheyanne lifted her chin into the air. "Why would I do something like that?"

Vivi's confidence faltered, so I grabbed her hand. It was a clear line drawn in the sand. Cheyanne looked at our joined fingers and frowned. Then she stood up. "Fine, let's go to your stupid diner."

9

Now: One Week, One Day After (Later That Same Night)

"Onion rings." I stand at the go-counter of Stan's Diner.

"Since when do you eat those?" Cheyanne cocks her head. "All I can remember is you and Vivi griping about it when I ordered them that first night we all hung out." She pauses. "I was such a bitch to her back then."

I shrug. That's water long under the dam. Cheyanne had apologized. Vivi had accepted. But the onion ring reality is I don't want to do anything I used to do. I don't want any of the things that were of me and Vivi. Thinking about ordering our favorite milkshake hurts. Memories become missiles and no amount of vodka can divert them.

The line waiter pushes our bags across the counter and wipes the trail of grease as he turns away from us.

"Come on. Let's eat outside." I lead them out the door away from the nighttime fluorescents.

Tonight's lucky. Stan's can be crowded with kids from school and hands, hearts, and hugs are definitely not what I want. Just food. Gross, greasy onion rings. We crawl on top of a picnic table, Cheyanne and Levi sitting back-to-back creating support for each other. I sit cross-legged and pull a ring from the waxed paper packet. The taste surprises me. Salty and savory and not the awful thing I'd convinced myself it was at age ten when I'd refused to eat them at a summer meal with Mom and Nina. "Bag." I hold out my hand for the vodka bottle, the rush from breaking the van's glass waning with the coating of grease.

We eat and I sip and eat and I sip and the buzz rebuilds. A car pulls into Stan's lot. A group of kids pile out, among them the mousy girl from the locker fight. Something familiar rises inside me, the urge to wound, to hurt, to hurl rocks. My hand twitches, a reminder to pick up the drawing pen not the sword, but lucky for me, my pens are at the house.

"What's up?" Levi asks, his doglike instincts detecting my shift in frequency.

"Nothing," I say, then jump off the picnic table. "I've got to pee."

I should stop. I should turn around. This is the point

when I can keep the anger volcano from erupting. But all I want is to let my dormant mountain blow and my body trembles with the need for it.

I push open the glass door. The group turns. The girl rolls her eyes at one of her friends and mouths something. My balance is the slightest bit unsteady but I hold it together and pass them on my way to the bathroom. I know their kind. Curious. Gossipy. Cruel.

No surprise at all when the bathroom door opens a minute after me. I wait in the stall, listening.

"I heard she had AIDS." The words are for my benefit.

"The world's better with one less of them. Although she was the nice one. The pretty one," another voice says.

"I bet having that dyke as her girlfriend is what did her in."

It's the comment I need. I bust out of the stall and am on the girl before my coping mechanisms can grab hold of reason. I pull back my arm and let it fly, feeling fist on skin, and hair in hand. Her friend starts yelling and opens the bathroom door. "Fight!"

There are fingernails and shoes on shins but I punch blindly, sometimes making contact, sometimes not. Whispers of sanity try to get at me, but my rage is louder and this girl said awful things and my hand is bouncing her skull against the door like it's that rock against windshield.

It's only a couple of minutes, if that, before strong arms pull me off and other arms carry her away.

The line cook keeps me in the back and then I hear sirens blaring in the distance. I hope Cheyanne and Levi have the good sense to ditch that bottle and get the hell out of here. My goose may be cooked but no reason for them to go down with me. Cheyanne will get that. She's a self-preservationist. But Levi, that kid is loyal to a fault.

After they've made sure the girl I punched is okay and they've taken her statement, the line cook leads me out to the front of the diner. It's always great fun to be taken down in front of an audience. The cops, a guy and a woman, aren't exactly kind. "Do you want to explain what happened here?" It's the guy cop and he's in-my-space close.

Though I want to be a smart-ass, the sting of my knuckles and the pounding of my kicked shins remind me to play it smart. The last thing I need is for my mom to have to call in her lawyer bosses on behalf of her troubled youngest.

"That girl said some crap in the bathroom and it pissed me off and we fought. I'm not sure who hit first." Vivi hated me trying to put off my bad behavior on other people. She always said blaming was for the unintelligent. But I'm not that intelligent and I'm not in a hurry to go to jail.

"Have you been drinking?"

"No, sir." Another lie for self-preservation. I doubt the vodka will overpower the onion rings.

He twists his lip into a kind of "sure" response, but doesn't push.

It's at that point I notice Levi talking to the lady cop near the cash register.

She walks over and says something to my interrogator, who stands and motions for me. "Come on, we're going to give you a back-seat ride to your mother's house. And call your school's resource officer." He hands back my license. "A few more months, kid, and this ride would be straight downtown. Got it?"

"Yes, sir."

I glance at Levi as I walk by and lift an eyebrow.

He waves at the lady cop. "See you, Aunt Rose."

Ah. I guess it's good to have friends in high places, or they might have taken me downtown anyway.

At home, Mom is grim disappointment and Nina is high hysteria. The officers are explaining that the SRO and the school will be notified, because both me and the skank I fought are at Grady, and in these types of cases there are school-imposed consequences. Emma Watson sits at the head of the hallway and watches it all go down with not so much as a tail-swishing hello. The vodka is starting to hammer my brain and the grease is roiling in my stomach. The bruises on my shins are starting to swell and throb and to be honest, I kind of like it. Anger wakes up my senses. Anger gives me excuses.

"Jess."

"Mom."

"Jess!"

"Nina!" I yell back. At some point, my sister's caring nature stopped being cool and started being overbearing and annoying. It was like she used an intense interest in me to avoid her own life and inability to have any sort of lasting relationship. Plus, she was twenty. Didn't most twenty-year-olds want to move out and have their own place?

"I thought we were finished with this." Mom.

"Seriously, what is the matter with you?" Nina.

"What is the matter with you?" Me.

How can I explain the anger and how it soothes? It's how I imagine heroin might be to someone after years of being clean. It's more than the burn of vodka. The anger volcano can go dormant but it never disappears. Especially now that Vivi is gone. Especially since my pens only pour out pain.

"Go to bed." Mom points to the hall.

I start toward Emma Watson, who rises as if to lead me on a path to redemption.

"Wait." It's Nina, rushing after me with a hastily poured glass of water and two aspirin.

"Thanks." My sister is always there. Even when I'm hateful to her. Even when I'm hateful to myself. But she doesn't see me. Vivi was the only one who saw me the way I wanted to be seen. Interesting. Artistic. Something more than a middle-class, if that, suburban girl. But now? I'm nobody.

10

THEN: Doves in the Pine Trees

"I've talked nonstop, it's your turn. Tell me something interesting." Vivi sat across from me on the teeter-totter at the park near school. She'd just finished making me listen to the doves in the pine trees above us, then recited every dove fact known to her and the entire internet.

"There's not much to say." Which was true, but also true was if I started talking, then I'd have to stop staring and think. And if I had to think, I wouldn't be able to focus on her lips and my dream of kissing them.

"Please. I think there are deep wells beneath that fetching exterior."

I forced myself down and she raised in the air, sticking

her legs up as she went. I'd forgotten how much fun a teeter-totter could be.

"How about I ask you ten questions in ten seconds like that magazine does with celebrities?" Vivi pushed herself back toward the ground.

I groaned, but smiled at the same time. Her enthusiasm for life was infectious. It was hard not to smile around Vivi. "Fire away."

"Where were you born?"

"Easy. Fort Bragg."

"Favorite television show?"

"*Game of Thrones*."

Vivi wrinkled her nose. "So violent." Then she shrugged. "But there are dragons."

I made a note not to invite her for pizza on Sunday nights when Nina, my mom, and I stopped everything for the show.

"M&M's or Snickers?"

"Skittles," I said.

She bounced me down for that.

"Ouch."

"Are you okay?" She gasped.

I loved that her face went from devious to concerned in a flash. "I'm teasing. Fine. Next question."

"How old when you started your period?"

"Twelve. No drama. I was at home on a weekend with Mom and Nina."

"Lucky. I was in math class wearing khakis. It was horrible."

"Poor thing." Then I pretended like I was looking at a nonexistent watch. "Ticktock."

"Right." She looked at her four extended fingers and opened out her thumb. "Celebrity you'd most like to hook up with?"

"Emma Watson."

"Nice." She held up a finger on her other hand. "Worst nightmare?"

"Dolls."

"Oh my god, me, too."

I shuddered. She lifted another finger. "Favorite animated movie?"

"*Coraline.*"

She laughed. "Thus the doll phobia. Those button eyes." She paused and thought for a second. "Dream college?"

"Don't have one."

She stopped and stared. "What? Seriously? Isn't that what high school is about? Counting the days until we go somewhere amazing?"

I shrugged and shuffled my feet. This is where things got embarrassing. My grades were in solid C to B- territory with the occasional D back in my messed-up middle school days. I was not college material. Community college, maybe, but what was the point of dreaming about out-of-reach things when you'd only be disappointed. "Fuck," I whispered under my breath, worried I'd inadvertently stumbled upon the thing that would set us apart. I knew she was into getting good grades and super smart, but I'd hoped the difference between us wouldn't be the wedge.

"Nope," she said.

"Nope what?"

"F-bombs. Can't stand that word. Or cursing in general."

My eyebrows raised.

"I know, I know," she said. "It sets me apart from the rest of the heathens, but there are so many other creative ways to curse. Like instead of saying that, say 'flibbertigibbets' or 'six sharp sheep' instead of the word that means going number two."

"Number two? You're serious?" It was ridiculous and adorable.

She laughed and bounced herself up again. "Try it."

"Um, farkelsnark?"

She laughed harder and hopped off her end of the teeter-totter and clapped as I ploomped to the dirt.

"Hey!" I jumped up and brushed the sand off my butt. "That was kind of mean."

She skipped toward me and took my hand and pulled me in for a front-to-front hug. I grew statue still.

"Is it still mean if I did it because I had to hug you for your effort?"

"Right here?" I asked.

"Right here." She looked around. "There's nothing untoward about a simple hug."

But it wasn't a simple hug. She pulled me in so close that I could feel her breasts flatten against me and her thighs push against mine and her hands on my back were like twin pulses of fire. Lightning coursed in my groin and if I'd ever had a doubt about my sexuality ever in my life, this moment cinched it. I pulled her closer and my leg wrapped around her calf in an attempt to get her close enough to crawl inside of her skin. My hands spread against her back, feeling soft flesh and bra straps, and if we weren't in a public playground they'd try to find their way to be skin to skin. We stood there hugging, if that's what you could really call it, until I audibly groaned.

It broke the spell because Vivi started laughing, but

her face was flushed and her eyes glittered and her breath was coming faster than before when she pulled out of my embrace.

"Wow," she said.

"Yeah," I replied.

We stood in awkward silence for a second until Vivi shook herself into the present moment. "I have two more questions."

"Pretty sure your ten seconds expired."

"You distracted me."

My face lifted further into the smile that wouldn't disappear. God, she was cute. I wanted to kiss her. Instead I nodded and looked at my fake watch. "Go." I held up two fingers.

"Do you ever dream about turning your doodles into something more? Like calling yourself an artist?"

This was not a Pepsi or Coke question. This was serious. But how could I answer, because allowing myself to imagine that I could be an actual artist was like having a dream. And dreams died. Like happy families, and fathers, and never moving from a house that was your parents' dream and a neighborhood you knew and loved. Calling myself an artist would make room for hope and I'd lived so long relying on my anger to make sense of things. My anger was comfortable and valid, and hope seemed weak and dangerous. Hope seemed like the kind of thing that would widen the cracks inside of me and let in way too much light.

"No." Even saying the word I knew I'd disappoint her. Maybe the idea of Vivi was stupid. She was so cheerful and happy and upbeat. She seemed to have an amazing life and knew nothing of hurt.

But she didn't even pause. "Wrong answer. I'm going to work on that and you're going to let me. You may think you're too badass to be a creative, but that's the thing, creative people are badass. It takes balls to put yourself out there in the world. Ask my mom about what it's like to be a chef. Not easy."

"You said badass. And balls."

She clapped her hands to her cheeks and her eyes widened. Then she giggled. "I did. Maybe you're changing me, Jess Perez."

I took her hand. "I don't want to be a bad influence." Then I didn't give her time to ask her tenth question. I pulled her toward me and leaned forward. My lips touched hers in a whisper kiss. Simple. Sweet. When I stepped back, she put her fingers to her mouth and smiled. The doves began to coo again.

Vivi and Jess. Jess and Vivi. Strong.

11

Now: One Week, Two Days After

My head jangles as the alarm starts cooing on my bedside table. Why hadn't I changed that stupid dove alarm tone? It makes my heart hurt as much as my head does. I slap it off, hoping to fall back to sleep, but the drumbeat in my skull is too loud.

"Fudgesicles." Vivi broke me of the F-bomb and the creative replacement comes naturally. I roll over and wipe the drool from the corner of my mouth onto my pillowcase. Emma Watson stands and stretches and gives me a widemouthed fishy yawn that brings bile to the back of my throat. "Damn, Emma. Warn a girl about the morning breath." But the cat's nose-wrinkle, in response to my talking, tells me I don't have room to complain.

I make the mistake of sitting up too quickly and immediately fall back to my pillow. Ugh. Then I remember—the vodka, the fight, the cops, Mom's disappointment. What a stupid flub-up. I am a complete and total idiot. The hollow rush of gravity and cavity swell again. How is it possible to be filled with so much void? Vivi would never have let me get so far on the anger volcano. She would have calmed me, cajoled me, talked me out of doing something so stupid. But then, she's kind of the cause of it all, isn't she? I curl over sideways and pull my knees to my chest, and hope that if I ball up tight enough I can stop the ache.

There's a knock at the door and the squeak of hinges. "It's past time to get up, Jess."

My mother's voice is hurt, filled with tension and frustration.

"I'm sorry."

"You get a strong warning from me—this time—but I'm not sure the school's going to be on board. I'm going with you. And we need to talk about you going back to counseling."

I squeeze my eyes shut again. Money is so tight right now between Mom's school, and Nina's school, and all the regular bills. Therapy is probably covered by my health insurance, but I don't want to start over. It was hard losing Samantha and even though she was there for me via phone those first six months after she left, it's not something she'd want to start back up.

"I'll be okay, I promise. It was, what's that word?" I rub at my damning skull. "An anomaly. I promise I can get it together. Use my tools." Then, "What time is it?"

"Past the first bell and the principal has already called. He told me about your first anomaly, too. Jess . . ." She sighs. "I thought we were long done with the fighting." Mom crosses the room and sits on the bed, causing Emma Watson to leap and run for the hallway. She puts a hand on my shoulder. "I know this is hard, hon. I know it hurts. But I need you to hold it together. And if you can't, we need to get you some help." She brushes the hair out of my eyes. "I love you."

That does it. Floodgates open. Tears and wailing. I'm flayed down the middle and falling into darkness, but Mom lifts me up and cradles me and rocks me until I'm gulping air and rubbing at my nose. "I'm okay, now." I roll upright and immediately clutch my head.

Mom stands and smooths the wrinkles out of her pantsuit. "Alcohol will do that to you. I may only be giving you a strong warning about your anger behavior, but you are grounded. Drinking is not tolerated, drinking on a school night, even if you are grieving, extra not okay. *Comprende*?"

"*Comprende*."

"Get dressed, let's go."

"Won't you be late?"

"I've called." Mom stands a moment longer in my room, her expression a combination of understanding and disappointment. "I'll be in the car."

At school, they are waiting for me. The principal. The school resource officer. The guidance counselor. The story unspools. I blacked the other girl's eyes but luckily, she did not have a concussion. Her parents are livid. They want to press charges. The school talked them down. My verdict? Alternative school for four weeks of in-school suspension to keep the peace and some kind of in-name-only mediated restraining order. My reputation has caught up to me.

Mom argues, but it's either hang out with the other lowlifes or a criminal charge. Grady High School does not tolerate violence between its students, either on campus or off.

It doesn't matter, the worst has already happened. Nothing else can touch me.

The SRO leads me to my locker and I clear it out to the movie score of whispers and stares. Books, papers, a few bags of unopened Flamin' Hot Cheetos that Levi brought me after I won some stupid bet with him. I can't even remember what it was about, only that he surprised me by remembering to bring me my spoils. I shove them into my backpack though my stomach lurches at the thought of them.

On the shelf, carefully placed, is a red portfolio with drawings I'd shown to the art teacher at Grady. I'd only gotten into one of her classes junior year, but she'd been advising me and letting me sneak in to work at lunch or after school when I waited for Cheyanne or Vivi to finish their extra-curriculars. Vivi was convinced I could get into the graphic design program at NC State, where she hoped to go. I toss it into the trash can. That part of my life is done.

Cheyanne looks up from the open doorway of her math class, her expression a question mark. I keep my head down and keep walking. I practice my breathing to bring myself down, but I don't really need to. I don't feel the anger today. Somehow this feels right, like the change I need. It's too hard to be in these halls without Vivi.

"Can I go back home?" I ask Mom as we walk to the car, my backpack overflowing with packets of work given to me by my teachers. "I can't do this today."

"Not on your life. Though I'm sure you regret last night's decisions and a good day's sleep would make *you* feel better, what's going to make *me* feel better is knowing you are getting the education you so rightly deserve."

Guess Mom is pissed after all.

"Can I at least get coffee and some breakfast?" Last night's onion rings haunt my mouth even after brushing and flossing twice.

Mom takes me to a drive-through and then speeds across town to the county's central school office where the alternative school is located. "Take the bus home. It's been arranged."

For the first time since the day began, I feel a flicker of fear. The alternative school is for the really troubled kids. The ones with ankle monitors and probation officers. The ones who punch doors and throw desks. It's not for girl-fight girls.

Mom and I wind our way through the old elementary school converted into the administration building. The hallway's fluorescent lights are dim and the student art framed on the wall looks like it's been here a good two decades or more. At the far end is a door. She says goodbye and I walk toward my fate.

I'm greeted by cursing.

The teacher, a man who looks like he could have been a Navy SEAL before he padded himself with a layer of break-room coffee and donuts, is in the face of some pocked-skin, buzz-cut kid I remember in the vaguest way from elementary school. Like a drill sergeant in his face.

Voice raised, finger-pointing, spittle slow-motion moving to the floor.

"Motherfucker, when I say sit down, I mean fucking sit down," he yells.

Mr. Alistair never talks like this. I stand, framed by the door, not moving, not knowing where to go.

A tall shadow steps in by my side. "This is nothing," the shadow whispers. "You're going to love McGovern."

"McGovern?"

The shadow nods. "Yeah, Mr. McGovern, Mac, Asshole."

"Asshole?"

"Better stick to McGovern."

"Thanks."

I watch Mr. McGovern, Mac, Asshole, stand down the boy until he practically topples into his seat. Then he notices me.

"You." He's talking to me, not the shadow.

"Yes," I say, then add, "sir."

"You're not going to cause trouble, are you? Not one of those girls to sashay her tail feathers and cause this neatly ordered platoon to fall ranks and drool on themselves as they writhe on the floor?"

"I'm pretty sure you can't say that to me . . . sir."

Someone yells from the other side of the disorganized

room. "He ain't no sir, that's McGovern."

"Shut it, delinquent," Mr. McGovern yells over his shoulder, then turns back to me. "I say a lot of shit I ain't supposed to in here, but then, so have you to get your ass handed to me. Well?"

"No, sir. I don't cause drama." I look around again and realize I'm the only girl in the room. There are maybe twelve guys and besides my tall shadow friend, they're all staring at me, waiting.

Mr. McGov . . . Mac . . . Asshole watches for a long second, then makes a throat noise to indicate he's done with me for the time being.

"Welcome to hell," someone yells.

"Nice ass," someone else yells.

I spin, my fists spontaneously clinching, a stab of excitement jabbing at some part of my reptilian brain before the weight of my mother's warning kicks in.

"Steady girl," my shadow whispers. "I got you." Then to the room. "Her ass will kick yours if you give her half a chance. This is Jess. She's my crew from way back. And she ain't into you. So leave it."

"I could have handled my own damn self." I turn to look at my mysterious backup. "Deuces."

"Sup, pussycat. Been a while."

Marcus "Deuces" Lamar was my seat neighbor all

through sixth grade. He was always good for a laugh or as a wingman in a fight. I glance down and see the bracelet on his ankle.

"Wondered what happened to you." Which is true, he was always one of my favorites but we just kind of lost touch.

"Corner work. They caught me holding for my bone-head brother. But that's old news. I'm out of juvie and working my way toward free. Seat's over here."

He leads me through more stares, but the other boys seem to be over the fact there's a chick in their midst and more curious about what I've done to land in hell.

What's left of the morning goes by in a blur that is painfully like regular school except without the switching of classes, gossip by the lockers, or, you know, girls. It gives me time to suss out my new environment. Blank cinder block walls interspersed with Chuck Norris posters. Things like "If at first you don't succeed, you're not Chuck Norris" and "Chuck Norris doesn't read books, he stares them down till he gets the inspiration he wants." There's a circular book rack in the corner of the room with graphic novels and comic books. A sad plastic bin with a handful of art supplies. The clock sounds an overloud and constant *tick-tick-tick.* No wonder Mr. McGovern breaks it up with an occasional well-aimed curse.

At noon, an alarm goes off from the front of the room.

"Starving," Deuces says.

"What do we eat?" I ask, realizing there is no cafeteria in the county administration building where we're housed. Now that my hangover is subsiding, I'm starving, too.

The pock-faced boy who I remember is named Israel thumps his hands on my desk. "One of only two good things about this hellhole. Mac takes us out."

"Out?" I repeat.

"Yeah, bitch." A boy with short dreads and huge zirconia studs in his ears stops and puts his elbow on Israel's shoulder. "He takes us all, prison style, to whatever shit-ass diner he's in the mood for. Pity for you if you're craving vegan gluten-free organic uptown sort of food."

"Fall out, men." McGovern pauses on his words like he remembers I'm here, but he doesn't modify his command.

"What's the other thing?" I ask Deuces.

"The other thing?"

"Israel said lunch was one of two good things."

Deuces's smile spreads slow on his face. "Oh, that. Guess you'll have to wait and see."

12

THEN: All Sparrows and Chickadees

It was bound to happen. All good things must come to an end, or at least, that's what they say. And I'd been good. So good. I'd held my anger like a precious thing whenever I was around Vivi. I'd been cautious and careful and aware of myself, but my prickly parts were still there, barely under the surface. I was like a porcupine, needles at the ready. All it took was the right sort of push and every bit of Samantha training I'd ever had flew out of the window.

"Douchebag." I twisted my torso so that my backpack knocked into the side of Daniel Lesotho, who'd just made a big show of sticking his tongue through the V of his forefinger and middle finger when he saw Vivi come walking up to my locker.

"Dyke." He shoved me sideways.

Rage kicked its way out from the tidy containment system inside of my chest and I slipped my backpack off, ready to swing it at him with the full force of my fury. "You Are My Sunshine" turned into "I Hate Everything About You." All I could see was Daniel's contorted face and the sweet metal of the lockers behind him. I was going in and he was going to pay.

Hands closed on my arm, pulling me back, and I turned, my backpack swinging wildly as it collided with Vivi's thigh, sending her falling backward onto the hard tile floor of the school's hallway. I froze. The raw energy drained out of me as quickly as it had come.

Daniel's laughter echoed off the ceiling as he walked away in the opposite direction and I stood staring at what I'd done, my hands over my mouth, my consciousness horrified.

"Oh, shit, I mean swizzle, Vivi, I'm so sorry." I squatted down to help her up but she scooted backward away from me and the anger that had triggered every cell in my body changed to shame and sorrow. I'd scared her. I never wanted to scare her, or hurt her, even if it was unintentional.

"What *was* that?" She crawled her way up from the

floor to standing and wiped the back of her skirt and leggings with her hands. There was a slight tremble in her fingers. "Why did you act like that? All he did was make some stupid hand motion. You were going to hit him?"

"I . . ." My face flushed and embarrassment mingled with the shame that then sparked more anger because I hated feeling this way. "Never mind. You know I didn't mean to hit you."

"All I know is you looked like you could kill that guy. Like a switch flipped or something. It was weird, Jess. And you did hit me. Whether it was intentional or not, it's not okay."

Cheyanne chose that moment to come walking up. There'd been an unsteady truce between my GF and my BFF since the night at Stan's. Both seemed to realize they were stuck with the other but it still wasn't a love connection.

"What's going on, ladies?" She placed her elbow on my shoulder and looked at Vivi. "You look like somebody stole your Lucky Charms."

Vivi kept her eyes on me, waiting for me to say something, anything. But I went into defense mode. "Daniel Lesotho called me a dyke."

"Uh-oh. Did you go all bruiser on him?" Cheyanne

karate chopped out into the hall, her stiletto boot almost nailing a group of junior girls in the process. They scurried out of the way.

Vivi crossed her arms. "This is funny to the two of you? Normal?"

Cheyanne shrugged. "Jess gets mad sometimes. So what?"

Vivi grabbed up her bag. "I've got to go to class."

This was not good. I needed to stop her. Explain. Tell her the truth, but I'd avoided it so far, skirting around the issue, only hinting that I used to be a bit of a bully in middle school. Who wanted to hear that your girlfriend was flawed and capable of whiteout rage where she ended up clocking you with her backpack?

"Vivi, wait . . ."

But my voice got drowned out by the bell.

I pleaded for forgiveness with an elaborate doodle of an owl that I tucked into her locker. On the back, I asked her to please call me. She did.

"We need to talk."

"Yeah," I said.

"My parents are headed out to the lake house tonight to fix something for next week's renters and they said you could come with us. It's a good place to talk."

Being invited to her lake house didn't sound like we were breaking up. I let out a huge breath of air I didn't even know I was holding in. "Okay."

When we got there, Vivi grabbed a couple of blankets and we walked out to the dock. We bundled up and sat facing the water.

"I'm really sorry about what happened."

"What did happen?"

I pulled the blanket tighter, cocooning myself in the threads. "If I tell you, you might not like me anymore."

"If it's that bad you should have already told me. I told you about my asthma."

"That's not something you can help."

She didn't answer. She waited.

I sighed and stared at the still surface of the water and our shrouded reflections. "In middle school all this anger inside of me boiled up and came out. I took it out on anybody I thought was weak or different. Mostly guys. Let me tell you, no eleven-year-old boy wants to have his butt kicked by a girl. I was a grade-A jerk.

"My therapist, Samantha, said I was a ticking time bomb. Between unexpressed grief from my dad's death and me figuring out I was gay, she said the two things built up inside of me—and mixed with puberty hormones, I went nuts. It took my mom about five months to actually take it seriously and get me in counseling."

"But you still have anger issues."

I glanced in her direction and she finally looked at me. "Yeah." Then, "I would never intentionally hurt you. I want you to know that. I'm not sure why that guy triggered me. I think I felt protective or something and then I hit you in the process . . . by accident."

"You didn't really hurt me," she said.

"But it's not okay what happened."

Vivi thought for a second. "I don't really see it as that different from my asthma. It sounds like it's something you can't help. A part of you. I mean, yeah, it's kind of scary, I'm all sparrows and chickadees, so it's hard for me to relate, and I don't want you to slug me with your backpack or anything again."

I reached my hand halfway across the gap between us. She brought hers to meet mine and we sat fingertip to fingertip. "You can help me," I said.

"I can?"

"Remind me of my tools. It's why Cheyanne was so nonchalant today. She knows about my song, my breathing techniques. She's had a couple of years of practice of helping me refind my center."

Vivi frowned. "I'll try, but I'd rather be your girlfriend than your therapist."

She had a point.

"Maybe you could just say something like 'use your tools'?"

She thought for a second. "Yeah. Okay." Then, "Does your art help?"

I nodded. "Yeah, the doodling really helps." I put my fingertips on top of hers. "I also use focus memories. Like this one Christmas from way back when my dad was still alive. We had such a great day. I remember being happy and calm."

"Do you have others?"

I felt heat rise into my cheeks. "Yeah."

She twined her fingers into mine. "Are you going to tell me what they are?"

I looked at our joined hands, too nervous to look in her eyes. "I think about you. Your smile. Your eyes. That day we hugged at the park. You do calm me. You're like a Vivi balm."

"Huh." Vivi gripped my hand tighter. "I like that."

Across the lake there was a "Hoo, hoo. Hoo, hoo."

"Great horned owl," Vivi said. "Like the one you drew for me. That seems like fate, doesn't it?"

It called again and I listened to the sound in a new way. Vivi wasn't running away from me. I'd told her my truth and she was still sitting here, holding my hand.

She pointed across the lake. "There." In the moonlight, I saw a great span of wings darkening the reflection on the water. "You know," Vivi said. "They are fierce protectors of their territory. Maybe instead of you thinking you have to protect me, I can help protect you?"

I squeezed her bicep in a "my, your muscles are strong" sort of way.

"Not like that." Vivi swatted me. "Like this." She placed her hand slightly above my heart. "I've got you, Jess. You're safe with me."

I knew the only person who could really help me manage my issues was me. But her intentions were pure and even though it was too soon to say it, I was in love with her. So I smiled, incredibly grateful for the chance to make things right, and laid my head on her shoulder, letting her wrap her arm around me as we sat watching the moonlight and the stars until her parents called us to leave.

13

Now: One Week, Two Days After (Afternoon)

A sliver of white moon hangs above the horizon as I walk out from the buzzing lights of McGovern's classroom, into a warmer October afternoon. Instead of the bus I was instructed to take, my sister waits in the parking lot.

"Mom told me what happened."

I get into the passenger seat, moving her papers and books to the back. "Yeah, whatever."

"Is it bad? Who's in there with you?" She looks over to where a bunch of the guys are filing onto the short bus. "Those guys? Jesus, Jess. How's sticking you in with a bunch of hooligans going to keep you from being one yourself?"

"Thanks for your vote of confidence." But I can see

how she'd think that. The guys are a combination of ankle bracelets, tough expressions, and bad haircuts. With the exception of a couple of ISS kids like me, they're all alternative school lifers.

She keeps staring. "I've got your back. But Mom's freaking out that you're on a rewind to ruin. And I'm kind of freaked out, too. I mean, I know you lost Vivi, but we can't handle losing you."

Using my thumb and forefinger, I press against my temples to keep myself calm. My sister's flair for the dramatic is undeniable. Sure, I'd had a moment or two of dark thoughts, but it wasn't because I was actually thinking of ending my life, I was just so sad I couldn't imagine how life was going to go on. But I guess it's right for her to worry and check in.

"I'm grieving, Nina. I'm not suicidal. I swear."

"Okay, I just, I was telling Benny how sad you are and how sad that makes me, and he was so sweet about it, such a comfort you know, saying I'd be okay." She backs out of her parking spot. "And I thought, you're right. I'll be okay, but not if my sister's getting into fights and stressing out Mom."

I reach for my phone, an automatic response to text Vivi and shout in all caps, SHE'S DOING IT AGAIN. And then I remember, no Vivi. I type anyway, but don't hit send. My fingers curl around my phone and cover the screen as I withdraw into myself and look out the window. Sorrow waves lash at the corners of my face. Vivi would type back and tell me it was okay and to cut Nina some slack, that she dealt with being a fatherless girl in her own way, which involved martyrdom and male approval, and somehow, I was her bellwether mark for martyrdom. I'd type back, I KNOW BUT SHE STILL BUGS THE SHINGLES OUT OF ME. And then Vivi would send me laughing emojis at my clever use of a non-curse word curse word on her behalf. The sorrow wave pummels me. There will be no more texts from Vivi. Ever. Again.

I click through the ones not deleted. They're nonsensical. Nothing of substance. Just meet me in the hall after 2nd block and k and a few pictures of her shoes, or her fingernails, or whatever other random shot she'd taken in the moment. It's the last one I read repeatedly. Mom's picking me up early, I feel like crap. And my subpar response. K, feel better, I'll call you later. Not even an I love you.

Nina interrupts my thoughts. "FroYo Mama? I got a coupon for buy one get one free."

I drop the phone in my lap. "Sure."

I'm not hungry. But sometimes it's easier to roll with Nina. And maybe, if I'm in a public place, I can keep the tears and anguish at bay.

When Nina brings our cups back from the toppings bar—hers piña colada with almonds, white chocolate chips, and pineapple, mine chocolate with crushed Oreos and strawberries—she slides into the booth across from me. I halfheartedly poke at my yogurt with the spoon she hands me. "I have an idea. Something to cheer you up."

How do I explain to her that grief is not really something you cheer up from? It's a quarry of dark rock walls and even darker water. It's the Upside Down or Shadowvale. But I just say, "Oh yeah?"

"I think we need to have a sister spa day. I've saved a bunch of money from work and we can go over to Asheville on a Saturday. We'll get a mani-pedi. I can take you to all those cool stores on Lexington that are more your style. We can eat from food trucks and go hang out at that hippie park and watch the drummers. I've already asked Mom, because she told me you were grounded, and she said it sounded like a good idea once you weren't grounded."

"You don't need to spend your money on me, Nina. I know you're saving that to help with your tuition."

She grabs my hand. "Don't be silly, sissy. This is totally worth it. Besides I would love a day in Asheville."

Of course she would.

"Yeah, fine, whatever."

She claps and grins and then pulls out her phone to

answer texts to Benny, the boyfriend, and picks a date for a few weeks off. "We can always change it if the weather's crappy." Then she's off on a verbal adventure filling me in on all the minutiae of her job at the chicken place and how she can't wait to finally get to do clinicals for her dental hygienist degree and how the extra year of hair stylist classes may have put her behind for graduation but at least she'd have two life skills. I play with my yogurt and insert a well-placed yeah, and uh-huh, until finally she's ready to leave.

When she drops me at the house before taking off for her job, I'm ready to collapse into a never-ending cry.

Emma Watson waits for me.

"Hey, cat."

Blink.

"Scoot over."

I climb under the covers and pull her to my chest. She's in one of her more helpful moods because she starts purring and kneading her paws against my sternum. With each press, I feel myself releasing. And with each release, I know it's coming. I roll sideways, still hanging on to the cat and let the sobs go. Emma Watson does not want to be in close range for that and wriggles away to the floor. I grab a pillow and hold it in my arms, squeezing and sobbing, until I'm spent. I can't believe this has happened. One minute,

Vivi was there. And the next minute she was gone. Is this how my mom felt with my dad? Does she regret the things she didn't say?

My phone rings. I'm not in the mood to answer it, but it's Cheyanne and I figure I owe her.

"Hey."

"Are you okay? Is your mom freaking out?"

"Yes. And yes. I'm grounded because of the alcohol and she wants me to go back to therapy."

"Might not be a bad idea."

"Seriously? I thought you were on my side."

"Jess." Cheyanne's voice is scolding. "Of course I'm on your side, but that girl you jumped looks bad. You messed her up."

I take some small measure of happiness from this until I think about how Vivi would react. She would have left me over something like a full-on girl fight. Hell, I might leave myself over it. It wasn't cool. I know that, but I couldn't stop myself. It just burned its way up and . . . slam. Done.

"My bad. I know."

"Alternative school for four weeks. Will that go on your high school record? Like for colleges and stuff? Will you have time to work on your portfolio over there? If I remember it's due in six weeks."

What Cheyanne doesn't know is I've tossed all my

drawings. Deleted all the digital images. Released, feather by feather, until each bird has vanished to a sky I can no longer reach.

"I don't know. It doesn't matter anyway."

"What do you mean it doesn't matter?"

Might as well give her the moment of truth, let her know how much of a loser her friend really is. "I'm not going to apply."

Silence on the other end of the line.

Then.

"Are you out of your mind? Do you know what your chances are of getting a decent job if you don't have a bachelor's degree at a minimum? You love drawing. It's the one thing I always loved Vivi for, goading you into realizing you had a skill. NC State will totally accept you."

"Cheyanne, stop. I'm not applying. I can't do it. I don't want to do it. Vivi's not going to be there next year, so why the hell should I be?"

"Good lord, would you stop with the pity party. You are not the only one grieving Vivi, and though losing your girlfriend seriously sucks, she would NOT want you to stop living your life. She would want you to apply."

I snug the pillow closer and fling my leg out from under the covers. "Chey, it's hopeless. Give it up."

"Not the answer I want to hear." Then, silence.

I try to outlast her but the mental image of her resting bitch stare pops up in my brain and I cave. "Fine. You can help me do college applications. But no NC State. No art portfolio."

"Better, but so weird, Jess. That artwork saved you from shit like last night. Listen to your mother and consider counseling. Then maybe you can talk to the guidance office, show you're doing the work for your fisticuffs and NC State might give you an extension."

"Not sure how that all works, but I will take your advice into consideration." I won't, but like with Nina, sometimes it's just easier to go along with Cheyanne.

"Good. Now take into consideration me coming over this weekend. Since you're grounded and I don't get to see you at school. Your mother loves me."

"Yeah, okay." An urgency to get off the phone and escape into the cocoon of my blankets strikes hard. "I'm gonna go. I'll talk to you later." I don't wait for her to say goodbye, just hit the end button. It's too much. I know they're all only trying to help, but it hasn't even been two weeks. It hasn't even sunk in yet that Vivi's really, truly gone.

14

THEN: The Patterns of Their Feathering

I was cocooned in my comforter with my sketchbook and pens when my mom walked into my room. "I have something for you." She slipped a white bag with string handles onto my bed. "They had a raffle at the office and I won. I could have chosen the laptop for your sister's college, but . . ."

I peered into the bag, not believing what I was seeing. It was not only an iPad but one of the big pro ones like illustrators used. It even had a digital pen with it. "Are you serious?" I couldn't believe it.

She sat down on the bed where I had my sketchbook open to a series of pencil sketches of owls in flight. She turned the paper toward her and smiled. "Of course I'm serious. It's nice to see you so engaged in something." She pulled me into a hug. "I want you to find your happiness. It seems like between having a girlfriend and your constant sketching you're well on your way."

It was nice the way Mom had gotten so cool about Vivi, even if it had given her a moment of pause. I knew other kids weren't as lucky as me, but ever since she lost Dad her whole outlook on life was what she called "now within reason." Which I took to mean, as long as we were happy and fulfilled, and didn't put ourselves or others in harm's way, then she was all for it.

"This is amazing, Mom." I wrapped my arms tighter around her, hugging back. "I'm going to draw something for you."

She patted her fingertips together in an excited clap. "And I'll frame it and hang it on the wall. Your artwork has definitely outgrown the refrigerator."

I was already pulling the cellophane off the box when she kissed me on the forehead and left the room.

Cheyanne found me first the next morning. I had huge circles under my eyes because I'd stayed up all night long working with the paint program, getting the hang of the tools, and trying to make a piece worthy of my mother.

"What are you doing?"

I twisted the tablet so she could see the image of the great horned owl like the one Vivi and I had seen at the lake a month ago. Instead of going realistic, like the fine-pen drawings I'd already done of the owl in my sketchbook, I went for something wilder with the marker brush tool. I'd chosen purples, blues, and lime green, varying the line widths, so it was more painting than drawing.

Cheyanne, who was rocking some serious cat eye makeup this morning, was speechless. Until. "Holy shit, Jess. When did you become a bona fide artist?"

I cringed. I'd only shown Vivi, Nina, and my mom my work. Showing other people transformed it. Made it available for criticism or praise and both were kind of the same. If you believed one you had to believe the other, and mostly I liked my doodles being for me. It shouldn't matter what other people thought, but a swell of pride filled me all the same.

"It's not that big of a deal. Well, my new tablet is a pretty big deal, but the drawing . . ." I lifted my shoulders in a whatever kind of move.

"Nuh-uh." Cheyanne took the tablet out of my hands and spent a long time looking at what I'd done. "I can adapt Bach cello suites to the string bass, but I could never do this." She handed back the iPad, then pinched me on the butt. "Girl, you've got talent!"

That was the moment Vivi chose to appear. She settled next to Cheyanne. "Right? I keep telling her she's good, but she says I'm *supposed* to tell her those things. Girlfriend law, or some crap like that." Vivi leaned across Cheyanne and scrunched up her face at me. "See, I'm not the only one who thinks you're a real artist."

I did like my drawings. I liked learning about birds from Vivi and then learning more by studying how they were put together, the patterns of their feathering, the variations of their beaks and wings. I liked finding out maybe I could do something after all. But still. "Y'all are kind of embarrassing me."

Cheyanne growled. "Get over it." Then, "How are you learning all of this? You're not taking art, are you?"

Vivi chimed in. "You should listen to your best friend. Sign up for art next semester."

After our big talk at the lake, Vivi had decided she was going to win Cheyanne over come hell or high water. Her tactic was simple. Pay Cheyanne as much attention as she paid me. Tell her how awesome her ideas were. Let her know in no uncertain terms that Vivi understood Cheyanne had best friend status and was willing to keep that space available even though she and I were a couple. Also, she wanted Cheyanne to know that she, too, understood about my triggers and wasn't going to run away from me if I backslid.

Lately, even though at first I thought Cheyanne would think Vivi was pandering to her, it seemed like it was starting to work.

"You know the makeup tutorials you're so into?" I said.

"Yeah."

"There are tons of art tutorials online, too. I've been following a few different channels and learning."

"Makes sense," Chey said.

Vivi looked at Cheyanne. "Is that how you got your eyes to look so amazing? They're cedar waxwing eyes."

"What the what?" Cheyanne looked at Vivi like she had lost it.

I pulled up a photo on the tablet. "You should know by now, Vivi speaks in bird. This is a cedar waxwing."

Cheyanne leaned closer inspecting the bird's black mask around its eyes. "Who knew, I always thought I was doing cat eyes." She looked at Vivi. "Will you please tell me what the hell is up with the bird obsession? Though I like it in Jess's art, it's seriously nerdy on you."

"Nerds are the best people. You are in the band. You should know this."

I held my breath. Vivi's teasing could go well. Or it could go south.

Cheyanne pinched Vivi's hip. A good sign. She only pinched the people she loved. "Answer the question."

Vivi shrugged. "I don't know, maybe I was a bird in my past life."

Cheyanne pressed. "There has to be something more than that."

I knew the answer but wondered if it would have the same impact on Cheyanne as it had on me.

"Okay, but you can't laugh."

Cheyanne crossed her heart.

"My mom's mother, GeeMa, loved birds. When I was little, I remember sitting on her sofa with a big illustrated bird book, watching the feeders she kept on the patio through the slider door. We would search the pages and I would match up the birds to their illustration. I loved learning all about them. I loved that special time with her. When I was eleven, she got lung cancer and died." Vivi paused. "I was pretty devastated because my other grandparents were in France, but a miraculous thing happened. When my mom and I went to clean out the things from GeeMa's town house, I went to get the bird book. On the patio, even though the feeders were low, there were more species than I'd ever seen at one time. And then the hummingbird appeared."

"The hummingbird?" Cheyanne asked, hanging on Vivi's words.

"Yes, it was late fall, way past time for a hummingbird to still be hanging around, but there she was, right outside the door, her wings beating for all her worth, and I swear, she was looking directly at me. She darted up and down and back, never leaving the door. It wasn't till my mom walked in the room that she darted off, but even then, she looked at my mom for a good thirty seconds."

"You think it was your grandmother's spirit?" Cheyanne asked.

Vivi nodded. "I did. I do. And I think it was her way of telling me the answer to everything is in the things and the people we love. So . . . birds."

Cheyanne smiled. "Excellent answer." Then she laughed. "Better than monster trucks or crossword puzzles."

Vivi frowned. "What's wrong with crossword puzzles?"

"Nothing, nothing." Then, to my amazement, Cheyanne linked her arm through Vivi's and leaned on her. "When are we going thrift shopping together?"

Vivi looked at me and winked.

Could it be that finally, after almost an entire fall

semester, we had achieved a GF-BFF solidarity coup? All because of a tutorial video and a heartfelt story?

But I didn't want them forgetting the most important person in this trio. "Hey, what about me?"

Cheyanne and Vivi grinned. "You?"

It was the best answer I could have gotten.

15

Now: One Week, Five Days After

"You have one new message." Our answering machine has an Australian woman's voice that's way more pleasant than the messages that get left. My mom has never succeeded at getting on the "no-call" list for solicitors and the like.

This time though, the caller's voice is hesitant as it fills the room. "Hello. Ellie. Jess. This is Abigail."

I freeze. It's Vivi's mom.

"I know this is last minute, but we got Vivi back yesterday. Well, her ashes. We were hoping the two of you can come to the lake tomorrow. For a private moment. The two of you, us, our priest, a couple of close family friends. We'll have lunch and say some things and let part of her go to the lake. Her father and I have decided we want to take some of them to France and booked spur-of-the-moment tickets. If this is a problem, let us know. Otherwise we'll see you at eleven? Okay. Thank you." Vivi's mom's voice breaks as the machine beeps the end of the recording. My mom stands frozen with me. Something in a grocery bag settles and the crinkle of the bag sounds like the air is ripping.

I split in two. This is it. The final goodbye.

"Oh, hon." Mom reaches for me and pulls me tight as my sobs ripple across my back and down my sides and into the very marrow of my bones.

"I can't. I can't. I can't."

Mom strokes my hair. "You can, sweetheart. We can."

"It's too much." There's no need to dam the river. Mom understands.

"I know it is. It *is* too much. But we'll go, and we will love each other. And you will share that love with Vivi's parents and you'll remember getting to be a part of letting her go to the bigger universe. And as cliché and unhelpful as it is for you right now, what you will remember in the years ahead is not this pain, but the beautiful moment of getting to be part of an intimate goodbye."

I'm being selfish with my incessant need for comforting. Mom didn't get this intimate goodbye. She got a military coffin and a folded flag and a slender tombstone for a veteran. There was no soft lake breeze or luncheon, or the love I know the Bouchards will shower over me and the others, even in their grief. I wipe my tears and nod. "Okay."

"That's my good girl. Why don't you go bathe and when you come out I'll have a little supper fixed for us?" She cups my cheek with her hand and holds it there.

The next morning the sky is overcast and gloomy. Nina makes a stink saying she wants to come, but I fight her and replay the message that clearly says the two of us, me and Mom. Nina wasn't invited.

"Jess," Mom says, but I stop her with a "No, this is my time. Not Nina's."

The issue is solved when Nina storms off to meet Benny for pancakes, which is fine by me. She'll get over it.

It takes about an hour to get to the lake house. Mom turns onto the long gravel drive. My stomach clenches thinking—*this is probably the last time I will ever come here.*

The car crunches over fallen twigs and leaves and I can't imagine opening the door or being able to use my feet to get to the house, the path, the dock, the boat. Because I know, without a doubt, that is how the Bouchards will do it. They will drive to an isolated cove and find a spot filled with birds and let Vivi soar.

"We're here." Mom turns off the engine.

"Yep." I stare up into the trees and push back the lick of tears and the stone of grief, and hope I can hold it together.

Mom hesitates a second, then takes out the keys and opens her door. The moment will never, ever, be right for me, but I might as well move the feet and take the walk and say the goodbyes. Breath catches in my chest and punches me. Mom walks down the path to the now open front door.

"Jess." Vivi's father says my name with a hint of his French accent and holds his arms open for me. He is handsome and still young and it does not seem right that he and Abigail should have lost their only child.

"Henri." I walk into his open hug and let him envelop me. It had taken a year before I'd felt comfortable calling Vivi's parents by their first names, even though they'd insisted from the start. But now it feels natural. He pushes me back and kisses both of my cheeks, then hugs me again. He reaches out a grasping hand for Mom.

"Ellie. So good to see you again."

Then Abigail is behind him. "Henri, bring them inside."

Inside we are introduced to Father Reinaud, the Bouchards' priest. There are also some neighbors, the Clarks who are older than my mom or Vivi's parents and acted as surrogate North Carolina grandparents. Henri leads us all to the boat. Abigail carries a book of poetry by Mary Oliver, Vivi's favorite poet. The Clarks and my mom are each given a single white rose. Father Reinaud carries a flute. And me, I'm given a small, lidded porcelain dish decorated with plumed-tailed birds. Vivi in my hands.

The outboard motor sounds subdued as we move slowly across the water. Luckily, the gray skies and chill turn to the temperature have kept other boaters off the lake. As if the world knows the gravity of the situation about to unfold on these waters.

When Vivi's father reaches the cove, he cuts the engine and throws out the anchor line. We sit in silence for a while, letting the symphony of the slight wind and the branches, and the birds, yes, the birds, be all our thoughts and conversation. Finally, Father Reinaud brings the flute to his lips and the melody he plays is both lyrical and haunting. A light, beautiful piece that fits the essence of who Vivi was. I let my guard drop and one tear after another rolls down my cheeks. Mom holds one of my hands. The other cradles Vivi.

When the flute dwindles away, Abigail stands to read, but then at the last minute shifts the book to Mrs. Clark, her tears streaming too intensely for speech to follow. In a musical, Southern voice Mrs. Clark reads a poem titled "Love Sorrow."

Love sorrow. She is yours now, and you must
take care of what has been
given. Brush her hair, help her
into her little coat, hold her hand,
especially when crossing a street. For, think,

what if you should lose her? Then you would be
sorrow yourself; her drawn face, her sleeplessness
would be yours. Take care, touch
her forehead that she feel herself not so

utterly alone. And smile, that she does not
altogether forget the world before the lesson.
Have patience in abundance. And do not
ever lie or ever leave her even for a moment

by herself, which is to say, possibly, again,
abandoned. She is strange, mute, difficult,

sometimes unmanageable but, remember, she is a child.
And amazing things can happen. And you may see,

as the two of you go
walking together in the morning light, how
little by little she relaxes; she looks about her;
she begins to grow.

Tears course my face as I listen. My relationship with God is questioning, but if he is a true and real thing, then I'd like to think that he is helping Vivi. By her side. Making sure she understands the new path she flies. When Mrs. Clark finishes reading we're silent again until Mom, after the trill of a wood thrush along the shore, stands and bends to the water, cradling her single rose in her hand and releases it as one might release a swan onto the surface. The Clarks follow in turn. Henri and Abigail hold each other, sobbing silent tears, the boat rocking us all in the rhythm of sorrow. Then it's my turn. I stand, my heart catching, a leaf twirling, a peek of sun between the clouds and I take the lid off the bird-covered dish. The breeze ruffles the surface of Vivi's ash. Grayer than I expected. Not as fine as I expected. I hold the dish to the sky, to the birds, and tilt it forward so that the wind pulls Vivi away from me and in the moment that ash touches the current, the thrush swoops out across the lake's surface toward the boat, then just as quickly swoops away.

I drop the dish and it disappears under the water.

"Oh." I turn, horror working its way up my face.

"It's okay." Father Reinaud takes the lid gently from my other hand and releases it into the lake with the sinking bowl. "It's okay," he repeats.

Now the boat is without ceremony. Just a sad boat on the sad lake, a collection of people only connected by the one released. Henri starts the motor and takes us home. We eat a quiet lunch. We drink our quiet tea. And then it is time for goodbyes. A hug. Another hug. A "please dear, keep in touch, we'll be in France for a month or so." And then I'm back in Mom's car, speeding away from the lake, away from life as I've known it for the past two and a half years, into . . . what?

16

Now: Two Weeks After

Sunday, I wake up too early. It's six a.m. and the world is still dark outside. I pick up my phone and go to my voice mail messages. I've been avoiding them. Scared what the sound of Vivi's voice will do to my heart, but I need her this morning. I need her to tell me something good. I start with the last.

"Jess, *cough cough*. Don't forget to bring those drawings in for Mrs. Thompson. You asked me to remind you. I love you so much. I'm so excited we'll be together next year at State."

If I'd known what that cough meant, I would have asked to talk to her mom, had them rush her to the hospital. Maybe she'd be alive if I'd been more in tune to the subtle changes of her breathing. I listen again and none of it seems relevant anymore. Applying to State is stupid. Art is stupid. All I can hear is that tiny cough and the thickness in her voice from a virus setting in.

I go to an earlier message. "Hey, lover. I'm just lying here on the dock watching the stars, wondering what my girl's doing." This had been a few weekends before. My dad's father had come to visit us from Texas and I'd stayed home to see him. If I'd known my weekends were numbered with Vivi, I would have fought my mother to be at the lake. Hindsight sucks.

The rest of the messages are part functional scheduling, part sharing silly stories, and part love songs. I transfer them to the cloud so they'll never get lost, then I grab my iPad for a bigger screen. I go to our Instagram feeds and save every silly video Vivi was ever in. I pop over to her Facebook page but the messages from so many kids who didn't even really know her start to piss me off.

Seriously.

Who are these people?

It's like the equivalent of a shrine but on the computer. There are teddy bear memes (she would gag) and flickering digital candles and wall posts with stupid notes like "Only the good die young, you were among the goodest—LOL, awesome thing I'm going to college" and "Rest in peace, you're in a better place now."

She's not in a better place. She's fucking dead.

I start to type that, but stop. Her parents might check this page and as much as I want to spew all over these imbeciles, I don't want to hurt Henri and Abigail. I want to remember the hope I had at the lake. But my hands flex instinctively. This crap makes me so angry. They didn't know her. They don't get to say whether she's in a better place or not. The more I look at the stupid screen the more I want to stick my fist through it. Instead, I stand up and pace my room, my hands pulling my hair toward the ceiling before I fling them out sideways like I can shoot fireballs from my scalp. I look around for something to destroy. In front of me is the canvas print of my first really good digital owl painting. Mom had it made for me last Christmas. But I can't stand to look at it. Birds are fucking stupid. Fucking. I said it. Fuck. Fuck. Fuck. I grab the canvas off my desk and stab the printed surface with my pocketknife until it's tattered.

I'm looking for what to wreck next when the doorbell rings.

There's Nina's voice, followed by another. Crap. It's Cheyanne. I told her she could come over but the last thing in the world I want right now is to hang out with her. She's going to be on me about the portfolio, bugging me, asking questions, telling me my grief shouldn't have power over me like it does. But she doesn't know. She doesn't know this hollowness.

There are footsteps and then a cooing as Emma Watson greets Chey. She enters my room with the cat draped over her neck like a blue fox stole. "Did you forget I was coming over?" Then when she sees my screen. "Ugh, that is so gross. Can you believe all those people? They didn't even know her. What is it about teenagers dying that gives randos some kind of weird death fetishization rights?" She turns my iPad upside down and flings a tote bag full of folders onto my desk. "You look like hell. What's up with your hair?"

I catch a glimpse of myself in the mirror. My hair on top is sticking out in a zillion directions. My eyes are puffy and swollen from crying off and on all night. Then there's my choice of comfort clothing—the Minion Snuggie Nina gave me as a joke for Christmas last year and fuzzy striped socks in metallic silver and lime green, both of which are oversized and make me look like an underfed orphan child. "I had to do something to keep from busting my device."

"So you tried to pull your hair out by the roots? Did you at least brush your teeth at some point this weekend?"

I breathe into my hand and sniff. "Roses."

From her other bag, Cheyanne pulls out two Starbucks

energy drinks in the big cans. "Vanilla or caramel?"

"Caramel."

"Where's mine?" Nina walks in from the hallway. She is fresh looking, in a soft pink T-shirt and gray jogger sweats. Cheyanne thrusts her own drink forward.

"Here, you can have this one."

"You've always been the sweetest thing." Nina takes it, even though I'm sure she realizes it's the one Chey got for herself. "What are you girls up to?" She pops the opening on the can and guzzles down a big gulp. I can't believe she just took Chey's drink. I honestly can't believe Chey gave it to her.

"I'm going to help Jess apply to schools."

"Oh, that's great." She leans over Chey's shoulder and flips through the catalogs. "Lenoir-Rhyne, Mars Hill, Elon. Aren't these all private schools?" Nina glances at me, her face saying what we both know. We are not private school girls.

"Yes. But they're all pretty easy for non-honors-track students to get into. Especially when they've chosen NOT to use their God-given talents in art for entry."

"What?" Nina looks at me. "I thought you were applying to some prestigious graphic design program at State."

I could kill Cheyanne.

My mom walks in from the hall. She's dressed in her

Sunday study clothes, jeans and a Harvard Law sweatshirt, even though her diploma's going to come from Concord Law, an online degree program. "Hi, girls, I'm about to head out. Everything good?"

Nina turns. "Cheyanne and I are talking to Jess about school. And apparently she's not applying to State after all."

Mom eyes me and gives me a questioning look.

"Just stop." I scrunch my hair in my hands like I'm trying to pull words out of my skull. "I don't know what I'm doing. I have a month still to apply for the program, but I can't think about it right now. It hurts too bad and y'all aren't helping."

None of them say anything.

Mom sips the coffee from her travel mug and blinks like she's thinking of the next right words. "Okay, Jess. We can table this conversation. But I don't want you to make a decision you'll regret in the fall. You don't want to limit yourself based on how you're feeling today. I'm the queen of bad decisions made due to grief." She waves her hand around to indicate our house, a move she's said over and over was her biggest mistake. But I don't see it that way. Moving is what brought me to Vivi.

But then, maybe she's right after all. If we'd never moved away from the base, I'd never have had a dead girlfriend. The thing is, I do want to limit myself. I want a tiny box of room, kitchen, room. I want a simple job where I talk to no one and meet no one and come home and sleep in darkness. I don't want light and lakes and depressing birdsong. I definitely don't want a sprawling college campus filled with excited freshmen who've never experienced the cut of loss.

Nina and Cheyanne nod along with her. "Yeah, take your time," Nina says. "You can always do community college first, like me."

Cheyanne slips Emma Watson off her neck and plops the cat in my lap. "We can just work on the easy stuff, save the essays for later. You know, practice, or something."

Mom squeezes my shoulder and the vision of ash blowing on breeze clouds my thoughts. "I'll be home around five. I thought we could have a kale salad and some grilled chicken with pomegranate relish." She spends Sundays studying at the law office where she currently works as a paralegal, in hopes of one day having her own corner office.

Nina scoffs. "Mom, it's *Game of Thrones* night. Pizza."

"One day your unhealthy eating habits are going to catch up to you." She looks at the three of our hopeful faces. "Fine. But no meat. A veggie supreme. Thin crust. And get a big side salad at least."

"Yes." Cheyanne fist pumps in a most un-Cheyanne-like way.

Mom leaves and eventually Nina leaves and finally it's me and Chey and her goals and aspirations for me.

"How are you?" she asks, her face solemn.

"Don't." I shake my head.

"Don't?"

"Ask that question. It's the stupidest question on the planet. How am I? Seriously?" I ball the comforter in my hands. "The girl I was certain I was going to marry and live a beautiful life with died. I suck. But when people ask me that, they don't want to hear the truth, they want to hear 'Oh, I'm fine. Hanging in there. It hurts, but I'll get over it.' I'm not going to get over it. I'm not okay."

Cheyanne moves her face back like I slapped her. "Excuse me. I'm sorry."

"And don't say sorry either. It's not your fault."

Cheyanne takes a breath. I'm not being fair to her but the hurt consumes me. "Ooookay. So, do you want to look at this stuff or what?"

"Why don't you just lecture me. It's what you want to do anyway. Just hold up the brochures and tell me what I should major in and exactly what I should write because I'm obviously a colossal screwup in your eyes and probably the only reason you're here is because you feel some obligation to the ghost of Vivi."

"I know you're in pain, Jess, but you're being rude. I'm just trying to help."

I ball up into my Snuggie and turn away from her. Being a douchebag feels so much better than letting the sad soak into my cells. "Whatever. This was your idea. I don't need your help." I'm pushing her, I know.

"We don't have to do this. Levi invited us to go see a movie later on. I was going to see if you wanted to go if we finished."

"So, are you going to lead him on forever, or what?"

"Jess." Her voice is warning.

"No, I'm serious. Because that boy really likes you and is really nice and I'm sick of watching you say jump and him saying how high. And it's disgusting how you are with him. You're a big fucking tease. You can't relate to my heartbreak if you can't even relate to your own emotions. You hide them in your schoolwork. Unlike me." I push Emma Watson off the bed. "I feel every single freaking one of them. Do you even have them?"

I find Cheyanne's limit.

"You, my friend, are being a class-A bitch. I'm going to leave now." She stands and hesitates, waiting on my apology no doubt.

It doesn't come.

"What are you waiting for? Go. Just get out of here."

Cheyanne grabs her bag and storms out of my room. I follow her to the front door. When it slams, I flip her the bird. And even though it feels righteous and alive, there's another part underneath that feels dirty. Like I was never worthy of a love like Vivi's.

On the way back to my bedroom, I stop in the kitchen. At the back of the fridge is a bottle of some fancy flavored gin someone gave my mom. I pull it out, pour a big glass, and top the bottle off with water. I push Emma Watson into the hall and shut my door so it's just me, the alcohol, and my memories.

And then I scream.

"Fuck!"

I scream it over and over and over again, my anger punching at Vivi in every direction. How dare she? How dare she die? When I can't scream anymore, and I've drained the glass, I curl into a ball and wish I could have died instead.

17

THEN: A Competition for the Ducks

"Wine?" Mr. Bouchard, I mean Henri, held up a bottle in front of me. My eyes widened. Alcohol seemed like something you snuck when your parents weren't around, not something they offered you.

It was my first overnight at the lake house and Vivi's mom had cooked beef bourguignon, which made the whole space smell insanely good.

When Vivi had whispered in my ear, "Want to spend the night with me?" my heart had stopped. But then she'd laughed. "It won't be like that. Because you're my girlfriend, we'll have separate rooms. But it's going to be amazing. We'll make cookies and drink hot chocolate and watch the wild ducks. Some varieties are only on the lake during winter months." I'd teased her about her obsession and she'd stuck her tongue out at me and her mom had called my mom and it'd all been arranged.

Now here I was, with a plate full of gourmet food, and an empty glass being filled with red wine. Abigail, Vivi's mom, must have noticed the shocked expression on my face because she laughed. "It's cultural. A little wine with a meal is normal for us. If you don't like it you don't have to drink it."

"Don't be silly," Henri said. "She will love it."

I envied Vivi sometimes. Her life was filled with trips around the globe and loads of international friends. Even though my dad's Texas family was an awesome mash-up of various degrees of Mexican and Texan, their lives seemed pretty much like mine. Suburban and boring. I tried to act cool though when I took the first sip.

Vivi giggled when she saw my eyes squeeze shut and my lips pull down into a puckering frown. So much for savoir faire.

She whispered, "You really don't have to drink it."

Abigail winked and passed me a basket of crispy bread. "Vivi says you are becoming quite the artist."

I scrunched up my face at Vivi. I knew she'd made the whole "Jess is an artist" thing her personal agenda, but it was still strange to talk about it so openly. But I nodded and tried a second sip of the wine after I swallowed the bite I'd just taken of the beef. It was pretty cool how its taste enhanced the flavor of the food but I didn't see myself becoming a connoisseur anytime soon.

"This is really good," I said before adding, "I like drawing and I'm definitely improving, but your daughter has a way of making me sound way better than the reality."

"That may be true, but she also has an eye for things. Our Vivi is a special spirit."

At this Vivi blushed. "Mom, stop."

"What? Can I not brag about my own beautiful daughter to the girl who loves her?"

Now we were both blushing furiously, because even though we were pretty joined at the hip whenever it was possible, we'd taken things very, very slowly on the physical and confessional part of our relationship. It wasn't that Abigail was wrong, at least where I was concerned, but the words hadn't been said between Vivi and me.

Fortunately, Henri jumped into the ensuing silence. "Did you see this?" He reached behind him and grabbed a folded newspaper section from the kitchen counter. "There is a competition for the ducks."

"What?" Vivi said. We both thought it was adorable when her dad sometimes said things that highlighted

English as his second language. "Are they going to have a beauty contest or something?"

He scoffed. "Not for the ducks. For the drawings. Here." He handed over the paper. "Take it with you downstairs to investigate, leave your mother and I to finish our wine. You can come back for the dessert and the dishes."

Vivi kissed her dad's cheeks, then her mother's, before grabbing my hand. "Come on." She pulled me down the steps toward the media room.

"Where are you taking me?"

"Didn't you hear my dad? He said go investigate." Vivi winked. "That was clearly a sign they're giving us solo time. I plan on investigating." Vivi tiptoed her fingers up the sleeve of my flannel shirt.

I glanced nervously back up the stairs. The last thing I wanted was any of our parents walking in on some scene they couldn't unsee, but the truth was I'd thought of nothing but kissing Vivi since we got to the lake house.

"Chicken," she teased.

It's true. I was chicken. For as much as I constantly longed for her, thought about her, looked at her, I was shy about making a wrong move or ever doing anything that would turn her off. I may have been confident about my sexuality in middle school but it didn't mean I'd had much chance at actual experience.

We went and sat side by side on the couch. Vivi faced me cross-legged with the paper in her hand.

"Can I see the paper?"

Vivi held it over her head. "You have to get it from me."

I tried to take it from her. She sat up on her knees and held it higher. I reached up more to try to get it. She moved her hand back and I fell against the front of her as I followed. Her softness and curves caught me and as my hand planted down to steady myself, I was in the perfect position for that kiss. Her lips parted and her eyes glittered, and I looked at the sweet bow of her upper lip and felt the clench in my body and I leaned in, but she wiggled away, leaped off the couch, and crouched down on the other side, taunting me with the paper.

"Oh, come on," I begged, groaning for show. Then I rolled off the cushions and went after her.

She jumped away again, running back to the front of the sofa. I followed but went wide, hopping over the coffee table and grabbing her before successfully tackling her to the couch. She kept the paper held high, her face flushed with the exertion.

"You have to pay the toll if you want to read the paper."

"The toll?"

Vivi closed her eyes and puckered her lips. At first, I thought she was going to mess with me again, but this time she didn't move as I pressed my mouth against hers. Her lips were always a surprise. Soft, full, warm. I kissed her top lip, then her bottom lip, then both. She dropped her hand with the paper across my back and brought the other one up and around. I let my body fall into hers, once again feeling the plush of her curves and the press of her breasts through her shirt. The next kiss brought more pressure and the pull of Vivi's arms against my back as she pushed up against me. Our mouths parted and between the soft push of lips came a warm rush of tongues and the sweet air of Vivi's breath. I cradled her cheek in my hand, kissing her again and again, my lips greedy and searching. An involuntary sigh escaped me. My hand, with a mind of its own, found its way to the hem of Vivi's shirt where it pushed aside fabric, seeking skin, heat, and more, more, more. That brought Vivi's hand to the top of mine.

"My parents."

I nibbled at her ear, my hand not ready to relinquish its newfound territory. "They gave us time to investigate, remember?" My voice grew deeper. "I'm investigating." I reached further under her shirt and found where her bra began and tentatively stepped my fingers under the side of the fabric, stroking the whisper of soft skin beneath. I was losing myself in the moment, the headiness of the wine making me bolder, and I started to push her shirt up so I could put my mouth where my hand had been.

Vivi wiggled out sideways from under me. "Jess." She glanced toward the steps.

"Too far?" I said as I sat back against the armrest.

She looked up at me from under bangs. "In this situation."

"But not always?"

She crawled toward me. "Definitely not always." She handed me the newspaper.

We cuddled together and read the article. It was a contest, held by the US Fish and Wildlife Service, to create a water fowl stamp and was open to kindergarten through twelfth graders across the state. North Carolina entries were judged against each other's age range and then those winners would go onto the national contest and eventually the US Postal Service would turn your artwork into a stamp if you won the whole shebang.

"The deadline's not till February. You could totally do this."

"I don't know. You're real sweet about my sketches, but this is serious competition."

"The worst they can say is no. Come on. Please? If you agree to do it, we can totally come back out to the lake house again. Maybe alone." She wiggled closer to my side.

"Alone?"

Vivi laughed. "You have a one-track mind, but yes. My parents can't bait you with a contest like this and then not give you access to your duck models. Will you work on a piece for it? For me?"

I read the article again. *No* could be hard to take, if you had your heart into wanting something. But learning to accept rejection without wigging out about it was definitely a positive step on the Samantha path. And with Vivi as my positivity coach, along with the promise of alone time, maybe I could deal with rejection. It was scary to put myself out there, to start to believe there might be something kind of cool inside of me, but since I hadn't been able to change my schedule and get into art class for after the break, at least this would give me a tangible goal.

I folded the paper into a neat square with the contest information facing outward. "Yeah, okay. A duck stamp drawing it is."

This time Vivi paid the toll.

18

Now: Two Weeks, Two Days After

My mom comes in when my third snooze goes off and hits the button on my phone. "Hon, get up."

"Don't want to."

She sighs and rubs her hand in circles on my back. "I know, baby. But sometimes putting one foot in front of the other, faking it through the day, is the only way to make it. I didn't want to breathe after your father died, but I had you and your sister to keep me going." She points to the framed copy of my winning duck stamp on the wall and another drawing I did that was chosen as a calendar finalist for the wildlife rehabilitation center contest. "You have something you love to do. Let your art help you find your way. It's always worked in the past."

I get out of bed because it's easier than telling her I'm not going to draw anymore. That it's too painful.

As I get dressed I think about Cheyanne. There's been no word from her. No texts on Monday. Nothing so far today. But then, I haven't really reached out to her either. Anyway, it doesn't matter. I'm not on main campus now and after this year we're going our separate ways. Maybe it was time for our friendship to end. Everything else has.

After lunch—the same nasty all-you-can-eat Chinese buffet from last week—we load onto the activity bus again. McGovern keeps driving west instead of turning back toward the county office building and our classroom.

"Where are we going?" I ask.

Before Deuces can answer, this pale-skinned boy, Levon, turns around from the seat in front of us. "We're going to get some edumacation. The great state of North Carolina has decided that juvenile delinquents need more than the three Rs. We need a trade." He looks over. "You're kind of small, but ripped, too. You'll do okay." He pauses like he's putting two and two together. "Are you that dyke whose girlfriend died? My cousin told me about some fight you were in. That's some sick shit."

I nod and Deuces gives me a little half slug on the shoulder.

Levon sticks his earbuds back in, turns around, and jacks his head from side to side, jamming to some silent tune as the activity bus bounces down a gravel road.

McGovern yells from the front of the bus. "All right, Grady's finest, we're here. Remember this is a fucking privilege."

"Is anybody going to tell me where *here* is?" I ask, stretching my legs after being cramped in the tiny seat.

"Cabinetworks," Deuces says.

"What?"

"Remember I said there were two good things? Well, lunch was the first and this is the second."

We file off the bus one at a time. McGovern stands at the bottom with a clipboard and a scowl. He counts us off into two groups of four, and one of five. I'm with Deuces, and two country-looking white boys that are alternative school lifers.

"Wood shop." He points to the largest group. "Finishing." He points to the next. "Forge." He points to us.

"Ah, man. I wore my nice kicks today. Can't I be in wood shop?" Deuces spills attitude all over the ground in front of McGovern. I have a feeling this isn't going to work in his favor.

"You will work where I goddamn tell you to work. Now move, pretty boy."

I follow Deuces, whose shoes are a blinding bright neon orange, across the parking lot and behind the large building in front, to a smaller one toward the back of the business site.

The buildings are prefab steel structures, some with doors open to the nice weather, the sound of machinery whirring from inside. It's obvious we're here as free labor under the guise of job skills training, but it's better than being stuck under the stare of Chuck Norris. The building Deuces walks toward has a smokestack coming out from the side of it that belches black clouds skyward. He's grumbling about his clothes as he goes. Two garage doors are rolled open wide and there are covered concrete slabs where a woman stands over an anvil, her hair pulled tight into a cap, safety glasses firmly in place, and the best set of arms I've ever seen on anyone, male or female.

The woman stops hammering and looks up. Her eyes skip over me, then skip back and there's the slightest raise of brow and lift of lip that tells me she's not used to having other females out here to work.

"You guys are my crew today?" The woman's voice is a normal voice, not the toughness I thought I'd hear; if anything it's a soft contrast to the hard metal and hot coals surrounding her.

Deuces nods. "Yeah. This is Jess, she's new."

The woman takes off her leather glove and pushes the bill of her Cabinetworks ball cap up, then down. "Not sure if that's good or bad."

I shrug. "Bad I guess. But, whatever."

The woman looks me over and it's like being naked under a microscope. Like she's trying to figure out what I'm made of at a cellular level or something.

Then the woman turns her attention to Deuces and the other anklet boy, whose name is James. "James. You and Matt can make the small hooks today since you know what you're doing. Kid," she addresses Deuces. "Why the hell did you wear those bright new shoes on Cabinetworks day? I don't want your attitude. Tell Mac that Greer sent you back over into wood shop."

"They're boss, boss." He wiggles his foot at her. "But I'm cool with wood shop."

I suspect he wore them to get out of whatever it is I'm about to get stuck doing.

"Just go." She glares and points in the direction we came from, but I can tell she's not really mad at him. He has that effect on people.

Deuces high-fives me on his way out. "See you later, lady lover."

I flinch out of habit. You never know how people are going to react to the gay thing, but Deuces seems to have no qualms about outing me whenever he gets a chance.

The woman, Greer, seems unconcerned by Deuces's jab. "You. It's Jess, right?"

"Yes, ma'am." I straighten up. If there's one thing my mother has pounded into my head, it's the old-timey Southern value of ma'ams and sirs upon first meeting someone more than a decade your elder. My cousins in Texas laugh their asses off every time I say it to my grandfather, but he always grins and pats me on the knee, so I don't stop.

Greer scratches at her pulled-back hair. "Though I appreciate the courtesy, if you call me ma'am again I'm going to put your pretty head on the anvil and have a go at it. Just Greer. Hartman if you need a last name."

"Uh, okay." Then, "Greer." The other thing I've learned is some people get pretty touchy about it.

"Follow me. I'm going to teach you some basics of the forge today. Let you get the feel for it, see if you can do it, and then we'll go from there. Ever worked in a forge before?"

"No, ma . . . Greer."

She sighs like this is the worst news she's had today.

But then she seems to get over it and smiles. "I hadn't either when I was your age, but I like it. It's good work."

"What do you make here?" I look around. It's gritty yet organized. Tools in neat lines. Anvils mounted on massive tree stumps. Fires going under metal vents.

"Hooks for coatracks and hall stands. Door pulls for cabinets. Part of the business's marketing is the whole 'all parts made in America' thing. Pretty damned expensive stuff, but then, we do have free high school labor." At this Greer winks and throws me a leather apron and a pair of gloves to match hers. "Put those on. I'll walk you through making a coat hook."

She shows me to a rack with a bunch of pieces of metal on it. "Steel, eight-inch piece of three-sixteenth round." She holds up a rod. "Tongs." She grabs these oversized tweezer things, grips the metal rod with them, then hands them both to me. She leads me and my extended arm over to one of the fires. "Let that rod heat up till it's red-hot."

The fire is sweltering and sweat beads at my hairline.

"What'd you do to land in the clink with McGovern?" Greer moves my arm so the metal I'm holding lies deeper in the coals.

"Fights." For some reason, I feel the need to explain myself fully. "I, um, lost my girlfriend."

"Breakups suck, kid, but not worth fighting about."

Greer motions for me to move the red-hot piece of metal over to an anvil, then hands me a massive hammer.

I lift the heavy tool, its weight grounding my arm.

"Put it on the edge here, now hammer so that top bit is flat." Greer points to the red tip of the piece of steel. "Whack the heck out of it. I want you to see how soft it's gotten."

"The fight wasn't over a breakup." I'm not sure why it feels important to correct Greer, maybe because I don't want her judging me like I'm just another wrong-track kid. "She died." The words leave my mouth as the hammer falls onto the searing tip. The metal moves like butter under the weight of it. It seems impossible for something so solid to move so fast. Impossibly fast. Like how Vivi died.

"Oh." Greer's mouth hangs open, as if she's unsure what to say next. I hold the hammer in the air. Then— "Sorry, kid. Hit it again."

I hit it. And hit it again. And a fourth time. It feels surprisingly good.

"Not bad. Now we reheat and repeat."

The boys are hammering on an anvil across the concrete pad but I stay focused in the circle of forge, Greer, anvil, hammer, forge. The red glow of the iron mesmerizes, then amazes as it becomes malleable.

"You're handy."

I swipe at a bit of bangs that threaten to get in my eye. "Handy?"

"Yes. You have a knack. You listen to the metal. You sure you haven't done this before?"

I shake my head but swell up inside. Then tamp it down. Nothing should feel good. Not even compliments.

"Sucks to be stuck in alternative school. Hard to get a leg up that way. But I'll tell McGovern I want you on the forge from now on if it suits you. It's hard to keep rotating these guys every week. They forget how to work the metal between shifts. Besides, it'd be nice to have female energy around. It's testosterone heavy here at Cabinetworks and I could use some solidarity."

"Yeah, sure." Then because I want her to understand I plan on doing my time and escaping McGovern, "I'm only here for a few weeks, so it's probably not worth it for you."

"Well, that's a drag. But leave the decision of what's worthwhile up to me. Or at least let me have my little fantasy of teaching another woman a male-dominated trade. Who knows, a few more weeks of whacking iron and you may be begging me for an apprenticeship."

I smile, and surprise myself by thinking she could be right. Something about the power over what, at first glance, seemed so immovable. When I was hammering, I wasn't thinking about anything other than the fluidity of my movement. It's like time stood still and every memory, every spiraling thought, simply disappeared. It's exactly what I need. A short circuit for grief. A channel for my rage.

19

Now: Two Weeks, Three Days After

The rightness of working the forge has drained out of me the further I've gotten from it. It was a fluke and with a week down on my ISS sentence, how many times will I actually even get to go to Cabinetworks? Loneliness drives me to think about Cheyanne. I poked the worst bear of all by teasing her about Levi and I should know better. But I guess that was the point of it. Find the thing to piss her off bad enough she'd leave me alone. It's the only place that makes sense to me. Alone. Miserable. Or at least not hanging out with people who are going to want to go deep into Vivi dying.

I'd rather lie in bed and keep taking tiny puffs of this joint Levon gave me on the sly. "My bro is starting a business," he'd said as we walked out of school. It's good and the mellow buzz is already spreading through my body but it doesn't block the bell ringing out a warning song. "Jess, you've been drinking a lot of booze since Vivi's gone. Jess, you're not into weed, remember." But my stupid period started and I have cramps and it's this or ibuprofen and at least this is natural. That's my justification anyway.

I scroll through the music on my phone but everything reminds me of Vivi. Nina and Mom are both at work. I have no homework. It's torture Emma Watson or find something to do. I can't text Vivi. I'm choosing not to text Cheyanne.

On a whim, I text Levi. He's a stoic guy and will respect my not wanting to talk about the deep issues. Besides, miserable, alone, and stoned seem like a pretty awful combination.

—What's up?

I hold the phone until it's obvious I'm not getting an immediate reply, then I get up and go rummage in the bathroom. I find an unopened jar of hair sculpting wax and twist it onto little strands of hair until I look like a hedgehog. Or maybe a brunette Bowie. I look pretty badass when I'm done. I find a tube of bloodred lipstick and finish off the look. I purse my lips and vamp through hooded eyelids and laugh at myself before rubbing off the lipstick. I leave the hair though. It's cool. Then I hear my text chime.

—Jess? You okay?

—I'm so bored. Let's go do something. Unless you're with Cheyanne.

—Like what? What do you mean about Cheyanne—she's not here.

—Forget I said that. Some guys from my new class were telling me about this community center they're going to be hanging out at. On your side of the tracks. I can find cash for booze if you want to go with me.

—Yeah. Okay. I'll see you in twenty at the tracks.

Levi may look like a straight arrow but he's just as up for anything to relieve his boredom as the rest of us. We've never hung out, just the two of us, but then I've never been without Vivi since Cheyanne brought him into our world.

I scrawl a hurried note to Mom and filch ten dollars from the cash envelope at the back of the silverware drawer. It's wrong, but I never needed much spending money with Vivi. She had a car and she'd take me anywhere. She had French grandparents who sent her cash and her parents were ultra-generous with us. At first it felt weird, letting her always pay, but over time we were such a couple it felt like ours not hers. So I'd never gotten a part-time job like Nina had at my age. But now, with my mom's hard-earned dollars in my pocket without her knowledge, I think I might need to remedy that.

I throw a hoodie over my flannel, tee, and jeans. I grab the forest green Docs that are my worn-in, favorite thrift gift from Vivi and then pause. Why is it like this? Why does every little thing stop me and threaten to break me down? I put the boots back in my closet where they don't threaten my emotions. Then I grab them again. It's stupid to attach feelings to objects. I tell myself they're only shoes, push my feet into them, and head out the door.

I bump my bike across the tracks to where Levi is waiting. Maybe a job wouldn't be the worst thing in the world. A car would be nice. But for now, my old Diamondback will have to do.

"Hey." He lifts a hand in greeting. "Glad you called."

"Yeah. Needed out of the house." Out of my head.

Levi stares at me.

"What?"

He lifts a hand to his head, then drops it, and I remember the Bowie look. "Oh, yeah, I was messing around out of boredom. Working a look."

"Wish mine would do that."

"Please. Come on." I jump back onto my bike and take off, Levi following. We skirt neighborhoods much like mine—small redbrick ranch houses with single-car carports, the occasional chain-link fence with ballistic dog behind it. We climb a hill and the pump of pedals burns my thigh muscles in a way that makes me feel useful and alive.

Finally, we end up at a squat cinder block building, a single light bulb over the door, a few scattered cars in the gravel-covered parking lot.

"Is this the place?" Levi asks. There's no sign on the street or above the door.

I look at the GPS on my phone. "Siri says yes."

We push through the metal door and faces look up. Mostly guys, a couple of girls.

"Wassup, kids?" Deuces prowls over and claps us on the back. He's strong with aftershave. "The hooch is out back with my man, Charles. Can't bring it inside. Come on."

He leads us through a tight hallway, lined with posters about upcoming community action meetings and a couple of people waiting on restrooms, to a small covered back patio. Charles, a guy I recognize from the regular campus, is holding court at a picnic table. Two girls, one with big boobs, one with braids, flank him.

Deuces points at us. "These two are with me. Hook them up."

Charles looks us over and I swear I can hear his mind scoffing about who let in the white dude and the dyke but

I just look back, needing the shot he's about to pour.

He tilts one of those industrial-sized thermoses and pours brown liquid into cups for the two of us, himself, and the two girls by his side. We lift our cups. "To getting turnt!" Deuces laughs and watches us get ready to slam our shots.

"You're not having one?" Levi asks.

Deuces points at his ankle. "Two more weeks. There's nothing going to get in the way of me getting this bad boy off."

I admire his dedication but all I want is the burn and the numb that will follow. It goes down hard. "Fuck." I was not expecting the smack of cinnamon and raw burn of whiskey. "That's good." I hold out my cup again. Four shots in and a soft, liquid heat settles over the mellow of my earlier high. The tension in my face leaves and I lean against Levi's mass. He drapes an arm over my shoulder.

"Feeling it, kid?"

"In the best way. Let's play some pool."

Somebody starts whistling across the room and I close my eyes tight for a second. Remembering not to remember. I can barely feel the lake anymore. Can't hear the whisper of birdsong or see the porcelain dish slipping from my hands to be swallowed by the murky blue-gray water.

I push any lingering sadness from Saturday out to the furthest reaches of my mind.

Deuces leads the way again and we get lucky. A game is breaking up at the back of the room. "Come on, we've got a table." He racks the balls and calls over another guy to play with us. "This is Monte."

Monte flips a coin and I call "tails" but it lands on heads and Deuces takes the break. He pockets a striped ball.

"Solid," Levi says. "That's us."

Solid. That's you, I think. The flare of annoyance rises again at Cheyanne. Or is it at myself for being such an ass to someone who was only trying to help?

Three balls in for Monte and Deuces and they finally miss a shot. Levi nods for me to shoot first. I line up the cue ball with the red solid and make the corner pocket. "Nice." Levi lifts a high five.

"You two boyfriend and girlfriend, or what?" Monte's scooted back onto a stool and is checking me out as he asks the question.

Deuces laughs. "No man, that girl likes girls, like us." Only Deuces can get away with sticking his tongue out and wiggling it for effect. The last guy that did that I just about clocked.

"I like girls." Monte's face screws up. "But that shit's nasty. The only going down happening is on me."

With the confidence of Vivi by my side, I'd have launched into a righteous debate about how you have to give to get in relationships.

Then he coughs in Deuce's direction. "And bro, if you're using your tongue, it ain't on no puss. You're all about the dick. However it's cloaked."

Deuces stiffens and I'm kind of taken by surprise, but when he only responds with a shake of his head, I keep my mouth shut and line up the next ball. I figure Deuces will tell me what I need to know and I damn sure don't want this dude ruining my sweet buzz.

But Monte's not done with me. He hops off the stool and comes to stand by my side. Too close. "So for real, you get it with the ladies? How do you hit it? You have a secret weapon?" He edges closer so that my elbow can't even move to line up the stick for my next shot.

"Get off me."

Levi adds a weak, "Yeah, man, leave her be."

"Naw, man. I want to know. Are you packing?" Then the asshole reaches his hand right up between my legs from behind and squeezes to see for himself if I have the fruit.

I. Am. Done. The building tension of the week busts through my control. I swing the pool stick back to the right, colliding with Monte's chest. Then I push against it and shove him back across the room and I hear words coming out of my mouth, obscenities, slurs, whatever my flip-switched mind grabs until I feel hands on my upper arms pulling me back. Deuces pulls Monte back. Somebody's yelling to get that crazy-ass bitch out of here.

And then me and Levi are outside by our bikes and I'm breathing hard and he's breathing hard and then he starts laughing. "Girl." He shakes his head. "Let's get out of here before we get our asses kicked."

"I want to break shit again."

We pedal off into the night, the sounds of the community center party fading away, leaving me with the circling thought of *I can't believe that guy fucking did that. I can't fucking believe I did that.*

Once we stop at the same store for the cheapest bottle of vodka and two jumbo Slurpees—mixed, bottle tossed, right there in the parking lot—Levi leads the way on his bike out past the tracks, past the junkyard of the other night, to vestiges of what must have once been an old farm. There are "No Trespassing" signs and a single strand of barbed wire surrounding the field, but he motions for me to follow him.

"Are you sure?"

"Yeah. This is my papaw's old place."

Levi, on occasion, lets his Southern roots show. And

we're far enough out on the edge of town that a few of these old places still exist, just waiting for the right stack of bills from the right developer.

"Your papaw?" I grin as I finally suck down a big draw of Cherry Coke and vodka Slurpee. "Seriously, you call him that?"

"Shut up. Are you coming, or what?" He unhooks the wire and lifts it so we can get our bikes underneath. We walk them across the field toward the old house and barn at the far edge. The windows are boarded up and there are more signs affixed to the structures. Levi heads toward the barn and puts his bike inside. He pulls out a bat and a ball and a glove. "I know you wanted to break shit, but maybe we can pitch a few to each other?"

I shrug and lean my bike next to his. "Yeah, sure, why not." There's a security light on the far side of the house that gives us just enough visibility to see each other out in the field.

We step apart and I pitch first. Levi cracks it out toward what would be right field and I have to run for the ball. I jog back, breathing harder than usual. "Dude, you're going to kill my buzz."

"I'll bunt from now on, I promise."

"Why don't we just toss the ball?"

"Fine." Levi puts down the bat and we stand a few

yards apart tossing the baseball back and forth. He speaks first. "I miss her, you know. Vivi."

"Don't. Please."

Levi nods. We throw the ball for another ten minutes in silence.

"I'm never going to get anywhere with Cheyanne, am I?"

"For a smart guy, you learn slow. No, probably not the way you want. Cheyanne is not into relationships beyond friendship. My observation."

Levi sighs. "Yeah. I figured. Come on." He motions for me to follow him and walks over to sit on the back steps of the old house. We sit in silence, sipping on our drinks. A rabbit runs up my spine and Levi scooches closer. "For warmth," he says. "Man, I wish I had a car. And a way out of my house."

I groan. "Oh my god. Same. Well, my mom's all right, but my sister drives me crazy. We both need to get out of there. Mom's still young. She should be dating."

"What's with the hair?" Levi turns his head toward me and I notice how pretty his eyes are. Bright blue with thick long lashes.

"I don't know. Can't a girl like me fix her hair? Maybe I wanted to look pretty." I make a crazy face and stick my tongue out.

Levi laughs. "You're always pretty, Jess."

"Oh, really. Why haven't you tried to kiss me? Isn't that what happens when a boy thinks a girl is pretty?" I'm totally messing with him, but also maybe not. I mean, yes, I am messing with him, but there's a part of my brain that's looking for any sort of distraction, even if it means turning down a one-way street in the wrong direction.

"What?" Levi moves away from me slightly.

"I'm serious. I've never kissed a boy. It's dark out, we're drinking. If you were into me, wouldn't that happen?"

"Um, no, because I know you're gay."

I look at the waning moon. "Yeah, probably. But how do I know if I've never tried the other side." This is a line straight out of Nina's playbook when she spent all my seventh-grade year questioning me and I spent all my time being pissed off at her. But my mouth is talking without much input from my brain apparently.

Levi shrugs and he's so red I can see it even in the moonlight. "I mean, I could if you want. But, I, uh, haven't kissed that many girls so I might not make a good impression."

The alarm dings on my phone. A warning that we better go if we're going to get back before my mom starts freaking out. I suck up the last of my Slurpee before answering. "I'm sure you're a natural, Levi." Then I lean over and kiss him on the cheek for fun. "Come on, I've got to get home."

I walk across the field to the barn on unsteady legs. Levi shuffles up beside me.

"You were joking, right?" he asks.

"One hundred percent." The only person I want to kiss is gone, gone, gone.

20

THEN: Brown-Eyed Birds

"I can't believe that's all the homework you have." Cheyanne rolled her eyes. "I want this to be over so I can be gone far away from Grady High School. At least until after winter break." Cheyanne and Vivi's textbooks were strewn across the table in preparation for first semester exams.

"There are some advantages to not being an honors student, oh wise ones." I grabbed a handful of popcorn and halfheartedly turned the pages of my history book.

Vivi smacked the top of my hand with her pen. "That doesn't mean you can't study. You still have to get your GPA up if you're going to get into State." That was Vivi's newest thing. Since my wood duck ink drawing had made it into the finals of the contest, she was convinced I could get into some fancy graphics program at NC State. Mostly because that's where she planned to go. It made me smile, because it meant Vivi saw us staying together all the way through high school. I was 100 percent okay with that.

I groaned for effect, though. "Both of you, total overachievers. We're not even done with sophomore year yet."

"Details. Simply details." Cheyanne started slamming her books shut.

"Where are you going?"

"My hair is not like this on a whim." Cheyanne had her sleek hair twisted into an elaborate series of spiral braids worthy of Cinderella's ball.

"Oooh, do tell," Vivi said.

I crossed my arms and rocked back in my tall kitchen chair. "It's not like that, Vivi. She's probably got to go to her brother's violin recital."

Cheyanne narrowed her eyes at me. "I'll have you know, it is like that."

I uncrossed my arms and kicked my chair down so all four of its feet were on the ground again. "It is?" I had to admit I was surprised.

"Well not *like that*, like that. It's simply an outing, but I wanted to look nice."

Vivi clasped her hands to her cheeks and leaned forward on her elbows. "Spill."

"Okay." Cheyanne organized her books into her backpack. "Remember how I told you that Mr. Lunesto recruited some band kids to join the orchestra class?"

We nodded.

"Well, there's this guy. He plays string bass, too. I agreed to go to a jazz concert with him."

"More," Vivi said.

Cheyanne tugged the zipper shut. "His name's Levi. He's actually a really good musician. Said his grandmother was a nightclub singer and played the piano. Anyway, he's cool and sort of shy and I said okay because it's a band I'd like to hear and there's no way my parents would let me go alone."

"You have a date?" I was shocked.

"No. We're going as friends. That's it."

Vivi pointed at Cheyanne's hair. "That's a date do."

"I knew I shouldn't have told the two of you. Even my closest friends just do not get it sometimes. Can I not go out for a night of music with a fellow music-lover and have that be all it is? Why does the world feel the need to pigeonhole me into some age-old stereotype of girl meets boy, or girl, then it's all Cheyanne and whomever with a baby carriage?"

Vivi leaned against me and grinned at Cheyanne. "Our little Chey has a date."

Cheyanne hoisted the massive bag on her shoulder. "It is NOT a date."

"Uh-huh." I winked to let her know I was only kidding around.

Cheyanne walked to the front door.

Vivi called after her. "You know we're teasing you. Enjoy the music."

All we got was a raised middle finger as Cheyanne walked out. We watched her leave through the window. Lucky girl had gotten a car for her sixteenth birthday. Not a new car, but it had four wheels and gave her freedom. She got in it and started to back out.

I turned to Vivi. "Have you . . . ?" I'd never asked her this. Fear of the answer, maybe?

"Have I what?" Vivi chewed her pencil in a distracted sort of way as she returned to staring at her American history book.

"Wanted to date a guy." It was stupid, but I got nervous waiting for her answer.

Vivi looked up and smiled. "Well, first. I have a girlfriend. And we are in love. And I don't plan on ever leaving her. But, if I were in an alternate world where I hadn't fallen head over heels for you, I might consider it."

"What?" I acted shocked, but wasn't really. Vivi was one of those bighearted, open-minded kind of people and if Vivi had to classify herself, I felt pretty sure she'd say it was all about the person, not the gender.

"Alternate world, not this one. What about you?"

"Please." I scoffed. "Never."

Vivi sat up at that. "Really. You're so absolutely sure? You're not at all curious."

"About dating a guy?"

"Yes." Vivi tapped her pen against my hand. "Come on. For serious. You've never once thought about what it would be like to be with a guy?"

"I think it'd be gross is what I think. I cried when my mom told me how babies were made. Told her I NEVER wanted that to happen to me. Are YOU curious about being with a guy?"

Vivi huffed out a breath. "Stop. I see you getting your feathers ruffled. We are having a theoretical conversation, not a planning meeting."

"Are you sure?"

She shut me up with a kiss. "I'm sure. Besides . . ." She winked. "They make substitutes for you to satisfy my curiosity."

That really shut me up.

It'd be weird though if I didn't wonder about the whole male-to-female mechanics. Maybe not curiosity about the physical part, but the societally accepted part. My mom, though totally cool with Vivi, worried about my lack of a father figure. She had mother guilt that my life would somehow be more difficult because of my sexuality. Nina complained that because I was gay she didn't get the full sister package, there would always be some woman that mattered more to me than her. And then society, for as much as things had progressed over the years, there were still plenty of people who only saw the word *sinner* stamped on my forehead. It would be so much easier if I could like guys.

Vivi pointed to the dogwood tree in the front yard. "See those dark-eyed juncos?"

Beady-eyed petite brown birds hopped around the branches, a constant flow of landing and leaving.

"Yes."

"They have a very strict social hierarchy. But as humans we have choices. Why would you want to limit yourself with labels? Say something happened to me and the next right person was male, not female, or even someone fluid, you'd limit yourself because of gender?"

I thought about it, but knew the answer. I'd never feel for guys the way I felt for girls. Just like Cheyanne would probably never want the romantic kind of relationship most people expected her to have.

"Yeah, I think I would. I mean, if I wanted a relationship

like this." I pulled Vivi's chair closer to mine and put my mouth on the side of her jawline and kissed the smooth skin covered in the finest mist of down.

Vivi's smile arced into my touch as I kissed up the side of her cheek and worked my mouth slowly to her lips. I brought my hands to Vivi's sides and pulled her closer. Kissing Vivi was like breathing. Necessary and life-giving. "You see," I said as Vivi softened against me, "I'm a girl's girl."

"Lucky me" had been Vivi's answer.

21

Now: Two Weeks, Four Days After

"Lucky me," I whisper under my breath as I walk into McGovern's room and try to ignore my hangover and the memory of the asshole at the community center. Chuck Norris greets me with a stare and an asinine comment. "When Chuck Norris crosses the street, cars look both ways." I plop my bag down on the desk behind Deuces and slide into the seat. "Hey, man."

I get an icy breeze in return.

"What's wrong with you?"

He twists in his seat. "I told you there was nothing I was going to do to jeopardize getting this cuff off"—he points at his ankle monitor—"and you had to go and pick a fight at my pool table? Monte was pissed, getting in my face, threatening to call my probation officer because I invited you to come hang at the hall. You emasculated him. You're lucky he didn't pull a knife on your skinny ass."

"God, don't be such a wad." The anger volcano flashes in my head but I hose it down. I shouldn't have done anything to put him at risk. Though that guy *did* grope me. What was I supposed to do, just let it go? If Deuces isn't going to speak to my right to defend myself, I'm not going to sit by him and help with his English homework. I grab my bag and move over by Levon.

"Sup, milkshake."

"I'm human not liquid."

Levon grins. "You're tight. I like you. How was the J I gave you? Good."

"Yeah."

"You're going back to the big school, right? You want to go into business with me and my brother? We could use a girl on the inside. Easy to hide stuff inside a makeup bag. Hook people up on the sly."

I'm about to circle my face with my hand and explain that this girl doesn't carry a makeup bag when McGovern slams through the door, a huge Circle K Styrofoam cup in one hand, a bear claw in the other, and his tattered marine corps carry bag over his shoulder. "Fucking fine day, miscreants, now shut the hell up so I can take roll."

Levon's still waiting on my answer. "What do you say? Are you in?"

I definitely need a job, but with a mom studying to be a lawyer, something legal is way more in my wheelhouse. But then I wonder, did I manifest this opportunity?

"I'll think about it," I say. "Still three more weeks to go before I make my escape."

"Don't think too long, opportunities like this don't come along every day. The pay's sick. Easy money."

"Perez." McGovern's voice booms and I snap my head up, worried he's caught wind of what we're talking about, but he's just checking our names off on his computer.

"Here," I reply.

"Tell you what," Levon's whispering again. "I got a sample package fixed up for you in my bag. You take it for free. Don't sell them for less than ten dollars, anything you make above that, you keep. See how long it takes you, then decide. Bet you can make fifty dollars in an hour or less."

This time when McGovern yells my name, he's pissed. "Perez, you said you were going to be no trouble. You're not doing much for your cause. Shut it. Do that work your teachers sent over. Now."

"Yes, sir." I walk over to the folder that's been deposited in the slot with my name on it and grab the packet of worksheets and review quizzes that have been sent over from the school. "I'm on it."

Becoming a drug dealer on a Thursday is perhaps one of the stupider decisions I could make in my short time here on the planet, but I could use some cash. If McGovern wants to lump me in with these guys, I might as well do something to get lumped. Except Deuces is a prime example of why I shouldn't even think about it. Not to mention how Vivi would probably bring a flock of ass-whooping angels down to whip me into shape. When I slip back into my desk, I lean forward. "Thanks, man, but I'm going to pass."

Levon scowls, then shrugs and goes back to the math worksheet he's pretending to attempt.

That afternoon, when I leave the building and turn on my phone—totally not worth it to risk cell phones with McGovern and Chuck Norris staring me down—there's a text from Cheyanne.

—I thought you might want to know that deadlines are approaching for some schools.

I have a choice. I could text her back, say I'm sorry, get on with it. Be back to the Jess who was Vivi's girl, Cheyanne's best friend, and loving daughter to Ellie, sister to Nina. But I hate the world right now. I hate it so hard I wish I could be a supervillain and burst random cars into flames. Cars with entire families. Moms. Dads. Little children. Even the family dog. The world forgets to wash its hands. The world forgets there are people out there with asthma, who might touch the same doorknob, and then die, all because you didn't wash your damn hands. And for some reason, Cheyanne with her "I'm grieving, too" and her "Vivi would want this" and her "Let's get on with the business of getting Jess over it" is the last person I want to be around.

No. If I text her back I'm liable to push her so hard and so far, I'll never hear from her again. I'm smart enough, and have had enough therapy, to realize that would be a mistake. I need to wait until I've made sense of myself. If she's really my friend, one day she'll understand. And forgive me for being such a dick.

My phone buzzes and I'm about to turn it off but it's my mom.

—Don't ride the bus. I'm picking you up.

Immediate guilt sets in. I got home on time last night, and she'd stayed in her room when I'd yelled to announce my presence, so there's no way she knows I was drinking again—and on a school night. But the guilt is there anyway. I know I'm messing up in a hundred little ways. Every minor step on this post-Vivi path is taking me deeper into some dark spiral, but I don't want to stop. If I have to feel,

I want it to burn me from the inside out, not drown me with suffering. I think about Nina's concerns. I'm not that girl, am I?

I text back, Ok

She shows up ten minutes later, looking sharp in her black linen pantsuit.

"Hey." I throw my bag in the back and climb into the front seat, buckling before she pulls away from the curb. "Shouldn't you still be at work?"

"They let me leave early for this."

"This?" My suspicion rises.

"Jess, you can't get in fights, get suspended, and expect no action on my part. If you don't want Samantha to help us find another therapist, fine, but I think a grief group would be good for you."

"Mom." I reach for my seat belt like I'm going to get out.

She hits the safety lock button and glares in my direction. "It's a group, Jess. At the VA. It's for kids who've lost their parents. I know you feel like you worked through losing your dad, but losing Vivi has to bring it back up, and maybe you can help some of these younger kids, and have a moment to breathe through your current situation. Please. Give it a chance."

It's not like I have a choice unless I jump out and run

at the next traffic light but she's already put a stop to that. Besides, she might have a point.

"You're the boss."

Mom looks at me and I can tell she wants something more but I slump in my seat and stare out the window. My life has gotten so fucked in such an impossibly short span of time. The flare of anger burns again and this time I'm mentally bursting Vivi into flames. Her dying was never part of our plan. Why did she have to die? What was she thinking?

I carry my anger with me down the overbright hall of the VA, into the double doors of the recreation room where the grief group is being held. Then it deflates. These are little kids. Seven, eight, nine maybe. They're squirming in their chairs or curled into the beanbags placed every so often in a wide circle. The therapist is a guy in his forties or so and he looks a little bit like how I imagine my dad might look now. How's that for a mind fuck?

"You must be Jess."

"Yeah."

"I'm Ben Alvarez. Everyone here calls me Mr. A."

"Whatever you want."

His smile straightens slightly at my tone, but it's the uncontrollable asshole force inside of me taking over. I can't turn it off.

"Just have a seat anywhere you'd like."

There's a little girl with short hair, bright red Skechers, and her arms crossed tight across her chest. I go sit in the chair next to her. "Hey," I say.

She shrugs and crosses her arms tighter.

"I'm Jess."

She shifts away from me.

"Okay, gang. Let's do a little warm-up activity so we can meet the new people today." Mr. A grabs a chair and turns it around so he's sitting with his arms resting on the back of it, his legs straddled to either side. "I'd like you to say your first name, and who you're grieving. For example, I'm Mr. A and I'm grieving my granddad."

He goes around the room and when he gets to me I get stuck. What do I say? Do I say my dad, or Vivi, or both? He waits and all the little kids look at me or don't, but I can tell they're all listening. I'm the oldest one here besides the therapist and they're curious about me, I'm sure.

"Um. I'm Jess. And I was grieving my dad, but now I'm grieving my, uh, um . . ." I decide to just say it. "My girlfriend, Vivi." My voice chokes on the last word and the little girl next to me uncurls and hands me the rock she has hidden in her hand.

"Hold this," she whispers. "It helps."

I take it and nod. Then she says, "I'm Darla and I'm

grieving my dad, too." She looks at my hands as I roll her rock in my palm, so I hand it back to her with a thank-you.

"See," she says.

"You're right."

She doesn't curl back up.

When the circle finishes with introductions, Mr. A asks us to stand up from our chairs and stretch to the sky, then stretch to the ground, then he has us stretch our fingertips into the center of the circle. "You feel that energy shooting out of your fingers? I think it's strong enough that those we are grieving can feel it, too." Twenty tiny hands wiggle their fingers with all their might.

He asks us to sit again and then requests volunteers, popcorn style. "If you have a picture you brought, or a memory you'd like to share, this is a good time. Remember, if someone else raises their hand to share before you, let's give them the chance to speak."

A little boy across the room holds up a framed military photo of his mom. "This is my mommy. She's not coming home." His hands tremble and his shoulders shake and my heart pounds. I want to hug him and tell him it will all be okay, but I know it's not true. He sits down abruptly, hugging the photograph to his body.

Mr. A puts a calming hand on his shoulder. "It's okay, Justin. This is a safe space to cry." Then to the rest of us,

"Raise your hand if you cried this week." All hands in the room go up. Justin lets the tears he was holding in his shoulders spill out onto his cheeks. Little sobs can be heard all around me. It is killing me.

A few more kids share stories. A girl named Destiny talks about a fishing trip to the Outer Banks and how her big brother taught her how to put a worm on a hook. A boy named Tyler shows us a toy truck in his bag that had been his granddaddy's first, then his dad's, now his.

I raise my hand.

"Jess." Mr. A nods for me to go ahead.

"Um, my dad died when I was closer to your age. He would hold me high up in the air to put the angel on the top of our Christmas tree. That's my favorite memory." I don't talk about Vivi, it's too fresh. But nobody asks me to either.

Mr. A, once satisfied no one else is going to share, pulls out a box of lap desks and paper, along with various supplies. "Everybody get a desk and paper and the drawing tools of your choice. Today we're going to create a picture of what we think the ones who are missing from our lives are doing right now."

The kids get up and grab what they need. I hesitate. The Sakura drawing pens haven't been out of my bag since the afternoon on the lake. But Darla is watching me expectantly to see if I'm going to grab markers, too. She's even brought me a piece of paper and a lap desk. My hands fidget with my zipper but I can't do it. If I draw, all of this sorrow is going to leak onto the page and I can't. I can't. I can't.

"I'm, uh, I've got to go." I grab my bag and run out of the room and into the ladies' bathroom. I stare at myself in the mirror and splash water on my face. My heart is beating out of my chest and it's taking every muscle I have to keep from breaking down. When I walk out, Mr. A is waiting for me.

"Are you okay?"

I cling to my backpack. "Yeah, fine. But I don't want to draw. I don't want to do this." Part of me wants to tell him the truth, that drawing, creating, is Vivi, is me, is life, is death, is everything all rolled away like a rock over a crevice. I'm not ready to let go of her yet. And if I start to find a way to live, to work on the work of moving on, she might truly disappear. Making art, even if it's stick drawings with little kids, is too close to allowing myself something good.

"You don't want to work with me and the kids?"

"I don't mind working with the kids. But I won't draw."

"That's fine. You don't have to draw. You can help the

others and wander around the room, let them tell you their stories."

I realize he's got some backdoor counseling going on with me, but I don't feel like a confrontation. I can commit, then back out later. "Yeah, next week. I'll do it next week."

"Here." Mr. A holds out his hand—cradled in it is Darla's rock. "She wanted you to have this. Said you might need it until next week."

Wow. I'm more messed up than the littles.

"Okay, yeah. Tell her thanks."

"Thursday?"

I stare at Darla's rock. He said I don't have to draw.

"Next week," I repeat. "Thursday."

"Good, see you then." He turns and leaves and doesn't insist I return because he knows the rock will bring me back. I find a chair in the lobby and curl up until I see Mom's car pull to the curb to take me home.

22

Now: Two Weeks, Five Days After

Friday afternoon, I stand at the forge, sweat dripping down my brow, feeling free. There's no room for misery when you're handling red-hot iron. The hammering is also a surprisingly effective way to work out any anger languishing in my cells. Death. Bam. Grief. Bam. Sorrow. Bam.

I feel Greer's approval as I bend the rod and put it in the vise, twisting the hot iron for the decorative part. Me and this coat hook thing are kind of natural. I stick the piece of iron back into the coal fire to heat the tip where the nail hole goes. Greer works by my side. The boys are across the room. I glance in her direction. "Remember what you said about me maybe liking this?"

She smiles. "Was I right?"

"Yeah. You were." I readjust my tongs to center the hook over the heat. "I never thought I'd do something like this in my life. I mean, I never even really knew it was a thing."

"It's a thing. And it's more than this and horseshoeing."

"It is?"

Greer motions for me to remove the hook from the flame and I do, moving it to the anvil where she uses an awl to punch a hole in the red-hot metal. When I quench it, she takes off her gloves.

"You know, I've been thinking, Jess. You said you were only with McGovern for a few more weeks. Which is good for you. But if you're really into this, I'd love to teach you the trade. That is if you're interested."

"Really?" My mind races. Then stalls. Because my first thought is I can't wait to tell Vivi about this.

"Yeah." She glances toward the boys and lowers her voice. "Look, it's not that I don't think all of McGovern's kids deserve a chance to learn a trade that can actually lead to a career. That's why I work with anybody he sends me, even if it's a pain to retrain some of them over and over. But you're the first girl who's ever landed here since they started the program. I've talked to my wife about how fulfilling it would be to train a female student."

I cut my eyes up quickly. So, Greer is gay, too. And married.

"If it's okay with your mom, you should come out to our house sometime. I've got my own forge set up in the back and I make stuff there. You could see how this works for something other than endless furniture hardware."

A rapid slice of excitement surges through me. Working with Greer, going to the VA, these are things that might help me get through the days. It's something my mom reminded me of. To get through the days one by one and eventually they'd get easier. If I can get through enough days, I might figure out how to be a person who can cope, without intentionally pushing her feelings, or her best friend, away. "Yeah, I'll ask her. Or you could. I can give you her number so you can talk to her. It'd probably be better that way. This whole thing"—I motion around the industrial site—"hasn't exactly put me in her good graces."

"Of course." Greer lifts her head and yells across the forge at Levon and James to throw some more coal onto their station. Then she turns back to me. "You've got a natural way with the metal. Have you thought about what you're going to do after high school?"

I look down before answering. Apparently, when you're

a senior in high school, having your shit together is what's expected. From everyone. I could give her the old story, that I'm applying for the graphic design program at State, but I don't. The deadline is in three weeks and there's no way I'll be ready.

"I haven't thought about much other than Vivi the last few weeks."

"Ah. Right. I can't even imagine. It must be incredibly painful." Greer puts a hand on my shoulder. "Come on, let's whack on some more iron rod, then when we take a break I'll show all of you some tech programs available here in our great state."

"In blacksmithing?"

"Some."

Inside I have a bit of a fight with myself. I'm supposed to be a hundred percent miserable, but the idea of continuing to blacksmith after Cabinetworks is over gives me a faint charge, despite myself.

When I leave school, I shove the pages I've printed about some of the programs into my backpack and turn on my phone. It lights up with texts. From Levi.

Hey. That's the first one.

Then.

—So, I'm guessing your phone is off or something?

Then.

—Do you want to hang out tonight? I was thinking we could maybe go bowling.

Then.

—As friends. Not a date, obviously.

I text the poor guy back to put him out of his misery.

—Yeah. Bowling sounds good. But nowhere close. I don't feel like running into kids from school.

The reply is lightning immediate.

—Sure. We can go down to Carolina Lanes. It's far. My dad's out on his big rig so I can use his regular truck tonight. Pick you up at 6?

I reply in the affirmative and climb on the bus. The only seat is next to Deuces. He shifts away from me when I sit down.

"Come on, man. How many times do I have to apologize?"

"More." Deuces talks to the window.

"I'm sorry. Okay? I know I put you in a spot, but your friend did grab my crotch."

"You didn't have to go all assault and battery on him. We could have dealt without me risking my parole."

"Yeah, I guess. But you didn't say anything either. You didn't tell him to stop. What if I were your sister or your cousin, would you have just stood there?"

"Of course not. But did you give me time to say anything before you started swinging your stick? I gave him my mind after you bolted. Told him it's shit to treat a lady that way."

"You did?"

"Just because I'm a parolee doesn't mean I'm low class. Of course I did."

I mutter, "Fine. Can we stop being mad at each other? You're my only bit of sanity in this hellhole."

Deuces lifts a closed fist and I dap his with my own. Then he hands me his phone. "Speaking of cousins."

There's a photo of one of the girls from the community center, braids not boobs. She looks like Zoë Kravitz. Pretty.

"Remember her?"

"Yeah."

"She wants your digits."

Though this would be the moment to make a completely inappropriate lesbian joke, I hold it inside. And feel a little sick. I'm not ready to give another girl my number. Even if she is gorgeous. "No, man. I can't do that. I don't know her."

"She's been driving me crazy. Won't let up talking some crap about you being such a stud and how she wants to start talking to you."

Gross. Now I definitely don't want to give her my number. But he hands me his phone with my name already in his contacts and points at his ankle monitor. "You owe me."

"I owe you nothing."

"True, but I'll be your BFF." He puts his hands up on either side of his cheeks and bats his eyelashes at me. It's so ridiculous, I cave.

"Fine." It hasn't even been three weeks since Vivi died. I could give Deuces the statistic I read about it taking at least a month for every year a couple has been together to get to a place of acceptance with the grief, but I figure he won't care. Or he'll feed me some bullshit about how the best way to get over someone is with a new someone. And I can't imagine being ready to date anybody new. Ever.

"Texting only."

"That's between y'all, but I'm sick of listening to her whine every afternoon."

I change the subject after I punch my number into his phone. Stupid it took a girl for me to do that. We should have gotten each other's numbers that first day at McGovern's. "So, was Monte telling the truth?"

"What truth?"

"That you're into dudes."

"It's not like that."

"Then what's it like?"

"I hook up with this hot girl in my neighborhood. Turns out she was born in the wrong body. You know, as a dude."

"She's trans?"

"Yeah."

I have to admit, I'm impressed. It's hard enough being homosexual in the South. Throw in gender issues and "the normals" lose their minds. Being straight and confidently dating a trans woman? That's hard-core self-confidence for a guy from a neighborhood like Deuces's.

"A few people have seen us out and I've been getting grief. I can tell you this because you don't care—I like her, but man, it's scary in my neighborhood to fly different."

"Scarier for her," I say.

"Yeah." He lowers his voice even further. "We talk all the time. I don't care what she's got going on. I'm chill with it. But we've got to watch ourselves around my neighborhood and keep it on the down-low."

I shrug. "I've never worried too much about what other people think. Figure living my truth and finding my happy place counts for way more than random opinions."

***

Turns out, those are words for me to prove. Levi picks me up and we go for pizza first—pepperoni, sausage, and green peppers—then head farther out to Carolina Lanes. It's a long way from home just like he promised, so when I go to switch my low tops out for the bowling shoes I always want to steal, I'm surprised to see this girl I sort of know from the Carolina Youth Pride events me and Vivi had gone to.

"Hey." The girl leans on the counter next to me. "I know you, right?"

"Uh, I think. Yeah. I'm Jess."

"You still dating that same girl?"

I do not want to open the can of worms that comes with telling a random person Vivi died. There are the sad eyes and the stricken face. Then the "Oh, I'm sorry, are you okay, what happened?" And my inevitable emotional reaction. So it feels wrong, but I shake my head. "No. Not anymore."

The girl looks at me a little more intensely. "No? Oh." Then she turns her body toward me.

Right then, Levi walks up. "Hey, got your shoes yet?" He leans on the counter, oblivious to the subtle scene playing out.

The girl looks past me to Levi, then back at me, and just as quick as she landed next to my counter space, she disappears. It gives me a weird feeling inside. Like she thinks I'm straight or something. I want to walk after her, grab her arm, tell her she's got the wrong idea. But Levi's bouncing in his shoes, talking smack about how he's going to break three hundred on the scoreboard, and I let it go.

Tonight, I'm here to bowl.

With my friend. Who happens to be a dude. Who told me I was pretty. Who reassured me this wasn't a date.

Why did he feel like he needed to say that?

23

THEN: Surrounded by Birds, a Pair of Binoculars in Your Hand

I wanted a date. A point in time that I could circle on the calendar with stars and hearts and exclamation points.

"What about our anniversary?" My hand, which was desperately trying to sneak beneath the drawstring waistband of Vivi's favorite cotton pajama bottoms, was being blocked at every entry point.

"Cliché," Vivi said. Then she grabbed my hand and pushed it away. "You're being sort of annoying."

"Fine." I opened my hand flat against the sweet curve of her stomach.

We shifted, lying nose to nose on the couch at the lake house, our legs twined like vines. Every part of me was alert with want. Our intimacy had grown over the past ten months, from subtle touches of hands, to sweet soft kisses, to kisses that felt like Vivi was engulfing my soul, kisses that burned and awakened parts of me and left me aching for so much more. Vivi, on the other hand, was not ready for anything below the panty line.

But, our one-year anniversary was coming up and I hoped that maybe, since it was such a monumental occasion, I could finagle some consent. "If that's cliché, then why not keep going right now? Your parents *are* gone for the day." I snugged Vivi closer so there was no space between us, and pressed the lower half of my body tight against her. Vivi let out the tiniest breathy cry.

I kissed her hard then, hoping she could feel the trueness of my love mixed in with the desire. I imagined my lips were hands, pressing and cupping and pulling back to the gentlest feather touch, then diving back, mouth to mouth, tongue to tongue. Vivi responded with her body, arching into me, gripping my hips and opening her mouth to take my wild need until she abruptly pulled away.

"Stop."

"Stop?" I wanted to cry. My lower extremities were on fire and it was all I could do not to stick my hand down my own damn pants and finish what I'd started.

Vivi scooted up on her elbow. "I don't want to risk

my parents coming home. I want it to be special. Okay, maybe cliché. I want a whole night. Time and space for it to unfold and be beautiful and if we're going to be together forever, why is there a rush?"

I spiked between hurt and remorse. "I'm sorry. I . . . It's just, you make me crazy. Your kisses carve tiny pieces of me and coat them in glitter or gold dust or that perfect organic raw sugar you love so much."

Vivi grinned. "Perhaps you should consider a career in poetry if the art thing doesn't pan out."

"Will it get me any further?"

Vivi's eyes darkened in a rapid flash.

I squeezed her hip. "I'm kidding, Vivi. Kidding. I'm okay with waiting."

"We're barely sixteen." She traced my lips with her finger. "What if we do go further? What if it messes up what we have? My parents aren't prudes but one of the things they both talk to me about is how sex changes things. That it both deepens the love, but can also create this whole other thing in the relationship to work through and around and with. We don't live together. We won't have parental consent. We said we didn't want to sneak around."

I traced the rim of Vivi's ear with my index finger. "You're right. We did say that. I agree."

"You do? Are you sure?" Vivi rolled the hem of my T-shirt between her fingers and kept her eyes focused there.

"I'm sure." I tugged her earlobe to get her to look at me. "But . . . maybe our second anniversary?"

Vivi cracked up. "Because we'll be total adults then."

"Come on." I hopped up and pulled Vivi with me. "Let's get the binoculars and go look at the kingfishers."

"Okay." She pulled me in for one more soft kiss. "Thank you. I know it's probably not rational, but . . ."

"Hey." I cupped her hands in mine. "You don't have to explain. You're beautiful. I love you. You're worth waiting for. Besides, do I look like the kind of girl who's going to run out and find some other girlfriend just because you have boundaries? I like that about you. Even if it does drive me to eat too many jelly beans and occasionally try to blind myself."

"As long as you're thinking about me while you're doing those things."

"Naked. On the dock. Surrounded by birds, a pair of binoculars in your hand."

"Awfully specific, Jess Perez." Then she giggled. "And duly noted."

"A girl can wish."

Vivi grinned and my heart tripped over itself. Being

with your high school sweetheart forever had to be a real thing.

As I watched her walk out to the dock ahead of me, I sent a little prayer out into the universe. *Please let us be the real thing. Please let us last forever.*

24

Now: Two Weeks, Six Days After

I know best friends aren't necessarily forever. And over the years, I've kind of been surprised that Cheyanne even stuck by me between my teasing, the girlfriend relationship with Vivi, and her utter so-much-cooler-than-me factor. But, I miss her. It's been almost three weeks since Vivi died, and though the black hole of awful still sucks me in at random moments, there are seconds of new normal laid out in between. I've composed about twelve different texts to her in my head. What happens if I reach out to Chey and the uncontrollable grief bitch rises up inside of me again? Will I ruin whatever thread is still connecting us? Better not risk it. I lie back on the bed and pull Emma Watson onto my chest. She purrs as I run my palm over the top of her head and only halfway down her back. Any farther and the purr will turn to a hiss and a good swipe at my hand with either teeth or claws. Guess I'm a lot like my cat. Vivi stares at me from my bedside table.

"What would you do?" I ask the photograph. I'd pulled it back out from the drawer last night. I desperately needed to see her face even though it made me sad.

I get silence and smiling eyes as an answer. It's not fair there's no cell phone to reach the other side. Vivi was not only my girlfriend, she was my other best friend. She'd know what I should do with my life. Cheyanne, school, therapy. Tears well and the cat turns heavy as stone on my heart. I move her to the side and curl into fetal position. When will this feeling stop?

I hear the house phone ring and my mother's voice talking, then there's Nina banging on my door.

"Get up."

The door opens without my invitation.

"Seriously, Nina? Did I say come in?"

"I'd be waiting for the rest of my life for that. Mom says get up. Some lady called from your school. Something about . . . blacksmithing? She's on the phone."

That pops me up and out of bed in a heartbeat.

Mom looks up from the phone, her books spread out on the kitchen table in front of her. "Here, get directions and work out the details. Your sister can take you."

"I can't. I have plans," Nina whines.

"You can. And you will. I have a massive read and brief due on Tuesday."

"Well, I have work and a date." Nina plops her hand on her hip as if her stance will make it clear to us her superior importance.

Mom gives Nina "the look" and I know I'm going. I grab the phone. "Hello?"

"Hey, didn't mean to cause a ruckus." Greer's voice echoes through the line.

"You didn't." I glare at Nina so she knows her selfish self was overheard.

"Your mom was fine with you coming over. Are you up for it? Happy to give you a ride back home if it's an issue."

I downplay my excitement. It still feels wrong. "I could come."

"Good. Let me give you the address. GPS should get you here, but you can call if there's a problem."

I scrawl the address and her number on a scrap of the napkin left on the table from Mom's breakfast. When I hang up, Nina's still scowling.

"You have five minutes to get your crap together, because I have to be at work at eleven."

"Fine. Don't be such a wad."

"Girls." Mom taps her pen on her books and we shut up. Mom going back to school to be a lawyer is something we all three agreed was amazing and necessary. Even if it means she's not available to us much anymore.

I run to my room to change, grab my phone and a jacket, and meet Nina at her car. Fortunately, Benny calls her within minutes of our leaving and she spends the drive talking on her Bluetooth to him instead of bitching at me.

"Hey! You made it." Greer pulls the garden gate open on the side of the house as Nina pulls away without so much as a see-you-later. A massive black-and-tan dog trots over and nudges his block-shaped head under my hand, his tail thwacking against the wooden fence. "That's Rufus. He's a big goof." Greer reaches for his collar to pull him back.

"It's okay," I say. "I'm owned by a cat, but I like dogs, too. Just don't tell Emma Watson."

"The actress?" Greer looks totally confused.

I rub the dog's ears. "Nope, my cat."

"That is an excellent name."

"Yeah." I nod as I follow her into the backyard. "Vivi thought so, too." And as soon as the words leave my mouth, the throat lump reappears. I try to swallow it down, but it takes some concentrated breaths and a discreet wipe of my eyes to get back to normal.

A slender woman who looks like a radder, pixie cut, petite version of Cheyanne pops her head out the back door. "Is she here?"

"Yeah, come meet Jess, the high school student I was telling you about."

Greer's wife walks down the back steps. Their backyard is the coolest thing I've ever seen. A riot of plants, mosaic concrete pavers, all sorts of metal sculptures, a hammock between two trees, and a mismatched assortment of patio furniture and umbrella tables that create the perfect atmosphere to throw a killer party. At the far end of the yard, a covered carport-type structure houses Greer's home forge.

"Hi there. I'm Eliza." She holds out her hand. I shake it and am surprised by the strength of her grip. "Greer's been so excited to finally have a girl working with her at the forge." She winks. "And a gay girl at that."

Eliza is super pretty and has these perfect tattoos of swans swimming up and around her arms until they disappear under the sleeves of her retro polka-dotted blouse. When I answer, I feel myself get kind of shy. "Yeah, I was glad for the invite. Thanks."

"Well, you two take your tour of Greer's metal utopia

back there and come on in when you get hungry. I picked up Thai food last night on my way home from the studio and there are a ton of leftovers for lunch."

"Studio?"

"I'm a tattoo artist."

It's there again. The flutter of life. The zap of being here on the planet and being excited and alive about something. It's not fair that I'm meeting this devastatingly cool couple, the picture of how I imagined my future life. It's all the what-could-have-beens punching me in the gut. But I manage to pull a happy face and hide the sorrow. "That's really cool."

"I like it. Enough about me though, you go have fun. We'll get more acquainted in a bit." She waves us off and disappears into the house. Rufus follows me as I follow Greer to the forge.

"Are these yours?" In the yard are flowers and rabbits and toads made out of metal and planted into the ground on rebar stakes. They're not typical though. More like twisted yard art babies produced in a marriage between artist Albrecht Dürer and Dr. Seuss. Way different from anything going on at Cabinetworks. An uneasiness settles upon me.

Greer glances over her shoulder. "Yep. Eventually, if I can get enough galleries to start carrying my work, I might leave Cabinetworks. But for now, this is my side hustle. With both me and Eliza being artists, I have to do the adult thing so we have decent insurance."

Artists. Art. Pens. Memories. A college career mapped out by Vivi with our future in mind. I didn't know Greer was making sculptures. I figured she was making fancier furniture or stuff for fireplaces. Is it too late to catch Nina's car? This does not mesh with my plan to leave my creativity behind. But I'm stuck here, so there's nothing to do but take the tour.

Greer shows off all the scrap metal she's amassed. Along with her coal forge, she shows me two welders and a plasma cutter, which she swears is the ultimate cool tool. There's a sandblaster for working the finishes off the metal and in a closed-off workshop room, a small kiln that Greer explains is for adding the glossy color to parts of her pieces.

"What do you think?" She holds up the body parts of a frog. "You think the guys at Cabinetworks would add it as decoration to the chests of drawers?"

I laugh, because the frog, though recognizable, is distorted and looks more alien than animal. The furniture at Cabinetworks is straight up mountain-cabin style. "Good luck with that sales pitch."

Greer grabs a metal box and pulls a bunch of enamel color tiles out and arranges them in a row. She picks hot orange and fuchsia samples from the pile and places them on the frog. "And these colors, opinion?"

"Very poison dart frog."

"I think it will look great in a bed of zinnias."

I nod, not sure which flowers are zinnias, but I guess it doesn't matter. The colors are wild and would look great in any garden.

"I've got something I wanted to ask you while you poke around in there." Greer motions for me to look through the scrap heap, which I guess she saw me eyeing as we walked in.

I pull a rusted chandelier from the pile and turn it sideways. It would work perfect as a flower for Greer's wild garden creatures. "Sure."

"I found out yesterday I got into this art show up in Raleigh and I'm going to have to bust my hump to get enough work together to fill a booth space. Do you think you'd be interested in a part-time job? I suggested James but Liza wasn't comfortable with the responsibility of dealing with him and a parole officer. But I can tell she likes your energy. Energy is very important to Liza." Greer laughs.

I put the metal piece down. "Work for you?"

"I mean, the money's not great. I could pay you nine bucks an hour cash, so no taxes taken out. And if you want, I could teach you how to use some of this other equipment. You could even do a few of your own creations for the show as a way to make up for the low pay, if you were into it."

I'm quiet for a long minute. I think about Levon's joint-selling opportunity I passed up and the money I've nicked from my mom's drawer. It would be nice to have a legitimate job. But this place, Greer and Eliza, they're going to bring up all my sad over and over and over again. I want the job, but I'm not sure I can handle the emotions.

Greer pushes her ball cap up on her forehead. "Damn. I guess I could go to ten. You'd be doing me a huge favor."

"I, it's not the money, I mean, yeah, ten's better. But I don't have a car, and you're too far for me to ride my bike and my mom works and is in school and my sister is temperamental."

"Well, if I could drop you back to nine an hour, and provide your rides, would you consider it? I'm thinking all day Saturdays or Sundays, your choice, and the two afternoons a week you come to Cabinetworks. You could ride home from there with me and work for about three hours. Fourteen hours per week. Cash money. We'd maybe start next weekend?"

I do a quick calculation—approximately five hundred a month. Maybe I could find a wreck to drive and not have to rely on Nina all the time. And I wouldn't have to become a drug dealer. And just because I'd be helping Greer with her artwork, didn't mean I had to do my own. Plus, Mom would be happy I'm involving myself in something other than pints of Ben & Jerry's and reruns of *Kim Possible.*

"Okay," I say. "Sounds like a plan." Then, "Wow, I have a job."

Greer twists both of her thumbs upward, then motions for me to follow her toward the back door and pulls open the screen. Rufus pushes past us into the house.

"Well, it's settled then," Greer says as she unlaces her work boots. "I've got an employee."

"And your long wished-for apprentice?" Eliza unfurls her legs from the sofa and I try hard not to stare at the sparrows dancing up her calves. Birds. It's the tattoo Vivi would definitely have wanted if she'd seen it. This job may gut me.

Greer props her elbow on my shoulder. "Yep. Going to bring another boss blacksmithing babe into the fold."

Eliza claps her hands. "Well, good. Greer needs the help. Are you hungry? Please tell me you'll help us eat some of these leftovers. I went overboard ordering last night."

"Yeah, sure." Since I'm reliant on them for a ride home,

and because Nina rushed me out of the house with no breakfast, I don't mind sticking around to eat. But sticking around to work? I'm a push/pull of thoughts and emotions. It's awesome. I can't. I could be a blacksmith. But the proximity to art? And a couple that reminds me of everything Vivi and I could have been?

I shove my racing thoughts away and bring up the me who hammers hot iron. Be in the now. Be happy about the opportunity. Be grateful.

"I'm actually really hungry," I say. "Thank you."

25

Now: Three Weeks After

My phone buzzes Sunday after lunch. It's Levi.

—You think you could help me later? I'm bombing my English class this semester. Could use a study date.

I move my phone from one hand to the other and think before answering. It's a lot of Levi time. I might have given him the wrong impression under the influence of vodka and Slurpee. I might have given him the wrong impression when I hugged him goodbye after bowling, and he kissed me on the cheek. But the alternative is a night at home, alone, again. Alone is the loneliest place to be.

Yeah, sure. I have to let my Mom know. Grounded. For studying she'll say okay, I answer.

Nina agrees to give me a ride on her way to work.

When we pull up, Levi's standing outside on his porch. Nina leans forward to look at him through the window, then pokes my thigh with her forefinger. "You didn't say you were studying with a guy. He's cute. In a down-home kind of way."

"It's not like that, Nina."

"It could be like that if you'd open your mind. If you decided to be straight, you'd never have to cheat on Vivi."

What's weird? I've had this exact same thought. But it left just as quickly, because you don't decide to be straight. "Decide? Are you for real?" I reach for the door. "Drop it, okay?"

She double winks at me as I get out of the car. "Call me if you need a ride home. I should be off work." Her generosity is only because she's curious about the situation.

"Thanks for coming over." Levi meets me on the bottom step. "My mom has a migraine. She was going to wait up to meet you, but her pills make her sleepy. So we've got to be quiet."

"Your dad's gone?" There's an odd feeling in the pit of my stomach. Levi's wearing cologne. He's standing very near. I feel a little out of control. Study date couldn't mean date, could it?

Levi leads me up the steps and opens the screen door,

then the front door. His house is the same kind of one-story ranch as mine. Just a little bigger and more lived-in, the difference between a rental and a home. Inside the house smells cleaner than I expected based on the outside. Like pine and bleach. His upright bass occupies a place of prominence in the corner of the living room. On the coffee table, Levi has an old vocabulary book open.

I sit in an armchair, not the couch. "Where are your cards?"

Levi sits wide-legged on the couch, edged toward the coffee table and his study notes.

"Cards?"

I pick up a pen. "Yeah, your index cards. For studying."

"You really do that?"

"Uh. Yeah. If I want to remember anything for tests. Cheyanne taught me in middle school and she was right. She didn't show you?" I rustle in the backpack I brought. "Here." I move from armchair to couch and hand Levi half the index cards. "First we write. Word on one side. Definition on the other. Then I quiz you."

"Okay." Then, "Thanks, Jess." He nudges me slightly with his shoulder. A liquid feeling flows through my bones. Not fireworks like when I touched Vivi, but something steady and warming. It feels okay to be hanging out with someone, doing homework, focused and quiet. Not thinking sad memories, curled onto my bed, my breath stealing away.

We take a break after writing out the words and Levi retrieves a bag of microwave popcorn and two Yoo-hoos from the kitchen.

"You remember my weakness." I let the chocolaty goodness slide down my throat.

Levi takes a big sip. "Mine, too. Love these things. You ready?" He sets the bottle down and puts his hands on his knees in preparation for me to quiz him.

"Yep." I pick up the stack of cards we created and read the first word. "Capitulate."

"To yield."

I read the next card. "Steadfast."

Levi pauses, his eyes searching skyward like the definition is written on his ceiling.

"You need a hint?"

He nods.

I think for a minute and the only thing I can come up with is the relationship I don't have anymore. But is it even that? It's not like the relationship is gone, Vivi and I will always be a we. Something about the thought actually makes me feel good. Like the over is only temporal.

"How I was with Vivi."

"Loyal. Faithful."

"That's right. You're awesome at this. You're so going to pass this test." I put the card in the "nailed it" stack.

Levi smiles, then falters. "You know, Cheyanne would never agree to study with me. One time we tried, but she got so frustrated because she's so smart. She didn't have the patience." He looks at his hands. "Or the patience to even try a second date with me. Vivi was really lucky to have you. It sucks what happened."

I lay the cards I'm holding in my lap. "Yeah. It sucks." And even though my moments-ago thought was soothing, I still don't want to wander into Vivi territory out loud. "You know, can we not talk about it? I'd rather just keep studying or watch the movie you threatened me with."

"*The Sandlot* is not a threat."

"No, but my tears are."

Levi scoots closer and wraps me in a strong hug. It's weird to be smaller than the person hugging me and not feel breasts pressed against my own. But it's not too awful terrible. He's warm and smells nice and his hug is surprisingly powerful. I don't try to wriggle free because I'm giving it two seconds of thought. Could I do this? Thought answered. No way, no how.

When the hug lingers on for too long, I break free. "Um. Movie?"

Levi wipes his palms on his jeans. "Yeah, okay."

My gut is telling me his feelings are mixed-up about me. I should set him straight—no pun intended—right this very second, but I hold back. He'd deny it, and then I'd look ridiculous. Besides, I don't want to give up his companionship, even if he may be starting to form the very wrong idea.

"This is one of my all-time favorite movies." He loads the DVD in his parents' player and tosses the case to me, then calls in for a pizza. "Same as the other night?"

"Yeah. Sounds good."

When he comes back to the couch, he sits next to me, close enough that from where I'm sitting cross-legged, I can feel the heat from his knee radiating onto mine. I should scoot away, but that might make things even more awkward. It's just a movie after all.

The pizza comes and we're eating slices over the box so the cheese doesn't get everywhere when my phone buzzes. "I better get that." I lean over and grab it out of the side pocket of my backpack. It's a number I don't know.

—Hey. This is Sahara. Deuces gave me your number. Text me?

I'm not sure what my face is doing, but whatever it is, Levi feels like he needs to check in on me. "Everything okay?"

"Uh, yeah." But there's a deep pit in my stomach as I shove the phone back in my bag, the text from Sahara unanswered. And when Levi slides even closer, close enough that his knee actually touches mine, I don't move away. Maybe Nina is right. Maybe I should give this straight thing a try. It'd be better than having to think about a girl other than Vivi.

26

THEN: Catbirds

Vivi's mouth was clamped in a thin, hard line. I knew I should try to appease her, but I wasn't feeling it. "Oh, come on. Stop. You know I never think about other girls." I reached for her crossed arms only to have her shrug away from me. A vaguely familiar prickle rippled through my veins. The annoyance materialized in my voice. "You're being ridiculous. Jealousy is ugly."

"You're calling me ugly now? Thanks, thanks a lot." Vivi unfolded her arms but only to storm off in the direction of the bathrooms. Great. The Youth Pride mixer swelled and throbbed around me, music playing, bodies dancing, people flirting. That's what had started this. Her thinking I was flirting. Did she not know that she was the only girl I ever thought about? I mean, sure, I could talk and laugh and be nice to other people. I could even have my Emma Watson free pass that she jokingly gave me for my birthday. But I would never use it, even if I had the chance. I was in love with her and for me that meant she was it. Lock, stock, and barrel.

"Shit." I rubbed my hand across the stubble of my newly shaved head. Then I dropped my hand. The stupid haircut was what got me in trouble in the first place. Some girl from another high school had convinced me to let her rub *her* hand over my shorn scalp. It just so happened to be at the same moment Vivi had bounced off to put in a good word for me with Grady High's art teacher, who was one of the chaperones.

Now I had hell to pay, because when Vivi turned around she'd seen some girl she didn't know giggling and stroking the top of my head. And okay, I was laughing, too, but it didn't mean I wanted to get with the girl.

There was no choice but to go after her. "Vivi, stop. Wait."

She kept walking, making a left to circle away from me. "No. I can't believe you. Why would you flirt with that girl like that? Especially when I was over there trying to convince Mrs. Thompson to give you a spot off the waiting list this semester."

"Babe, please, I'm sorry. I shouldn't have let her touch my hair." My blood started to boil in old familiar ways, and I counted my breaths in a one, two, three, deep pattern. It had been a while since I'd had something trigger me into rage, but I could feel it coming. I knew it wasn't logical, but that didn't always help me shut the valve.

"Oh, what? Is your grief *expressing* itself again? Nice avoidance."

And spike. I counted harder, closing my eyes to do it. When I opened them, Vivi was gone. I spotted her across the room talking to a guy from Grady. Try as I might to catch Vivi's eye, she was resolutely not looking. And I was having a hard time stopping the spiral of anger. I could stay and risk really losing it. Or I could leave.

I walked out the door. Luckily the mixer was close to home, so I hoofed it through the muggy late August heat. I texted Vivi to let her know.

—I'm going home. Don't come after me. I wasn't avoiding. I'm sorry, but shit got weird for me. I love you.

Then I turned my phone off. If she called or texted there was a chance I'd still blow and I wanted to process through whatever set me off. Vivi's dig at the end was because she was hurt, I knew that, but it wasn't cool for her to make light of my diagnosis.

I walked through the front door and threw my keys on the bench.

"Shit." Nina's voice was panicky.

I looked toward the source of the sound and saw my sister's arms flailing back into her shirt, then her head popping up over the back of the couch, followed by the face of the latest, Enrique somebody. Lovely. Nothing like walking in on your older sister sucking face on the couch.

"You're not supposed to be here!"

"It's my house, too." It'd be so easy to let this can of steam blast at my sister but instead I stomped to my room, opened the bird field guide Vivi had given me, and flipped pages looking for something to draw. The breathing and the walk home helped but losing myself in a new drawing would let me find my way back to the moment and the normal me.

The yellow-bellied sapsucker page caught my eye, both because the name and the bird were interesting. Compact, a longish bill, feet for gripping the sides of a tree. And the name, yellow-bellied, which was another word for coward, which I guessed I was for running off, but sometimes it was easier to deal with myself in quiet spaces. As my pen drew in the basic starting shapes and shading began to form, I calmed down. And as I calmed down, I realized what a jerk I was for leaving Vivi there. I turned on my phone. There were texts but I didn't read them before sending my own. Easier to just say what I wanted to say, than read and have a potentially bad reaction.

—I'm really sorry. Can you stop by my house before you go home?

Vivi's reply was swift. Be right there.

I had to walk out through the living room again, but with Vivi standing in the front doorway, Nina and Enrique had to at least act human. "Hey, Vivi." Nina fake smiled and acted like she hadn't just had some boy's hand up her shirt. But I didn't want to linger for small talk.

"Come on back to my room." When I closed the bedroom door, I reached for Vivi to give her a hug but Vivi placed her bag in between us. "Not yet."

My heart dropped, worried that Vivi wouldn't forgive me for walking out of the mixer. But Vivi had a huge grin on her face.

"Look in my bag."

I pulled the handles apart and peered down into the shiniest eyes I'd ever seen. A tiny mew followed. I looked up at Vivi with my mouth dropped. "How?"

"Right? I was upset after I got your first text because what I said was so wrong. It's stupid how jealous I got and

I should have never thrown your issues in your face like that, but you're smoking hot with your hair buzzed and that girl knew it and I just wigged out. And then when you started counting I thought you were faking, and oh, none of this matters because something amazing did happen. One, Mrs. Thompson said she had a space in Art 2 this semester after I showed her some of your drawings on my phone and that she'd let you skip Art 1. Apparently, your level can be at her discretion if you can prove you're ready. You just have to go change your schedule on Monday. And two, I went out behind the building through a back exit to call you. There's a Dumpster there. That's when I found her." Vivi looked into the bag, too.

I reached in and pulled out the smoke-gray kitten. "Hey there, kitten." Then to Vivi, "Are you going to keep her?"

Vivi put her bag down and glanced at my open sketchbook. "Can't. Dad's terribly allergic to cats. I can't even take her home for the night to keep her until the shelter opens."

I held the kitten up and made kissing noises at her. "Shelter? I won't let that bad lady take you to the shelter."

"Have another bright idea? Funny, this bird you're drawing, the yellow-bellied sapsucker? Its call actually sounds like the mew of a cat." Vivi whirled and her mouth and eyes grew round. "It's meant to be. She's meant to be your cat."

I kept talking to the kitten. "Are you meant to be my cat?" The kitten answered with a swipe of claws at my nose. I laughed. "Yep, you're my cat, all right."

"You came home and drew?" Vivi kept staring at the drawing.

I cradled the kitten in the crook of my elbow and stepped over to stand next to her. "Yeah, I didn't want to be mad. I got triggered, I guess, and didn't want to lose it with you. So I came home and started sketching."

"Did it help?"

"A lot. I'm really thankful you pushed me to turn my doodles into something more. That's amazing what you did with Mrs. Thompson."

"I'm sorry I got so jealous. Next time I'll be more chill." Vivi threaded her arms between my arms and waist, the cradled kitten between us. "There's one more very important question, though."

"Oh yeah?"

"Yeah," Vivi said. "What are you going to name her?"

I looked down at the kitten and laughed. "You sure you won't get jealous again?"

"Um . . ." Vivi raised an eyebrow.

"I only know one other person with eyes this cool color of coppery brown."

Vivi let out a slow breath. "Soooo . . . you're going to name her Hermione?"

"Nuh-uh." I grinned. "I'm going to name her Emma Watson and then she'll be in my bed and when you call and ask me what I did during the night, I can say I spooned Emma Watson, and there's nothing you can do about it."

"Hmmm, maybe this was a mistake." But Vivi's eyes were laughing. "I think I'll have to tell your mom how you're not responsible enough for a cat."

"See, that's where you'll get derailed. My mom is helpless when it comes to kittens. And when I tell her it's us or the shelter, well, this beauty won't be going anywhere."

"Emma Watson." Vivi lifted the kitten's little face. "Have to admit, it's a pretty cool name for her."

I leaned forward and kissed my girlfriend. "And you're a pretty cool girl for bringing her to me." I brushed my nose against hers. "Are we okay?"

Vivi wrinkled the tip of her nose against mine. "The best. Do you accept my apology?"

"Duh." Then, "You never have to be jealous of me. I'd never cheat on you. I don't even think about other girls.

Even if I am seriously cute with this haircut."

She shoved me backward onto the bed and Emma Watson jumped sideways onto the pillow in a tremendous huff. Then Vivi kissed me, long and slow, and any anger I'd felt melted away as my body molded into hers and the kitten's purrs filled the room.

27

Now: Three Weeks, Two Days After

I can't decide whose stare is worse, Emma Watson's, Chuck Norris's, or Levon's. But, since he's the one in front of me . . .

"Look," I whisper. "I see the same six or seven people all the time. I'd be the worst salesperson ever." Convincing him I'm not up to being his and his brother's mule is getting annoying.

"Miscreants," McGovern growls in our general direction.

I bow my head to my work and ignore Levon for the rest of the morning.

At lunch, we're at Carport BBQ. It's literally in someone's carport, a take-out window set up in their kitchen and a big smoker going in the backyard. Deuces plops down on the bench next to me. He's got a full rack of ribs on his oversized plate. "I'll miss these lunches if they send me back to the big school."

"Will you get to go back once you're off probation?" I use a fork to eat the pulled pork off my sandwich. It's too much meat to pick up and eat with my hands.

"Maybe, but I'm good with McGovern. Figure I might put in at Cabinetworks when I graduate."

I nod and chew.

Deuces points at me with a rib held between sauce-covered fingers. "How come you never texted Sahara back?"

"I gave you my number to give her. That was the only agreement."

"Ah, man, she's still driving me up a wall about it. Throw the girl a bone, or whatever it is you got."

I steal his pickles off his plate. "Fine. I'll text her." There's a pit in my stomach as I say it. Texting another girl feels like cheating. Even if I know Vivi is dead, gone, not of this world. Logic doesn't rule over feelings here. And I'm pretty sure Sahara is simply curious. I'm not some big stud. I'm a one-girl girl. And currently, that girl is a dead girl.

That afternoon, after Cabinetworks, I ride with Greer to her house. Her truck is a three-quarter-ton blue Dodge that's seen better years. The floor is covered with mail, coffee to-go cups, and empty plastic gum dispensers. I have to shuffle stuff aside to make room for my feet.

"Sorry about that," Greer says. "I'm a hopeless slob except with my tools." She turns off the road into Bea's Donuts. "Want a coffee?"

"Yeah, sure."

She orders three coffees and a baker's dozen of mixed donuts. "Have you had these before?"

"Nuh-uh."

"Eliza's going to love us for bringing her Bea's. Cream and sugar?"

"Just sugar."

When we get to the house, Greer parks on the street and I carry in the donuts and drinks. We go up the back steps into the kitchen. Rufus wags his tail from his bed next to the table. Apparently, he's not an evening dog because he's not even bothering to get up. "Hey, buddy." I slide the donut box and drink tray onto the table, then squat down to scratch him on the belly he presents me.

Eliza emerges from somewhere in the back of the house. "I thought y'all would be here earlier." She slides in next to Greer and leans in for a kiss. "Hey, babe." Then she plops into a chair, all push-up bra and tattoo-shop-tight T-shirt and I stare harder at Rufus.

"Ah, nectar." Eliza lifts the to-go cup in my direction. "How are you, baby babe?"

"Good." It's a dead-end answer and stops probing questions. Plus, Eliza is really pretty and I get nervous in front of her. Even if she is ten years older than me and married to my boss.

"What are y'all working on tonight?" Eliza grabs a rosemary batter donut with lemon-curd-and-blueberry filling from the box.

"Forging frog bodies. Maybe show Jess here how to do some enameling. Then I'm going to let her see which of my scrap metal pieces speak to her so she can start working on a creation of her own."

"What?" I feel the same panic that started in therapy with the kids. "I don't want to make anything of my own." My voice is too sharp.

"Oh my god, this is insanely delicious." Eliza licks filling off her fingers, oblivious to the panic on my face or the rattled look on Greer's.

"Yeah, okay." Greer's voice has a kind of "Chill, kid" sound to it and she watches me as she leans in and takes a bite of the donut in question. "Mmmm." She motions for me to take one and I grab the chocolate cayenne with vanilla glaze.

Eliza wipes her hands on one of the cloth napkins piled

on the table. "Greer told me about your girlfriend, Jess. Such a terrible thing. How are you holding up? Are you okay?"

I hate these moments, but something about Eliza makes me open a crack. "Some minutes. Some days. I don't cry as much."

Eliza nods. "I lost my mom suddenly, I know it's not the same, but I understand the spiral." She leans forward and grabs my hand. "Listen, you're safe here, when the waterworks come, just let them fall. We get it, we won't ask questions, and we'd love to hear all about her. She must have been special to pick you."

I feel the prickle on my cheeks that precipitates tears and do a quick inhale, exhale before I respond. "Thanks. She was. I mean, not because she picked me, though that was pretty awesome, she was just so, I don't know, herself. Always herself."

"Good quality." Greer grabs another donut from the box. "How long did y'all date?"

"A little over two years. An intense two plus years."

Eliza laughs. "Guess you couldn't U-Haul since you were both still in high school."

"U-Haul?"

Greer puts her donut down. "Seriously?" Then she looks at Eliza. "Honey, we got old."

"Speak for yourself, Over Thirty. Twenty-eight is not old."

Greer turns to me. "U-Hauling is when two lesbians meet and immediately move in with each other."

I nod. "Oh . . . right."

Eliza laughs again. "She has no clue. Man, things have changed since we graduated from high school."

I scramble to let them know I'm not clueless. "No, I've heard that, I think. And we sort of did. We were always together. School, after school, weekends. We were lucky because our parents were cool and everybody really liked each other." I sigh. "It's why it's so hard. I miss having that one person who totally gets me." The prickle intensifies.

Rufus sits up and rests his head on my thigh like he senses my uneasiness.

"What happened?" Eliza asks. "If you're okay rehashing it, that is."

I rub the dog's ears. "It's okay." Inhale. Exhale. Talk. "She had asthma and it got aggravated by the fall pollen, or something. Then she caught a flu sort of thing . . ." My voice catches remembering how I didn't get to say goodbye to Vivi at school that last day.

"Eliza, damnit." Greer grabs a box of tissues from the counter and puts them on the table. "Look what you've done."

I clear my throat. "It's okay. She just got really sick and stopped breathing." What's weird is how comfortable I am talking to them about it. Way more comfortable than talking to Levi, Cheyanne, or even my mom. Maybe it has to do with Greer and Liza being in a same-sex relationship. They get it. Maybe not the grief part, but they can understand how much I loved Vivi. Sometimes I wonder if straight people think gay relationships are as valid as theirs. I know it's a paranoid thought, especially when it comes to those who were closest to me and Vivi, but it doesn't change the connection and solidarity I feel to Greer and Eliza.

Eliza comes and hugs me. "You poor kid. And her parents, too. What a tragedy. Do you see them?"

"They left for France to see Vivi's grandparents for a while."

Eliza lets me go. "Well," Greer says. "We'll give you both of our cell numbers and if you need to midnight text or chat or whatever, you've got yourself some understanding big sisters." She takes my phone and adds Eliza's number to her contact info then hands it back.

I slide it in my pocket. "Thanks, y'all." And I realize I mean it. As hard as it is to dredge up Vivi thoughts, Vivi pain, Vivi memory, at least with Greer and Eliza there's none of the baggage of my angry years. And they get it. As long as I can stay clear of the making of art that I associate so fully with Vivi, I might be okay. I can use my hands to help someone else and that will be good enough.

Greer stands. "You bet. Now, Eliza, if you're quite done with making our Jess cry, we're going out back to get some work done."

Eliza closes the box of donuts and waves us out the door. "Make pretty."

"Always do," Greer replies.

I give Rufus a final hug and follow Greer to the forge.

28

Now: Three Weeks, Four Days After

It's Thursday, which means afternoon therapy with Mr. A and the littles. I'm having to catch a ride on the bus from school to connect with the city bus. Too much time to think.

As I watch suburbia give way to city streets, my mind wanders to Vivi. I wonder if she'll always appear so readily to me. Out of habit, I look at my phone, hoping to see that she's texted or dm'ed me but, of course, there's nothing. I lean my forehead against the window and feel my hollowness bounce against the glass. There's a *shush, shush* sound filling me that is reminiscent of shell against ear and the sound of the ocean. I try to put a name to the sound. Loneliness. *Shush, shush.* My heartbeat pulsing. *Shush, shush.* Nobody.

My fingers open my texts and I see the unanswered one from Deuces's cousin and habit or impulse takes over. My fingers type on automatic pilot. Nothing much, a simple hello. Then, regret. Then even more regret when I see the bubble and dots pop up to indicate she's responding. They disappear and no text comes. Then they appear again and suddenly I'm invested in this moment and I know it means nothing and that it's only to stop the loud echoes of my heart and my loneliness. Still, I will a text into being. Just someone, anyone, communicating with me.

Hi, she says.

Then, more dots and bubbles.

Then they disappear.

It hits me she's nervous or something and now I feel really shitty because I don't want to lead anyone on and I'm not even in the zone of thinking about dating, but I promised Deuces I'd respond and now I have. And I don't even fully know why or how this has happened.

Another text appears. Sorry I missed the fight the other night.

This feels safe. I can talk about the asshole at the community center. I text back, You didn't miss much. My friend hauled me out of there before we got our asses kicked.

—So . . . he's just your friend?

This doesn't feel as safe. I hesitate. Yes, of course Levi is just my friend and I don't want to pretend I'm straight, but man, it'd be a convenient way to extricate myself from this situation. But I don't want to lie.

—Yeah.

Cool, she responds. Then, You want to maybe hang out sometime? I was looking to find somebody to go with me to this new club I heard about.

Club scene is definitely not in my cards right now. But then I remember I'm grounded, kind of, and that is not a lie.

—Kind of grounded. Definitely can't pull off late night right now.

The bus takes the final turn toward the VA building so I add another message. Gotta run, at my appointment. Nice to "meet" you.

She texts back a thumbs-up emoji and I don't know why I feel bad, but I do. Like I shouldn't be blowing her off so easily. She is Deuces's cousin and I could at least tell her my story, or get Deuces to, so she understands it's not about her. And then there's the *shush, shush* of my heart that makes me want to reach through the phone and pull any friendly voice close to fill the cavernous spaces carved out by loss. So I text her back.

—Maybe once I'm not grounded.

As soon as my finger sends it off into space, I want to reach through the phone and pull it back. What the hell was that? Why did I feel the need to leave the door open? I don't want to go to a club and I definitely don't want to go with some girl who called me a stud. What does that even mean anyway? I close my eyes and pull Vivi up so she inhabits my senses. I picture every lash, the freckle at the top of her left earlobe, the strong line of her clavicle bone and the way it tied into the softness of her chest. I listen to her laugh and her ugly tears and think of the way her nose was always slightly running in cold weather and how I'd get so grossed out when we kissed. I'd kiss her winter nose a million times if it would bring her back.

I hate thinking of her in the past tense.

The bus stops and as I wind my way into the building toward the meeting room, I've worked myself up into a state. My chest feels like crowbars are working from the inside trying to spring my rib cage open and someone has poured wet cement into each of my limbs. My face must look wild because when I walk into the room toward last week's seat, little Darla flinches.

I turn and hoof it to the bathroom again so I can get my shit together. This time I do something I haven't done in over a year. I panic dial Samantha. I know my mom had emailed to fill her in on what was going on with me, just in case this moment came, and lucky for me, she answers.

"Jess." Her voice is warm and familiar and I'm able to release my death grip on Darla's rock.

"Hey," I say, not totally sure why I even called her but glad to hear her voice all the same.

"You need me to walk you through the steps?"

I look at myself in the mirror and notice that my biceps have gotten more defined in my little bit of time working the forge. "No," I say. "I'm not spiraling up. I'm spiraling down."

"Ah, okay. Tell me about that."

My voice cracks a little but I hold it together. "I know Mom told you about Vivi. It's just I miss her so much and I'm messing up. At school, with my friends, life."

"Jess. You're old enough now for me to tell you this is normal. What you are feeling, the pain, confusion, even anger. All normal stages of grief. And you've got compounded grief. Which challenges your coping mechanisms. Tell me how you're coping."

I blurt it out. "I just texted a strange girl who told a mutual friend that she thinks I'm cute. I don't know why I did that. It's making me hyperventilate that I did that. I can't start talking to another girl already, it hasn't even been a month since Vivi died."

"I think that's a positive thing."

"You do?" I stare at my face in the mirror, my surprised expression stuck in wide-eyed mode.

"Yes," Samantha says. "It's important for you to continue to live. There is no timeline for grief. And there's nothing wrong with talking to a strange girl. I think people come into our lives at moments when we need them. Don't attach values to this new friendship. Just take it for whatever it is. Whatever it may have to teach you. Nothing you do now has any bearing on the very real love you felt for Vivi."

There's a silent pause that's not uncomfortable. I'm thinking, she's waiting.

"Do you believe in heaven?" I ask.

"What do you believe?" Samantha volleys in classic therapist turn-it-back-on-the-patient mode.

"I hope it's real. I mean, I don't really think there's some dude and pearly gates and angels with harps riding around on fluffy clouds. But maybe it's more like our essence, soul, whatever, is energy and when we die it gets released into a bigger world. Has to be some other dimension, right? Otherwise this life would be pointless."

"Tell me more about life being pointless."

I sigh. "I'm not thinking my life is pointless if that's what you're worried about. I'm just happier with the thought that Vivi is out there somewhere. That she's guiding me. Like the way I feel about my dad. I even like to think maybe they're hanging out together sometimes. That there's more beyond our physical beings."

I hear Samantha's smile in her voice. "That's a beautiful image, Jess. One you should hang on to. And hey . . ."

"Yeah?"

"Don't be so hard on yourself. It probably is too soon for any kind of lasting relationship, but there's nothing wrong with new friendships. And this is a very cliché thing for me to say, but Vivi would want you to keep living all of life's complexities. Speaking of which, how's the artwork going?"

Talking to Samantha about my artwork is complicated. How do you tell the person who suggested you draw in the first place that your pens drip poison? Especially when they're your former therapist. Especially when they might try to reason you back into something that you're nowhere near ready to be reasoned into. I bow out. "Um, listen, thanks for taking my call, but they're calling for me to come to the room. I'm at my VA therapy. Have to go."

She buys it and when I hang up, I take a last look at myself in the mirror. The face is calmer, probably won't scare children, but I still think about ditching. I wish I could go to the lake. Maybe there I'd be able to talk to

Vivi, feel her presence, know how the heck I'm supposed to live life in all of its complexities.

There's a knock on the door and a tiny voice. "Jess?"

I open it and Darla looks first at my hand holding her rock, then up at me. "It's time for us to start." She holds out her hand. I take a deep breath, grab it, and let her walk me down the hall.

29

THEN: Eagles Mate for Life

It wasn't hard to convince Vivi to ditch school for our anniversary. I'd simply taken her hand as we'd walked toward the school and whispered, "Come on, I have an idea" before leading her away for the day. But it was way harder to convince Nina to give us a ride out to the lake house.

"You're where?"

"At the Circle K four blocks from school. Come on, Nina. It's a special day. Please."

Vivi looked around. Her eyes darted toward every car that pulled in and she flinched at every door chime. She whispered, "Maybe we should go back. We're going to get in trouble."

I held up one finger and kept begging Nina. "I swear, I'll totally cover for you if you want to sneak out with Enrique."

"I'm dating Javier now. But fine, I'll pocket this favor."

My sister showed up about six minutes later, which gave me enough time to buy an anniversary feast of beef jerky, Flamin' Hot Cheetos, Sour Patch gummies, a package of powdered sugar mini-donuts, bottled water, and two convenience store cappuccinos. Vivi threw a package of spearmint gum onto the pile. She nudged me. "A feast."

"For a queen." I glanced sideways at her and tried to hide the hopeful smirk but she saw it all the same.

When we'd stepped away from the cashier she whispered, "We talked about this, remember?"

"I know. I know." But a girl, who was wildly attracted to her girlfriend of a year, couldn't help but wishing.

I let Vivi ride up front with Nina so she could give directions. When we pulled down the long gravel drive to the lake house, Nina whistled. "Damn, this is awesome. Maybe I could hang out with you guys and go swimming?"

My no was instantaneous. Vivi's was guiltier but there all the same. "Maybe another time?" she said. "Or when you come to pick us up?"

Nina turned around and stared at me. "Do we need to

have 'the talk'? Is that what this skipping school is about?"

"Oh my god. Would you stop?" But even though the last thing in the world I wanted was my straight sister to give me any kind of sex talk, there was a part of me that hoped maybe Vivi would change her mind. Of course, I wouldn't pressure, but if she gave me the green light . . . I was all in.

When Nina drove away, Vivi smiled at me, the plastic convenience store bag swinging against her thighs as she rocked back and forth. "So . . ."

"Our anniversary," I said.

"A whole year."

"Amazing."

"You want to swim?"

It was a blazing hot, Indian summer day and I hoped before it was over we'd jump in the lake. I also kind of hoped maybe nobody would be around and we could do it sans suits. But I had something else on the agenda first. I'd learned about a pair of bald eagles building a nest along the lake and wanted to find them to show Vivi.

"Eventually."

"I'm melting."

"What if I told you there was a report of a pair of nesting bald eagles on the lake?"

"Shut up."

"It's true. I saw it on the news and I think they're only a few coves over. Are you up for a hike?"

Vivi closed in for a hug. "Here I was thinking you were going to try to convince me to have sex with you and instead you brought me out here for eagles. Now I know you love me."

Okay, so this made me feel the tiniest bit guilty, but I'd grab on to the glory if she was giving it to me.

She pulled the spare key out from a crevice between two rocks. "Let's put our feast inside. We just have to be sure to put everything back exactly like we found it so my sweet Henri and Abigail don't suspect we've been out here without their permission."

"Yes, ma'am," I said.

Twenty minutes later, we were chugging the water and I was questioning the sanity of looking for an eagle's nest that could be anywhere. My internal GPS was not so great, and traipsing across people's properties and traversing the woods was getting kind of old. Plus, it had to be one hundred degrees in the shade.

"Maybe we should go back. It's ridiculous out here."

Vivi scowled. "Quit complaining. I swear they have to be over in the next cove. It's quiet and there are really tall trees and you will be as excited as I am when we find them. Besides you're the one who came up with this idea."

I shut up because she was right. It would be cool to see bald eagles in the wild, but if I'd been smarter, I would have just downloaded the news section I saw and shown it to her on my iPad. Some other ornithology geek besides Vivi had no doubt blogged all about them, including coordinates to find the bloody birds.

The trail took a steady uphill turn. Vivi climbed ahead of me and suddenly her breath became labored.

"Hey, Viv. Slow down, you sound like a freight train."

"I'm fine."

Shit. What was I thinking suggesting we hike on such a hot day? We were at least three miles from the house and in an area of undeveloped lots and conservation land. Not a good place to be if she had an attack.

Her breathing got worse and she stopped and bent forward. "Jess." Her voice was strangled and harsh.

I rushed to her.

Vivi kept her hands on her knees and gulped for air.

I dug my hand in Vivi's pocket praying she'd remembered her inhaler, then breathed out a sigh of relief when I felt the hard-plastic edge against my fingers. I pulled it out and held it up toward her mouth. "Here."

Vivi grabbed it and sucked in as she pumped. After a minute, she stopped gulping and took a couple of real breaths. She crumpled into a cross-legged heap in the middle of the trail.

"Super fudge. Are you okay? Look at me."

Vivi looked up. Tears tracked her cheeks and with a ragged voice she answered, "That was scary."

I sat next to her and pulled her into my arms. "I was so stupid. I should have known."

Vivi cried. "Don't be mad. I hate being a fragile flower. I didn't want to stop. I wanted to find the eagles."

I wiped tears from her face. "Shhh. Are you crazy? You think I'd be mad because of your asthma? You can't help that." I paused. "But can I be a little mad when you know you're pushing yourself too hard? If you don't tell me it might be too much, I won't always know. I want to keep you around for a long, long time."

Vivi shrugged. "You're just so . . . naturally athletic . . . and I don't know, sometimes I want to best you. To get up the mountain first. To be the one to make the discoveries."

"Really? Are we going there? Because if I recall when we lined up our report cards you'd bested me on every single line. And when we had that fake cooking contest with your mom and dad as judge, you totally won. And you can water-ski in circles around me."

"But you're totally healthy."

I squeezed her. "Yeah, my body. But what about all my therapy? My tendency to use fists instead of words? That's not totally healthy."

Vivi snorted back tear snot. "Oh yeah."

"See?" I pushed the loose strands of hair back behind her ears. "I love you. Heavy breathing and all."

Vivi's eyes held light again and danced as they looked at mine. "Now about that heavy breathing . . ." She waggled her eyebrows flirtatiously. "If you help me find these eagles, we might be able to work something out on the anniversary front."

I groaned. "I can't even believe I'm going to say this, but there's no way I'm letting you hike anywhere but very, very slowly back to the lake house. So, it's a hard pass on finding the eagles."

"But don't you want a special anniversary prize?" Vivi pecked me on the lips and pocketed her inhaler.

I took her hand and twined my fingers through hers. "You're already my prize. I don't need a thing from you until you're truly ready. What we have is about this." I placed my palm on Vivi's heart. "Not about this." I dropped it to Vivi's breast, then pulled my hand away, laughing before growing serious. "I love you, Vivi. I don't want anything bad to happen."

"Don't worry," she replied. "We're going to be like those eagles. Mated for life."

I wanted to believe her, but the memory of her struggling for air stayed stuck in my mind the whole way back to the lake house.

30

Now: Three Weeks, Six Days After

I'm at the lake, walking through the woods, stepping over fallen branches, and my throat starts to close in. There's a beeping, but I can't find my phone, and I'm immobilized by my lack of air. The beeping gets louder. My air constriction tightens.

I startle awake from the dream, but even though my eyes open, there's no light. Only an opaque gray. Like I'm going blind. I panic for half a second, then . . .

"Emma Watson," I mumble. "Get off my face."

There's another beep.

My actual phone.

Hey, girl. Been hoping I'd hear from you. Still grounded?

I stare at the screen, hit with a weird combination of

feelings—partial fear, partial excitement, partial curiosity. What do I say to her? How do I proceed? I think about my conversation with Samantha and what she said about people coming into your life when you need them. With Cheyanne currently gone from mine, and Levi an odd substitute, maybe a new friend wouldn't be the worst thing. Just because we're texting, and just because she said she was interested, doesn't mean that's the way it has to go down.

—Yeah, but I might be able to talk my mom into a reprieve.

—So, there's this new gay club that opened on the south side. Eighteen and up. The bouncer's from my neighborhood. We'll get in no problem even if you're not eighteen yet. You in? Please say yes, I've never been to one and I really want to check it out.

I must be the first queer girl her age she's ever met. She'll be plenty disappointed when she figures out that I know gay clubs about as well as she does. Vivi and I had each other, Cheyanne, Levi, and a handful of other peripheral friends. We didn't do much scene.

—You still there? You in?

—Yeah. I'm here. Let me check with my mom. But, I should let you know, I'm not really thinking about this as a date, if that's cool with you.

I see the dance of bubble and dots appear and disappear

and then a text finally comes through.

—Yeah. That's cool. What? Do you have a girlfriend or something?

—Just keeping it single for now.

—But you'll still go?

I can't believe I'm even thinking about it. But I guess there's a teeny, tiny part of me that even though I'm not interested in being with anyone else now, thinks someday I might be. Besides, dancing seems like an excellent way to be in the moment, instead of the past.

—Yeah, I'll still go.

Mom agrees to unground me, not that it's been too strict anyway, and in a rare spurt of generosity, even offers up her car if I swear on her life I will not drink. It turns out Sahara lives in an apartment complex not far from Deuces's community center. What would Vivi think about all this? Samantha's right. Vivi would want me to live. To be happy. It's just so hard to figure that part out when it hurts so bad. I take a deep breath.

Vivi was always an optimist when it came to people. I should be, too.

When I pull up and park, I get the stare down from a bunch of guys shooting hoops. Sahara emerges from a door and the guys' heads turn and though I can't hear what they're saying through the closed window, I can tell there's an exchange of smack talk going on. A nervous wave ripples in my stomach. Maybe there's the tiniest smidge of attraction, coupled with outright terror.

"Hey." Sahara jumps in. "This is your car?"

"My mom's."

"Nice." She laughs and kicks her feet up. Her toenails are painted a glittering bronze that looks good with her skin tone.

I quell the impulse to tell her to take them off the dashboard. "So, do you have directions to this place?"

"Yeah." She punches them into her phone and I pull out onto the road. Since I don't drive a ton, I have to concentrate, which seems a good enough excuse to keep the small talk small. I learn that Sahara goes to Jefferson Christian, that's kind of a surprise, and that she hates it, not so much a surprise if she's actually questioning her sexuality. But then she starts asking me questions.

"How come you're not looking for a girlfriend?"

And here I am again. Do I tell the story or let it lie? "I'm just not."

"What, did somebody break your heart?"

"Something like that."

"My friend Zach told me girls like you are kind of soft

inside and that might be why you said that to me over text."

Girls like me. What the hell?

She keeps talking. "I told him I bet you weren't that soft. That you were just using that line to keep me at a distance. I get it. That's cool. But a girl like me won't wait around forever."

Holy cats, this brave adventure of mine is starting to feel like a wrong turn down a bad road.

"Once you see me dance, you'll be all in." She winks at me when I make the mistake of glancing her way. "Next road on the right, and we're there."

The bouncer waves us in when she sees Sahara, even going so far as to give her a little booty pop as she walks through the door. Then she bro-nods at me and raises a fist for a bump. I don't raise mine.

"You want a drink?" Sahara asks.

"Um, yeah, sure. Coke, I guess."

"That's it? I bet I can get us some alcohol." She scans the room and it doesn't take more than five minutes before she's pushed herself up against some older lesbian with a ball cap and piercings, batting her eyes and motioning for me to hand her my money. Here I thought I was going to be like the Greer and Liza of first gay experiences but

Sahara obviously doesn't need me to figure her way around the room.

"What do y'all want?" The woman places a hand on Sahara's hip and tilts forward to listen to our answer.

"I'll have a White Russian." Sahara leans into her hand.

"And you?"

"A beer is fine." I'm not a huge fan of beer, but I swore on my mother's life I wouldn't drink, and with a dark bottle, I can fake it.

The woman returns moments later with our drinks and a beer for herself. "Sorry, girls, my risk, your tax." She doesn't hand us any change.

Sahara's already sipping through the miniature red straw and looking around the room with big eyes, so I let the money thing go. "Come on." I push my way toward the stage. A girl band is tearing at their guitars, but most of the club seems like they're waiting for the DJ to take over and get things pumping.

Sahara is suddenly close. In my comfort zone close. She's staring at me with a half smile, practically begging for me to check out the details. And they're there. Massive liquid brown eyes, hair slightly shaved at the sides with tight cornrows that disappear into a high ponytail, a shirt that dips low enough to show the slight swell of breasts underneath a black bra. The girl is definitely pretty. But she's also not Vivi.

"What's your deal?" I figure the direct approach is best. I take a fake swig of the beer.

"What do you mean, what's my deal?"

I have to get close to make sure she hears me—the guitars are shredding. "Wanting to hang out."

Sahara turns it on then. Leaning in so her chest rests against my arm, grabbing my wrist with her non-drink hand, being all coy and flirtatious. "I've been curious about girls, you know, like you. That's why I told Deuces to hook us up. You're glad he did, right?" She does some kind of ponytail flip, chest out move, that I'm sure works on guys, but seems a bit too calculated for me.

I don't answer her last question. "So, you think you're queer? Is that what you mean when you say girls like me?"

"All I know is I think you're cute. Labels are stupid."

It sounds like what Vivi would have said. All kinds of feelings assault me. Embarrassment, the warmth of flattery, need, hunger, the want for warm lips and soft arms, but she's also not the girl I want. All I manage to squeak out is, "Thanks." But I don't tell her she's attractive. One, she already knows it, and two, I don't want to do anything about it.

The band is wrapping it up and the DJ seamlessly flows into the space and the dance floor fills. Sahara pulls me into the crowd of bodies. At first, we're kind of awkward shuffling, but then the song changes and Sahara jumps and squeals and plants her feet firmly and starts shimmying her ass. She turns and backs it up to me and the music is good and dancing feels safe enough, so I open my arms wide and shimmy forward with my hips. I'm not really thinking about it when my hands land on Sahara's hips. I don't mean anything by it other than dancing, but Sahara leans her head back against my chest and moves her body so I feel it against me.

Suddenly, I'm so aware of Vivi. She's like a shadow, standing in the corner of my mind, watching this all go down. Whatever release the music was giving me ends. I jump backward away from Sahara.

She turns. "What? Why are you stopping? Am I doing it wrong?" In that second, Sahara looks vulnerable and uncertain and I feel like shit. She's at a Christian school. That's got to be hard if she's uncertain about her sexuality. The desire to protect her and validate her questioning surges inside of me. But it doesn't last long, because she comes back at me all sexed-up. "You know you like this."

It's too much. It's the opposite of sexy. It's the opposite of anything I want. I exit the dance floor. Sahara follows me, grabbing at my arm.

"What'd I do? Why are you acting like this?"

I walk into the bathroom hallway, where the music is slightly subdued.

"It's not you, okay?" I pace in the confined area, avoiding Sahara's eyes, freaking out inside, needing to leave. The only thing Sahara could possibly have come into my life to teach me is that I'm in no way ready to be out on a Saturday night with a girl at a club.

"You seriously don't like me?" Sahara grabs my hand and tries to pull me close. "I thought this would be easy?"

"Get off me." I have no clue if Sahara is gay or bi or simply questioning, but just because I'm a girl, and just because she's a girl, doesn't make it easy. You can't just text a girl and have instant romance. I feel it rising, the fury, my old friend anger. I start counting breaths. But then Sahara mashes herself against me in a weird combination hug, almost kiss. It's too much. I shove her backward to the wall. "I said get off!"

The drink dyke happens to walk into the hall as this is all going down. "Hey now. Don't be treating your lady like that." She holds me back with an arm across the chest and addresses Sahara. "You okay, darling?"

Sahara's eyes flash from super hurt to her own rage. "Yes." She steps next to drink dyke. "As long as I leave this hall with you instead of this rank-ass bitch."

Drink dyke releases her arm from me and my anger drains, replaced by the tremble of spent emotion. "No hard feelings, right?" She winks at me, snugs Sahara around the waist, and leads her out of the hallway.

"I need to give you a ride home," I shout after them.

Sahara turns. "You don't need to give me anything. The bouncer will make sure I get home safe. Thanks for nothing." Then she disappears back into the pulse of purple and blue lights on the dance floor.

I slump against the wall. I can't believe I shoved Sahara. I can't believe she tried to kiss me. What girl just throws herself at someone else without an emotional connection? It's not me. I can't. I won't.

Instead, I text Levi.

—You doing anything? Need a friend.

—Tracks?

—Yeah.

31

Now: Three Weeks, Six Days After (Late Night)

Levi is waiting for me by the time I park the car in my driveway, grab my bike, and get to the tracks.

"You okay?" He doesn't stand up from where he sits, dangling his legs out over the road below, his head bobbing to whatever's playing through his earbuds.

"Extra weird night. What are you listening to?"

He hands me the right earbud and I put it in my left ear. It's something instrumental that has kind of a rhumba beat to it.

He pulls a pipe out of his pocket. "Wanna blaze? It's the weekend."

"I shouldn't, but I will."

He lights the bowl and inhales, then hands it to me. "Cheyanne called me."

"Oh yeah?" I perk up a little, curious as to what they talked about.

"Yeah, it was about something for the orchestra fund-raiser, but then she asked if I'd seen you. Told her we'd been hanging out more. She acted kind of surprised. Then she told me y'all hadn't been talking since you switched schools."

I hang my arms on the crossrail and lean against it. "It's my fault. I can't seem to stop being angry at the women around me."

"Not really hard to interpret that."

We stop talking again, both of us getting into the groove of the drums, passing the pipe till it's empty. We move our shoulders with the beat in a lazy swish and swim our hands against the air and I don't think either of us really connects the vibration we're feeling to anything other than the music until the roar gets louder than the tunes.

"Train." I twist quick toward the oncoming headlights. I know we're safe, but it's always scary as hell to be on the tracks when it roars past. Plus, it's illegal and if the conductor notices us, there may be cops waiting at the end of the overpass by the time all the cars pass us by.

"Duck," Levi says and pushes me into a huddle.

The engine is roaring up on us, the light not really hitting us directly, but making the woods on my side of the tracks glow. Levi grins at me from inside our huddle of shoulders and arms and hoodies and I start laughing. We keep hanging on to each other while the train rushes next to us, the sound blending with the music still playing in our ears, and the whole overpass rumbling with the tremor of train. The track switches on the album and the music plays in time with the train and Levi and I do this modified, cross-legged, hoodie-huddled, groove dance with just our arms on each other's shoulders. Maybe about the thirtieth car is when things get weird. Levi's arms circle me more fully, and because I don't want to fall off the overpass or fall under the wheels, I scoot closer. Then he puts his forehead against mine and it's like we're in a bunker during a war or something with all the noise and spark. I lift my face a little and the next thing I know Levi's lips are on mine. But instead of pushing him away like I did with Sahara, I kiss him back.

He kisses me again then and I feel his hands spread open against my back, pulling me toward him, and the music is still playing in my ear. I'm not really thinking about the what of this thing I'm doing, rather I'm experiencing the sensations. Train rattle, percussion, wind, flesh.

My mouth opens to his tongue and now I'm exploring the inside of his mouth and it's warm, kind of wet but not really. He tastes like chocolate and I'm surprised by the scratch of stubble near my mouth.

The train cars keep coming and Levi's mouth is getting bolder against mine and his hand starts to slip around the edge of my shirt and that's when I realize, shit, he's actually into this. Levi's getting worked up and I'm just stoned. My brain wakes up and shrieks at me. . . . *Stop.*

I shriek at him. "Levi, stop."

He looks up and his eyes are glazed, like one of those cartoon animals in love. The last car finally rattles past.

"I need to go home. I can't get caught if the conductor called the cops."

"Yeah, okay. You're right. I'll walk you." He puts a hand on my shoulder. It feels proprietary.

I need to cut this cord right here and now. "Levi, I, about what just . . ."

He shakes his head. "No, don't say it. Let me hang on to it for a little bit. I need the fantasy. I need to wake up tomorrow morning with a smile on my face and the memory of kissing a girl I think is super cool and that I really like."

"I like you, too, Levi."

"You do?" His smile is hopeful, his eyes crinkled, and

the music just smooth enough that all I manage is a nod, even though I should be adding the necessary "as a friend" statement.

When I'm shut safely into my room I grab up Emma Watson and the photo of Vivi. "I am messing crap up left and right."

Vivi's smile is enigmatic. But I think she'd agree with me.

Emma Watson purrs.

I pick up the phone and text Cheyanne one word.

—Sorry.

Because not only have I totally pushed her out of my life when all she wanted to do was help, but it seems like I may be doing the same thing I've accused her of doing all this time, leading Levi on.

32

Now: Four Weeks After

I'm getting dressed so Nina can drop me at Greer's house when my phone buzzes. I grab for it.

It's not Cheyanne.

—Hey. Last night. Kind of wack, right?

Ugh. Levi. Last night was so bizarre. Between Sahara, the train, the kiss. I want a rewind button. My chest aches because none of it feels like me. None of it feels like the me that Vivi loved. I'm scrambling and reaching and I feel like I'm trying to dig myself into a hole while at the same time hold on and get myself out. It's apparent this text is his way of checking in on what happened last night. Do I answer him? Or ignore it?

I go for ignore but then I opt for a simple thumbs-up emoji.

He texts back right away.

—Um. You want to meet up tonight?

I need to put a few days between me and Levi. We've been hanging out a lot and even though having a bunch of nights to myself is a sure invitation for the wallow of Vivi thoughts, it might help set him straight on the "just friends" thing again.

—Can't. Have to work. A bunch going on this week.

Oh. Sure thing. Had fun last night. He adds a train and a lips emoji, followed by the goofy closed eye, tongue out smiley face.

If I were to emoji interpret, he's bringing up the kiss and then giving me, us, an out with that smiley. I scroll through and choose the one with angle eyes and tongue out. Hopefully he'll read it as "yeah that was left field, we were totally messed up, and omg."

Before I stick my phone in my pocket, I check to see if Cheyanne has texted me back.

Still nothing. My heart sinks a little, but at this point I get it. If it were me on the flip side, I might hold out. Make me wait to prove a point of what a bitch I was.

***

Greer puts me straight to work. I mastered the welds she needed to connect the rebar rods to her garden creatures and I'm working through the group of them. The welding helmet protects my eyes from the flash of light and the leather apron keeps any stray sparks from popping holes in my clothes. Soon I find a rhythm, sanding the weld spot, brushing it clean, lining up the rebar, hitting it with the weld. The sound, kind of like the bug zapper my neighbors have hanging in their backyard, is as satisfying as watching the welding wire melt and fuse the pieces together. Once I have all the welds done, I move the pieces to a big table and plug up the handheld sander to clean up my work a bit.

Greer comes over from where she's been forging to check out what I'm doing. "Nice job." She holds up one of the rabbits, its ears longer than its body, its face a cartoon menace. "I like this guy. Hopefully there are art buyers out there with an imagination as twisted as mine."

I wipe the grime from my hands onto the apron. "He's not that twisted. He just has character."

"Thanks." She inspects the rest of my work, then motions for me to follow her. "Come on. I'll show you how to work the plasma cutter. It's how I cut out these flat pieces."

We walk to a machine that looks similar to the welders

but says PlasmaPro on the front of it. Greer hooks it up to the air compressor. It has a handle that reminds me less of a torch and more like a glue gun. A flat sheet of metal is edged out over the concrete floor and Greer has drawn the outline of one of her creatures in chalk on its surface.

"It's pretty amazing, this thing. Draws in metal and cuts it right out. Only thing to remember is to keep a steady hand and keep it about a forty-five-degree angle, like so." Greer hits the trigger and a bright flame lights up that she lowers onto her drawn line. The plasma cutter eats the steel like it's butter.

As I watch the machine cut out perfect metal reproductions of Greer's surrealistic creatures, I think about birds. How my drawings might be interpreted in metal. And then I shut it down. Because making art is another way of cheating on Vivi. It's moving forward. It's picking up the pieces. It's saying I can still find passion and joy in a world without her and it feels so, so wrong. Despite what Samantha might say.

When we're done for the afternoon, Greer invites me in for a cold beverage. Their house is decked out in Halloween finery. There's even a full-sized coffin crawling over with stuffed spiders in their den. "Whoa." I look around, my eyes not even able to take in all the details.

Greer laughs and hands me a Coke. "Yeah, Eliza and

I are sort of obsessed with Halloween. We have a massive party every year. Bunch of tattoo folks and lesbian ladies. I would have invited you but it's Thursday and that's the day of the kid therapy gig you told me about."

I don't want to seem pushy, but I actually want to go to this party. Otherwise it's me, dressed up in my Minion onesie with only the littles from VA therapy as my witnesses. And also because Halloween was something Vivi and I loved. Even though being out with Sahara was not what I wanted, I actually didn't mind the dancing and the people watching. It made me forget myself for a minute. A party at Greer and Eliza's would be safe, nobody trying to know too much about me or dancing too close, just a bunch of undoubtedly freaky cool people.

"I'm done by five. I could come. I mean, if you were thinking I couldn't."

"Settled then. Come. Bring a plus one, if you want. Won't be many folks your age here. And there might be some drinking going on. Not for you, of course."

"Of course," I say. Then I remember what I'd decided to ask Greer. "Hey, um, I was wondering when I might get paid?"

Greer kills the rest of her soda. "Won't be till the end of next week. Have to wait till Cabinetworks pays me. Is that going to be okay?"

I clench my feet and my big toe's knuckle hits the steel toe of my boot. "Yeah, sure, that's fine." Hopefully Mom won't notice the money I've been nicking from her cash envelope before I have time to replace it.

"Cool beans." She pauses. "You know, the invitation's still open if you want to make a few of your own things to sell at the show. It'd be a way for you to pad what I'm paying you on the back end. Give yourself a little extra holiday money or put it toward the wheels you said you hope to buy."

My fingers itch when I think of it. My grief is lonely and when I'm working with metal, my mind is free of anything but the work. I can see the way my drawings will transform. There are pieces in the scrap pile I want to claim for my own. Nests and feathers and elongated beaks out of discarded industrial parts. I clench my fingers into fists, but my mouth opens and speaks without me, "I'll think about it." Try as I might to hold back the want, it's there.

33

THEN: Bird of Prey

My locker was a disaster. I had a binder between my knees, my latest English assignment in my mouth, and my elbows blocking the avalanche of donated Halloween makeup that Mrs. Thompson, the art teacher, had put me in charge of. I was trying to hold it all in but it was barely working. I grunted as I shoved my massive algebra book in sideways under the bags, but as I almost had it in place, hands snuck around my waist and I jumped, spilling art supplies, lotions, and potions all over the hallway.

"Vivi." I turned to face her. "Maybe give a girl some warning?"

She laughed and started picking up the things that had

fallen. "It's way too early to get scared. We haven't even done our makeup yet."

Mrs. Thompson had stayed true to her word and let me switch my schedule and take Art 2. As part of it, I'd been wrangled into doing face painting at the local arts council center for their Halloween celebration. After the elementary trick-or-treaters had cleared out, the art students and plus ones were going to participate in a zombie crawl down an alley behind the building, where regular people would pay good money to walk through and have the ever-loving crap frightened out of them.

Vivi rode the bus with me to my house so we could get ready there before Mom gave us a ride to the event. I instructed Vivi to sit at the vanity chair in Mom's room. In addition to the makeup Mrs. Thompson had collected, we'd gathered all kinds of abandoned makeup from Cheyanne, Nina, and Vivi's mom, and even bought a bottle of liquid latex for creating realistic wounds. The arts council was providing most of what was needed for the kids' face painting, but Mrs. Thompson had suggested we bring whatever we could to add to the tools available.

Vivi, of course, hadn't made it easy. She wanted to be a zombie bird of prey. I brandished a makeup brush and a beak I'd crafted out of toilet paper rolls.

Vivi raised her eyebrows, her look skeptical. "That is what?"

"Your beak. You say I'm an amazing artist, now you're going to have to trust me."

Vivi grinned. "I like the new confident you. Have at me."

I placed the cardboard beak of the small falcon onto her nose and applied layers of latex and toilet tissue to hold it in place. Once I was satisfied it wasn't going to fall off, I sponged a layer of white base makeup over Vivi's whole face, then slowly built up the layers of black, rusty browns, and golds, and the touch of blue gray that made the bird so beautiful.

After about forty minutes, Vivi looked transformed enough for me to swivel the chair toward the mirror. "What do you think?"

Vivi touched the beak extending from her face. "This is amazing." She tilted her head in quick birdlike movements as she looked at herself. From her bag, she pulled out the wig she'd made from feathers and a shower cap, and tucked it on over her hair. "What do you think? Am I a fearsome zombie falcon?"

"I need to blend in the shower cap line, but then yes. Fearsome."

"Okay, blend, then one thing before I do your zombie face."

I dabbed at her hairline. "Vivi, I can't kiss you now, there's no way."

Vivi swatted me. "No, idiot. You have to take a photo of me. For your portfolio. I was looking on the site for State's graphics program, very prestigious by the way, and they want a well-rounded portfolio. This"—she circled her face with her hand—"is excellent."

"You really think so?" I knew I was fishing for a compliment, but at the same time I was thinking about Vivi's words. I'd never thought of myself as one of the four-year college people. But my mom did it as an adult, and now she was applying to law schools. Maybe I could do something awesome, too. Maybe Vivi's dreaming for the both of us wasn't out of reach. Maybe I actually had what it took to be that girl.

"Finish me up and get your mom's good camera. We'll let the photographs answer that question. Okay?"

"Deal."

When Vivi's makeup was complete, and we stared at the images on the back screen of Mom's SLR, I finally agreed with Vivi. The transformation was unreal. I'd figured out how to take the flat image of the falcon and turn it into something three-dimensional. And awesome.

"Now do you believe me?" Vivi asked.

I nodded and kept staring at the image on the tiny screen.

"Please apply with me. When I'm studying my butt off you won't be bugging me to go for pizza, because you'll be busting your tail in the art studio. Then we'll graduate together, move off to somewhere like the Outer Banks where I can work for the Park Service and you can work from home and take care of our many cats."

I looked up from the camera. "Indoor, of course. We don't want them hunting the birds at our many feeders."

"True." Vivi grinned. "I solemnly swear to clean the litter box a zillion times a day."

Emma Watson appeared in Mom's doorway meowing for effect. Vivi squawked at her and the cat took one look at the makeup on her face and bolted back out into the hallway.

"Big, bad bird girl."

"You know it." Vivi winked. "Now let's go scare some civilians."

34

Now: Four Weeks, Three Days After

"Damn civilians," McGovern grumbles as he walks away from whichever not-ex-military school staff member has knocked at the classroom door, then calls my name. "Perez. Hallway." He jerks his thumb toward the door, but doesn't get up. Everyone turns to look at me, but I don't know what's going on any more than they do.

I step outside. Mrs. Swaley is seated at the bench by the door. She stands when I come out.

"Jessica, how are you?"

"Fine." Suspicious.

She has a folder in her hand with my name on it and a laptop in the other. "Have a seat." She pats the bench next to her as she sits again. "I would have waited until you return to main campus next week, but Mrs. Thompson seemed to think time was of the essence and was concerned you'd slip through the cracks. I promised her I'd check in with you since I was going to be at county office anyway."

"About what?" I ask.

She opens her laptop and the page for NC State pops up. "She gave me the impression you were going to apply to a program with a very specific deadline date. I believe the fifteenth?" She looks to me for confirmation.

I shrug. I'm conflicted, yet not. I know for sure I don't want to go to State, but maybe . . . somewhere else?

She keeps going. "In looking at the requirements, it seems as if your grades and test scores are close enough in line you have a chance to get in. But for this program there's also a portfolio requirement."

"Yeah," I say. "I know." What I don't say is all the pieces that were good enough are gone. I suppose someone with enough technological savvy could retrieve them, but why bother?

"Are you able to get online at home? Is there someone there to help you with the application if you have questions? I'm happy to work with you now to get done what we can get done." She looks at her watch. The offer doesn't feel genuine and judging by how many times I've seen her walking through the halls of Grady with a Starbucks cup in her hand, I feel certain all she wants to do is leave so she can sneak over to the drive-through on her way back to main campus.

"Yeah. I have people to help me." I do have people. Everyone wants to help me. But what I'm figuring out is I have to wade through it myself. My fingers twitch. Like the flick of wings. I stuff them into my back pockets as I stand and return to the classroom.

I go home to an empty house. It's me and Emma Watson and the sound of nothing. My feet take me from bedroom, to living room, to kitchen, and back again. In the past, I'd be talking to Vivi, or working on sketches, or doing homework. But life tastes like cardboard and I don't want to do any of those things. I consider going and sneaking from the gin bottle again. But then I think about Darla from the VA group and getting buzzed doesn't feel like who I want to be. I also don't want to cry tonight. I don't want to dredge up memories that make my chest fill with shards of glass or my limbs grow heavy with ache. I open my computer. I pull out the brochures Cheyanne left for me. I start flipping through. There are clean-cut students with dentist white smiles and books under their arms, there are handsome guys with legs lifted onto brick steps and pretty girls seated on the step wall next to them. Some photos are diverse. Most are not. But college doesn't seem like the place for a Vivi-less me.

Out of curiosity I type in "blacksmithing + North Carolina + school" to see what I get. The first several links are for short-term schools where you can go to learn to put shoes on horses. Though it's interesting, it's not for me. My Texas cousins never could get me past my fear of the massive animals. Until they start putting shoes on cats, that is not my kind of blacksmithing.

I read some more and stop when I come across a school up in the mountains. It's a craft school that teaches all kinds of things, blacksmithing included. I follow the links and click through, looking at pictures. The people in the classes are all different ages, ethnicities, but they each have a certain cool factor, like Greer and Eliza. Loads of tattoos, not so shiny as the kids on the college brochures. I'm disappointed when I read it's not a place where you can get degrees, rather, a place where you take specialized classes for a few weeks in the summer. I wonder if Greer has heard of it. I bookmark it and go back to my search bar.

When I take North Carolina out of the equation, a few other things pop up, including a school in Carbondale, Illinois, that offers a fine arts degree in blacksmithing. A strange feeling comes over me and I pause. I'm not supposed to feel excitement. But there it is. My finger hovers over the trackpad, suspended between stepping forward and holding back. I don't know why I can't just press the link but something stops me. It's knowing I'll be moving ahead while Vivi stays suspended in time. It's my changing course and moving to unknown terrain without her knowing. If ghosts are real, and I'm gone from here, could she find me?

I shut the computer lid. I'm not ready to risk it.

Instead I take a different risk.

"Hello." Cheyanne's voice is laced with caution.

"Hey," I say. She's quiet. I plow on. "Did you get my text?"

"Yes."

She's not going to make this easy on me and honestly, I don't blame her. I was an ass, even if my grief made me do it. I take a deep breath. "Cheyanne, I'm sorry, okay? I know you were only trying to help. It's just been really hard and I haven't handled it well."

"Understatement much?"

At least she's talking.

"I know." I flick a laser light beam across the bedroom floor. Emma Watson doesn't budge from where she's sprawled on top of my clean clothes laundry basket. "I was hoping I could make it up to you. I've been invited to an amazing Halloween party tomorrow night. You could come."

"Oh, I could?"

Sarcasm spills into my ear.

"Please come?"

She's quiet again. Finally, when I'm about to beg, she speaks. "I'll see if I can make it. I have to take my brothers trick-or-treating. What's the address?"

I sit up and quick shuffle the scraps of paper on my bedside table and find Greer and Eliza's street number and give it to her. "I'll be there around seven . . . as a Minion."

She's laughing as she hangs up.

I'll take it as a good sign.

35

Now: Four Weeks, Four Days After

I come out of the bathroom, slipping on my Snuggie over my school clothes, when I bump into Deuces. I was worried he'd be mad about Sahara, but he was totally cool. Apparently, she'd had a good time after I left and met someone else to be her LGBTQ guru.

Deuces takes one look at me and starts laughing. "Girl, what the hell is that?"

"My Halloween costume."

The only acknowledgment McGovern made about the holiday was pulling out a special Chuck Norris poster that he hung on the front board. "Chuck Norris got all of your candy." Pretty sure he made that one himself.

"You going to Chuck E. Cheese or something?"

I'd like to invite him to Greer's party, but I figure if Greer had wanted anybody else from school to be there, she'd have done the inviting herself. Besides, there was the chance Chey would show up and Greer hadn't told me to invite a posse.

"Something. It will involve little kids."

"Good thing. Otherwise you'd look like a damn fool."

"Thanks for the vote of confidence." Hopefully the people who show up to Greer and Eliza's won't be as judgmental.

He high-fives me as I walk by and head out to the car where my mom's waiting to give me a ride.

"You look cute," she says.

"Tell that to him." I point out the window where Deuces is getting on the bus. His ankle monitor doesn't go unnoticed by Mom.

"I hate that you're here, Jess. I hope the fighting is done now."

"It is, Mom. But here's not so bad." As I say it, I realize it's a thought that's been tickling the sides of my brain. It's only another week before I'm released back to main campus. Which means no more Cabinetworks. And even though I'm working for Greer on the side, it still bums me out to think I'm going to lose my hands-on afternoons and chilling with the guys in alternative school. Would it be so bad to stay here until I graduate? It's not like I loved much about Grady High other than Vivi, Cheyanne, and Levi. Maybe I could do online classes next semester like some of the guys do.

Mom interrupts my reverie. "It's not great, Jess. This is not the place to be if you want to get into State." She glances my way. "The deadline's coming up, isn't it? Two weeks?"

I wish everyone could leave me alone about it. State was Vivi's dream, then she made it ours. In all my thoughts, I'd imagined myself there with *her*. I'd picture *her* walking across campus to meet me for a meal, *her* smile lighting up her eyes when she saw me. Never, not even once, did I picture myself on that campus, in those classrooms, without Vivi nearby.

"I know." I work hard to keep the irritation out of my voice. "The guidance counselor stopped by yesterday to see me. She's going to help me with the application."

"Won't I have to do the FAFSA form? I know you're eligible for benefits through the VA, but it wouldn't hurt for us to be prepared. Pretty sure my salary is low enough still for us to qualify for some help if we need it."

"Yeah, sure. I'll get you the link." There's no harm

done in her filling it out. Even if no other application ever gets filled out or submitted.

We drive across town to the VA building. Mom tells me to take a cab service to the party and she or Nina will come pick me up at ten.

"Ten?" I start to give her grief, but she silences me with a swipe across her lips.

"It may be Halloween but it's still a school night."

"Fine."

Inside Mr. A is waiting for me. He's wearing a firefighter's jacket and hat.

"Nice costume," I say.

"I'm glad you keep coming back, Jess. The kids seem to really connect with you."

I don't answer but it does make me feel good. It's not so long ago that I was just like them, squirming on plastic chairs or beanbags, trying to make sense of a life with my father gone. Just like I am now, without Vivi. I dig in my pocket and find Darla's rock that she'd let me keep again last week. "Here."

He shakes his head. "Give it to her yourself."

The kids arrive one by one. There's a cat, a Spider-Man, two Supermans, one fisherman, a few other random costume jumbles, and Darla dressed up like a soldier. After we do a quick fashion show, we sit in the circle like last session. This time we're sharing favorite Halloween memories, or favorite candy, or favorite fandoms of those we've loved and lost. It's much like last time, except this time there's no one new to the group. And this time when the circle gets to me, I share two memories.

It takes a little digging to bring the first one into focus, but when I pull it up I'm smiling. "In first grade, my sister, who was in fourth grade, wanted us both to dress up as this singer, Selena. Our cousins in Texas had introduced her to the movie and she was completely obsessed with the story. But I didn't want to be Selena, because I never really liked wearing girlie clothes." Darla sits up straighter in her chair next to me. "I wanted to go as Mater from *Cars*." I laugh. "My sister was so mad at me. She said I was a girl and it was stupid to want to go as a boy tow truck and my costume would look dirty. My dad, he stepped in. He put a hand on her shoulder and suggested she go as Selena if it was so important to her but if I wanted to be Tow Mater, then Tow Mater I would be." I glance at the ceiling and a wash of warmth floods me. We may not have had enough time, but when I think of him now it's these beautiful snippets of life. I realize maybe I'll get there with Vivi one day. So I keep going.

"The other person I lost, my girlfriend, she wasn't in the military like the rest of our lost loved ones, but she was very special to me. It's still pretty new. And it still hurts pretty bad." My voice cracks and I squeeze the rock in my palm. Darla edges her chair a little closer to me. She raises her hand.

Mr. A nods and she asks, "What was your favorite thing about her?"

I smile as I wipe away the tears forming in my lower lids. "Her smile. Her infectious love of life. Her obsession with birds. The way she believed in me."

Another boy raises his hand. "What do you think she would have gone as for Halloween this year?"

I know the answer. "Fawkes. The phoenix from Harry Potter. I was going to go as Dumbledore."

"But you're a Minion?" someone else said.

"Too sad to go with the old plans," I answered. At this, all the little kids kind of nod and squirm.

"What should we say to Jess? She really opened up to us," Mr. A addresses the group.

"You are loved," they say and then I'm engulfed in hugs as they swarm me. I don't bother to stop my tears, but in short order tears turn to laughter as the littles pile on top of me in more of a wrestling heap than a hug. When we return to our chairs, Darla takes my hand and her rock is cradled in our joined palms. It feels like a step in some kind of direction. Which way I'm not sure, but my heart, for just a moment, feels full.

36

Now: Four Weeks, Four Days After (Night)

The driver has to creep down Greer and Eliza's street. There are still trick-or-treaters out en masse, and loads of cars parked along the curb. Even from here I can see the insanity that is their front yard. Gauzy cobwebs strung from all the trees, huge black spiders caught in the film, the house festooned with indigo and orange lights that don't blink so much as pulse. I have the guy pull over and tell him I'll walk the rest of the way.

It's obvious their house is popular with the kids because tons of them spill up and down the steps and they're talking about it as they pass me on the sidewalk.

"That dragon was rad."

"I heard one of those ladies is a witch."

"They gave us full-sized candy bars!"

The last comment lets me know just how into Halloween Greer and Eliza really are, like Vivi and her over-the-top costuming needs, and wham . . . the warm heart feeling is replaced by the jackknife of loss. Grief fucking sucks. Sorry, Vivi. Forking. I gather myself in and breathe deep. I check my phone to see if Cheyanne has texted to let me know if she's definite or not. Nothing. I turn around to see if my driver's still close by but he's long gone. Looks like I'm in this thing. Alone.

I push open the metal gate at the front of their sidewalk. It's new, obviously Greer's creation, and ridiculously awesome. It's all bones and skeleton heads and even a "Keep Out" sign incorporated into the metal design. I need to remember to tell her she should totally make some of these to sell.

I shoulder in with some trick-or-treaters and make my way up the front steps, ready for the full #GreerLiza experience. A kid dressed like an EMT knocks on the door. There's a blast of fog, the sound of trumpets and creaking doors, and then the door opens revealing Eliza in a skintight red bodysuit covered with orange sequined scales, thigh-high studded boots, and a pair of massive outspread wings attached to her back. She has a wig on that makes her hair look like a geisha and it's stabbed through with a zillion decorative chopsticks. I hope Cheyanne shows up if for nothing more than to see Eliza's costume. She will die.

The kids gasp and the dragon smiles. I guess even though Eliza's costume is fierce, it's better not to scare the pants off your neighbor's children. Behind her, Greer's done up like a circus ringmaster, and costumed people mill in their small living room.

"Jess." Eliza spots me and when the kids pass, their candy bars safely in bags and plastic pumpkins, she gives me a quick hug. "So glad you're here." She turns back for the next group of trick-or-treaters and I slip past her wings into the house.

"Jess!" Greer holds her arms wide and bows, flourishing her hat as she does. "We need a Minion for our circus."

My face goes hot under the warmth of the Snuggie. Vivi would never have let me get away with this level of Halloween lame. But I squeak out a thanks all the same.

"Come on, I'll introduce you to some folks." Greer drapes an arm over my shoulders and leads me through clusters of people, saying names as I take in details. Their friends are as eclectic as they are. Straight, gay, with kids, without, black, white, Hispanic, and Asian. But the unifying factor is the costumes. Everyone's spot-on amazing.

We wind up in the kitchen, where Greer points me to

the under-twenty-one beverages. "Came solo? I hope we're not too boring for you."

"Are you kidding? I'll have fun just watching how people dressed." Right about then my phone buzzes. I glance down.

—We're out front. Is this rad house where we're supposed to be?

I flash my phone at Greer. "Not sure who the 'we're' is, but I did invite my friend, Cheyanne."

"Well, invite her in."

—Yes. There's a dragon named Eliza at the front door. Who's we're?

There's no answering text as I hear Eliza saying, "Come in, she's back there somewhere."

At the front door, I see Cheyanne, dressed like Levi. And Levi, dressed like a girl. That's the "we're." Cheyanne invited Levi? My stomach drops. Did he tell her about what happened? I imagine Levi having this moment of fantasy where he thinks he can finally get over Cheyanne now that we've locked lips, and turning to her as a friend for advice. As Greer slips away to greet other guests coming in from the back door, I sneak a splash of the vodka on the counter into my fruit punch, for fortification.

"You came."

Cheyanne looks at me through narrowed eyes and I

know, in that moment, Levi has told her everything. "I called Levi for a ride because my car's in the shop and he was super excited to get dressed up and come out and find you. Isn't he pretty?"

Cheyanne should be the one dressed as a dragon because there are flames shooting from her nostrils. She may be here, but she's definitely still pissed. I gulp the fruit punch. I look at Levi. His eyes are amazing with makeup, I'll give her that, but just because he's dressed like a girl, doesn't mean I want to kiss him again.

"Hey." A tattooed girl interrupts our conversation. She's young but not as young as us and she's totally checking dude-drag Cheyanne out.

Cheyanne barely turns in the girl's direction, her eyes are so intently boring into mine. "Hey," she answers but it's dismissive and the girl walks away.

"She was checking you out," I say to break up the tension.

"Good for her. I'm superhot tonight. Doesn't mean I want to do anything about it."

"Are you going to be pissed at me forever?"

Before she answers, Levi sidles up closer and props his arm on my shoulders. "Whatcha drinking?"

"Fruit punch." I nod to the counter. "It's over there."

"Southern fruit punch?" he asks.

"I made it that way, but don't be obvious. Greer's my boss and I'm pretty sure she realizes you're still in high school, too." Cheyanne's stare hasn't eased and I'm breaking down waiting on her answer.

Finally, Levi walks away and she hisses, "I'm more pissed than before. I canNOT fucking believe you. You kissed him? You know what he's like. At least with me, I never gave him a physical reason to get his hopes up."

"Cut me some slack. It was a mistake after a really weird night. It just kind of happened. It didn't mean anything. It was a nothing. He knows that."

She throws up her hands from where they've been crossed. "Listen to yourself, a nothing? What kind of toxic friend are you? Between the crap you said to me and now kissing Levi right after Vivi died? Your grief card's running out. We are here, Jess. We want to support you. We are your friends. But we have limits, and in case you've forgotten, it sucks for us, too."

Levi returns with two cups and holds one out for Cheyanne as he moves back in next to my side.

Cheyanne sips her drink and rolls her eyes like I'm lower than the sole on her shoe, but she doesn't say anything else with him here.

"Um, do y'all want to go out back and see where I work?" Anything to avoid Chey's scorn.

"Yeah." Levi smiles all the way into the corners of his eyes when he looks at me.

Hot fudge sundae, have I screwed up. I thought he got it. I thought when we walked away from the railroad bridge that I had made it pretty clear, except then he shut me up, but I've avoided him ever since. Shouldn't he have gotten it?

I drain my cup as we walk down the steps. Rufus ambles over, wagging his tail. He's wearing a tuxedo shirt. "Hey, buddy." I ruffle his ears, assiduously avoiding conversation with Cheyanne or Levi as I lead them across to the forge.

"So, um, this is Greer's studio." I fling my arm out with a flourish and practically wipe out Cheyanne's cup. She hop steps sideways and bumps me into Levi, who uses the moment to drape his arm over me again. I wiggle out from under it and keep pointing out equipment and Greer's work.

Cheyanne's glare softens, but only slightly. "You're making art again?"

At this I stiffen. "No."

"You should be," she says. "It'd be way healthier than whatever else you've been doing to occupy your time."

"Like hanging out with me?" Levi flips the wig hair over his shoulder.

There's another eye roll. "You said it, not me." Then, "Levi, could you refill my drink, please?" Cheyanne hands him her cup. "Just plain is fine."

When he walks off with all three cups she lays into me again. "You know how he is, Jess. He's sweet and good and he deserves a girlfriend who's going to really love him. Not me, and certainly not you. You're being selfish because you're sad and bored and he's easy to take advantage of. The minute you find some girl you're into, you won't have the time of day for him. Believe me, I remember."

"I never stopped hanging out with you when Vivi and I started dating."

"No," she says. "But we went from two to three. And now that she's dead, you've pushed me out of your life and snagged Levi as well. You're not the only one grieving her death, Jess. She was my friend, too."

I lean back against the workbench, a wash of self-pity rushing over me until I shake it off and find my words. "Leading him on was not my intention. Neither was pushing you away. It's just hard, Chey, it's so hard." All of my carefully cultivated party facade melts away and I fall onto her shoulder sobbing. I feel Chey's arms wrap around me. I am loved. I am lifted. Why can't I act the way I'm supposed to?

37

THEN: Scattering Robins

Waking up at seven a.m. on Saturday morning was not the day I wanted to be having, but self-pity would get me nowhere with my GF and BFF. Today was the first ACT opportunity for Grady High School juniors and there was no way Vivi or Cheyanne was going to miss it. And hoo-rah for me, they'd insisted I sign up, too. "Just in case we have to retake," they'd said. It was really a reference to *my* unlikelihood of making a college-worthy score on the first try. But at least I knew they loved me.

I downed a swig of coffee, grabbed two number-two pencils, and my ID. A horn sounded outside and I stuffed them in my back pocket.

“Good luck,” Nina said as she stumbled out of her room into the living room.

“Thanks.” I bolted for the door before she could enlighten me with test-taking tips, but when I hit the front stoop, I stopped. Parked at the curb was the shiny burnt-orange Honda Element Vivi’d been begging her parents for ever since she saw it sitting in the used lot at the dealership. I ran across the lawn and Vivi leaned over from inside and pushed the door open.

“Welcome to my car.”

“No way.” I ran my hand over the dashboard, opened the glove box, then moved my seat back. “When? When did this happen? Why did you not call me immediately?”

“Last night, and I wanted to surprise you.”

I tapped on the satellite radio console. “You are so spoiled.”

“There is nothing about that statement that upsets me. But it is awesome, isn’t it? Dad got a royalty check from some song lyrics he wrote for a friend, ages ago, and surprised me. It’s seven years old, but this makes it smell new.” Vivi reached out and flicked the new car deodorizer hanging from the rearview mirror.

“You need something classier than an air freshener for your car bling.”

"That's what artist girlfriends are for. To make classier bling." Vivi leaned over and kissed me, letting her lips linger and tease before pulling away.

I grinned. "Hmmm, new car, hot kiss. Makes getting up at the booty crack of dawn almost worth it." I rapped on the dashboard with my knuckles. "Onward, Jeeves."

In the school parking lot, Cheyanne did the same double take I'd done. "Nice ride. You've bested me in style."

Vivi linked arms with Cheyanne and dragged her to look at all four sides of the car. "I could never best you in style overall, but I definitely win the car category." Cheyanne's car was a standard issue four-door used sedan in a dull dark gray.

Inside the school, we looked up our names and the printed lists and found the classrooms we were to report to. Vivi and Cheyanne were in the same room since their last names were close in the alphabet, but I was in a room in an entirely different wing. "Good luck." Vivi leaned in and kissed me on the cheek.

"You, too," I said, but I knew they didn't need it.

In the room, we had to hand over our cell phones and wait for the official intercom announcement that testing could begin. A cold prickle of sweat worked its way onto my palms. Why had I let them talk me into this?

Halfway through the test at one of the breaks, I knew it was a disaster. The math was insanely difficult. My heart rate picked up a beat. I tapped my pencil on the table and ignored the glares of the people sitting around me. My good friend, rage, slipped into the corner of my brain and waved at me. He pointed at the glaring girl to my left. I drummed harder with my pencil, letting the thrill of pissing her off take over my actions. A cough came from the front of the room. The proctor held up her own pencil and made a slicing motion across her throat with it. Oh, how I wanted to leap out of my desk and let it scrape across the floor and make a big show of storming out of the room. The test would be a misadministration. All these people's tests . . . invalidated, and I'd be at fault. I stopped drumming my pencil, closed my eyes tight, and clicked through the possible outcomes. Nothing good. I opened my eyes, sighed, and remembered—Vivi believed in me.

The next several problems I darkened in the letter C and prayed at least a few of them would be right.

After the test was over and they released us from our classrooms, I met Chey and Vivi in the parking lot.

"Joyride?" Cheyanne asked.

"Food?" I added.

"Picnic," Vivi said, pointing at the blue sky.

We stopped at DaVinci's Deli and gathered sandwiches, water bottles, and an entire bag of mini-donuts. When we got to the park, Vivi pulled a blanket out of the trunk. She held it up. "Dad's emergency kit proves itself useful."

Once we were sprawled out in a patch of sunlight, I told them what I'd been holding in during their comparisons of feeling confident. "I bombed the test."

"Bombed it?" Cheyanne asked.

"Total failure. The math was so much harder than I thought it would be."

Vivi put her hand on top of mine. "I bet you did better than you think."

Cheyanne garbled through a mouthful of donut. "I think you need like a twenty-five composite to get into State."

I flung a pinecone, inadvertently disturbing a flock of robins. "There's no way. I'll be lucky if I got an eighteen like Nina."

Vivi leaned in for a side hug. "You can take it as many times as you need and we're here to help you. Right, Cheyanne?"

Cheyanne nodded. "Yup. Here to help."

Sometimes it was easier when I was angry Jess and

could bury myself with harsh words and fists. Meeting Vivi was the best thing to ever happen to me, but it also made me the most accountable I'd ever been. And the most studious. But then I thought about the test. Rage had come to visit and I'd dealt with it. I hadn't reacted. I hadn't blown up. I'd filled in every bubble and left the room with everyone else. Maybe I wasn't a total failure.

"Do y'all really believe I can do this?"

They nodded and crossed their hearts.

I lay back and stared at the sky. They believed in me. What if I could be a college girl?

"Okay," I said. "Study dates. See if you can transform me from average into State material." I still doubted that was possible, but if your best friend and girlfriend thought you had the goods, the least you could do was try.

Cheyanne chucked a donut into my hand. "Now can we talk about something else? Like when Vivi's going to let us drive her car? Or how many band instruments will fit inside of that thing? My brain still hurts."

Viv jumped up. "Let's go swing."

I stood up and watched them run across the park, scattering the flock of birds as they passed. The moment locked in my mind—a beautiful image for my sketch-book later that night. Then I thought about the image of me . . . making art, going to school, my mother, my sister, my girlfriend proud. My smile lifted and I leaned back, welcoming the warmth of the sun and the warmth of my thoughts. I'd come so far since Dad died. Then I smiled toward the sky, because I knew, if he were still around, that he'd be proud, too.

38

Now: Four Weeks, Six Days After

I'm not too proud to admit that the only reason I agreed to hang out with Nina for the day is my trying to avoid something else. In this case, it's hurting Levi's feelings. After Greer and Eliza's party, Cheyanne texted me a warning. I'm going to post that Levi is your new boyfriend if you don't tell him in VERY CLEAR terms that you are friends only. Instead of following through I was avoiding, hoping he would get the hint on his own, though judging by the number of hey what are you doing? texts, it hadn't quite sunk in yet.

Nina was blathering on as she spread butter on her toast. "I've got us booked for a mani-pedi at a salon on Wall Street and then I got us reservations at the pinball arcade because that seems like something you'd like and after that I thought we could find someplace extra cool to eat, a friend told me about this crepe place that has amazing skinny French fries, and then we can go to the shops down on Lexington, those are always fun, right?"

"A mani-pedi?"

"I know, I know. Not your thing. But you don't have to get polish. They massage your hands and your feet and put lotion on them and it just feels good. A relaxing start to our day. I figured relaxing would be good for you. You have to admit you've been kind of tense."

"Nina. My girlfriend died."

Nina sighs. "Still? It's been over a month, Jess. Shouldn't you be snapping out of it?"

There's no explaining it to her, even though she should know grief doesn't work that way, so I don't answer. She finishes eating and we head to the car and before long we've made the junction with Interstate 40 and are hurtling westward.

"How's it going with that guy you've been studying with?" Nina asks.

"He passed his vocabulary quiz."

Nina stares at me for a beat too long and I scream. She snaps her eyes back to the road and darts around the eighteen-wheeler she's coming up on too fast.

I press hard on my imaginary passenger's side brake.

"Could you please slow down? You're driving like an idiot. How did you ever even get a license?"

"Nice change of subject." But she slows down. "I need more information. Since when are you palling around with guys?"

I shrug and look out the window at the passing farmland. "Can we just drop it? You, Cheyanne. Everybody's making such a big deal about who I'm hanging out with."

Then I start crying again, totally unexpectedly, and it comes out of me like a freaking gusher. Nina looks panic-stricken and pulls off at the next rest area.

She tries to dab at my face with a Kleenex. "Did I do something? I'm so sorry. I didn't mean to ruin our day."

"Stop." I push her hand away and unhook the seat belt. "I'm going to go pee and then we can go. I just cry now, along with getting into the occasional fistfight. I make stupid decisions. Welcome to the new Jess."

I leave her sitting in the car while I go in. There's immediate relief when I let the stream out of me. I sit for a minute and stare at the drab green door of the stall. It was always easy with Vivi. I'd ask her what she thought, what she'd do, and then I typically took her suggestions. It never bothered me that I relied so much on her, but now that she's gone, I feel untethered. Lost. I think maybe I'm ready to find myself. To stop feeling this way.

Tourist brochures catch my eye on the way out. There's one with an anvil on the cover. I pull it out. "Southern Highland Craft Guild," I say to myself as I read the lettering.

"Have you been?" This hippie-looking dude with a long braid smiles at me, a tiny white-haired woman by his side.

I shake my head. "No."

"It's all kinds of crafts from around the area. You can see our work there, too." The woman's voice is high and chirpy and enthusiastic. "I think today is a demonstration day." She grabs a second brochure and flips it over. "Yep. Blacksmiths, potters, maybe even a weaver."

"Blacksmiths?"

"Yeah." The guy smiles. "You know guys, and girls, who beat on those anvils." He points to the illustrated anvil on the paper.

I smile back. "Yeah, I do know." I thank them for their input and get the name of their craft company so I can see the glass and metalwork they do.

When I get in the car, I hand it to Nina. "Slight change of plans. If I do your mani-pedi, can we go here instead of shopping?"

My sister looks at the brochure, her eyebrows quirking just like Mom's. "Yeah, I guess, if this is what you really want to do." I can tell it's killing her because shopping is way more her speed, but this day is supposed to be about me and I know she feels bad because of my tears.

"Awesome." I don't complain about her driving the rest of the way.

When we've finished Nina's list of to-dos, I have to admit I am feeling more relaxed. I even agreed to let the nail guy put polish on my toes. Black, like my soul, but it looks cool. And my manicured nails look trim and tidy, all the little loose skin clipped away. The vintage pinball arcade is amazing and we find the crepe place where we gorge on herbed French fries and ham and cheese crepes.

"You seriously want to go to this art place?" Nina looks longingly at the clothing shop next door to the restaurant.

"I seriously do."

"Okay, then, we should get going."

We flag down the waiter and pay, then head to the car. I punch the address into the GPS and Nina drives away from downtown. The craft place is off the Blue Ridge Parkway so it takes us a couple of "make a U-turn" commands before we get sorted. When we pull into the parking lot there are a bunch of cars and a few white tents set up near the front doors.

"This is the place."

A few little birds flit in and out among the trees.

"Look." I point. "Those are dark-eyed juncos, you only see those in winter near us."

Nina pauses and looks. "Vivi taught you that."

A sad smile comes with my agreement. "It was unreal all the facts she knew. Those look plain but they're like the British royalty of birds. If you're a low man bird, you stay low man bird. Every bird in its rightful place." Vivi would have said my rightful place was at State, by her side. The reality is, the chances of my getting in, even with an intact portfolio, would be slim to none. No matter how many times I took the ACT, I could only manage to squeak it up as high as a twenty-one. Not shabby, but not top state school standards, despite Mrs. Swaley's encouragement.

As Nina and I wander around the tents, I look at all these people making cool things, fireplace tools, hooks, there's even one woman, really tall and blond, who's forging curled iron legs for tabletops made out of tree slices.

"Do you think they earn a living doing this?"

Nina shrugs and tries on a woven scarf at the weaving demonstration tent. "I don't know, ask." She puts the scarf back and looks at her phone. "But do it quick, we need to head back. I have a date with Sid tonight."

"Sid? What happened to Benny?"

"He had commitment issues."

I bite my tongue because the real answer is probably

the exact opposite, that Nina had the commitment issues, but I won't argue the point with her. We've dealt with our daddy grief in different ways.

I approach the blond woman. She smiles and quenches the metal she'd been hammering. I swallow my nerves and say the first stupid thing that comes to my mind. "Do you make all of this?"

"As my mother would say, God makes it all. But I take the raw materials and craft them into something more. Are you interested in blacksmithing?"

I nod and even though I'm nervous and a little embarrassed, I go for it. "Yeah. I just started learning how to work on the forge through a work-study program with my high school."

"How about that? I didn't know there was a program like that around here."

"Not here. In Charlotte. Can I ask you something else?"

"Shoot." Up close the woman is older than I'd thought. Maybe in her sixties, but she's in amazing shape and has young energy. More reasons to keep hammering.

"Can you make a living from this?"

She laughs out loud. "Now that's a direct question. You sure you want to know?"

"Yes." Then, "Please."

"Depends on the kind of life you want. If you think you have to have a brand-new car, and a big fancy house to survive, then probably not. But if you prefer a life of making your own rules and living simply, then yes."

I think about Greer and Liza's life. Small house, big hearts, awesome friends. "I think that sounds good."

"Then go for it," she says. "Here." She hands me a business card. "If you have any questions along the way, feel free to be in touch. It's always nice to meet more women interested in the craft."

"Can I have another card?" Maybe Greer doesn't know about this place or this lady's work. She hands me one and I wave bye before threading my way through people and booths back to my sister and the car.

Once we're buckled up, I turn to her. "Hey, Nina?"

"Yeah?"

"Would you think it's weird if I tried to stay at the alternative school?"

"Maybe a little. But you've always been different than me. I'd have died on a social level if I'd had to leave the main campus, but it seems like you're doing okay there and it's pretty cool you've gotten into this." She gestures toward the blacksmiths. "One thing I've learned at hygienist school is having a trade that can get you an actual job is good. What does Mom say?"

"No way, José."

Nina laughs. "Yeah, I can hear her. Do you want me to talk to her?"

I consider it for a moment, but sometimes what Nina says, even if she thinks she's being helpful, can twist in ways I might not expect. But it's pretty cool that she'd offer. "Nah, it'd be better if I did it myself. But thanks for offering." I pause. "And thanks for today. It did make me feel better."

"Yeah?" She smiles and twists a strand of her hair around her finger.

I nod, then give her a hug. "Yeah. You're not bad for a big sis."

She pushes me back. "Go on with your bad self. Now who's going to cry." When we get on the highway, she drives a whole lot calmer. Kind of how I feel after talking to the blacksmith. Calm and like I might have found a new way forward. One I never saw coming. One I never wished for. But one that, maybe, I need.

39

Now: Five Weeks After

There's no more putting it off. I text Levi. You want to hang out?

The immediacy of his affirmative reply makes me feel like a dick. I should not have kissed him. I should not have held back on what I wanted to say that night when we were leaving the tracks. Cheyanne's right. I know how he is and if I'm honest with myself, I did string him along. Not consciously, but with my sad inner self who wanted someone to comfort her. We make plans to meet again at the tracks after lunch.

Mom's studying at the kitchen table when I walk out from the back.

"Will you be here later?" I ask. Figure if I plan on laying down truths with Levi, I might as well lay down truths with her as well.

"I will. Is there something you need, sweetie?" She pauses her highlighter and looks up.

"Want to have a talk, that's all."

Mom closes her book and motions for me to sit in the chair next to her. I hadn't planned to do this now, but the opportunity is presenting itself.

"Remember how I asked you about staying at the alternative school and doing online courses for next semester?"

Mom frowns in response. "I don't remember any such thing. You might have hinted you liked it there, but staying?"

"Please, Mom, listen. You of all people have got to understand. I'm comfortable there. My grades haven't sunk too much lower and it's not like any of the classes I had scheduled for next semester matter besides the last science I need. And it's available online."

"Jess. You can't avoid life forever."

"No, it's not that, please, listen. I love working at Cabinetworks. It helps me be in the moment and not be sad and not be thinking about Vivi every second of every minute." Working with my hands, being covered in soot and sweat with the ring of a hammer in my ears, is the only thing since Vivi died that gives me a purpose I feel good about.

"You can't run from the grief, love. It doesn't work that way." Even after all these years, a tear still springs to the corner of my mother's eye.

"I'm not running." My voice is a low whisper, maybe because even as I say it I'm wondering if it's true. It seems like that's all I've been doing for the past month, pumping my arms away from pain toward any other emotion I could find.

Mom sighs. "I'll be honest. I don't want this for you. I'm digging in, trying not to be judgmental about the types of kids over at that building, but I'm struggling. I don't want you messed up with drugs or more fighting or whatever emotional problems that are sheltered there."

At this I get angry. "Mom, I have emotional problems."

Double sigh. "Please let me finish."

I nod.

She folds her hands together on the table, her future lawyer pose. "I am open to considering this."

I sit up. "Really?!"

"On one condition."

I sit back.

"You need to apply to State, as planned, along with at least four other four-year programs that fit your test scores and GPA. I don't expect you to be unrealistic in your choices, but I want you to have them. Even your sister plans on going back to get her four-year technician degree after she's worked for a couple of years." She reaches out and cradles my cheek. "And Jess, I do know how hard it is to walk through the grief of losing a loved one. But what choice do we have? Life is a gift. Don't turn a blind eye to it."

A few weeks ago, it seemed like I had limited choices. Alcohol. Fights. But now I feel as if I'm getting a clue. And I'm not wrong about staying at the alternative school. I know I can make it work and stay on track. Besides, most of those guys, except for maybe Levon, are hoping to stay on track, too. "You know, it's kind of disrespectful to assume I would cave so easily to peer pressure. And disrespectful to assume all the guys there are on a path to trouble. Maybe by staying at the alternative school, I'd be part of the solution. Someone serious about graduating and doing their work. Dad always said a good work ethic was a person's golden opportunity."

Mom smiles. "He did, didn't he?"

I smile back hoping for the yes.

Mom spies the subtle manipulation. "Though I love sharing memories with you, and though they do make me feel warm inside, I don't plan on changing the conditions

AND even if I come around to your way of thinking, we will still need to meet with the school and your guidance counselor to see if it's even possible."

It's my turn to sigh. "Fine." I stand up and kiss her on the forehead. "Thanks for thinking about it."

She opens her book and waves me out the door.

The next talk won't be so easy. What's Levi going to say? He can't admit he was thinking about it because then he'll look bad. Which makes it weird for me to say anything. But if I don't say anything, then it will linger, even if Cheyanne doesn't make a big deal out of it. For as much as I have no problem jumping into a physical fight, hurting someone's feelings, especially someone you like and respect, is way tougher.

Of course, he's waiting for me since I stopped to talk to Mom.

"Hey." I sit down next to him on the tracks and damn if his expression isn't all soft and hopeful. I drop my face into my palms and rub my thumbs on my temples, then look back up. Do this quick. "Levi . . ."

One word and his expression shifts and I feel like the biggest heel on the planet. What was he supposed to think? We went from never hanging out just the two of us, to suddenly being buds and confidantes. He's straight, why wouldn't he think I was into him? It's no different from when I used to crush on straight girls. Better spit it out. "You know what I'm going to say. I tried to say it the other night but you stopped me. I'm a lesbian, Levi. I'm not into you."

He plinks rocks down onto the road below. "Yeah. I figured."

"But you're hurt. I can tell." It's too bad Cheyanne's not into him, I'd love to be able to give him some sort of hope.

He shrugs. "Doesn't matter. I'll move on. It's just . . ." He looks up at me. "The kiss was good, right?"

I smile and put my hand on top of his. "You are an excellent kisser, Levi. Soft lips, fresh breath. You're not even pushy with your tongue. If it hadn't been for the shave stubble, I might have thought you were a girl, your technique is so impressive."

"Pshew." He leapfrogs with his hand so his rests on top. "At least there's that. If I ever actually find a date, can you testify to my prowess?"

My eyes go wide. I don't really want the world to know about my lapse in judgment.

"Right," he says. "Then you'd have to say you kissed a boy and didn't like it."

"Going for the gold star, you know." I nudge him, then

gasp as a car emerges from under the overpass as I let a rock fall. We both hold our breath, but luckily it misses the trunk by a hair. "That was close." I grow serious. "It was good though. Hanging out with you. Getting into the community center situation. Buzzed bike riding. You've helped me a lot."

He squeezes my hand.

I keep talking. "After Vivi died, those first couple of weeks I felt like my insides might self-combust. I couldn't be around my mom, or Nina, or Cheyanne without a zillion reminders. I hated bursting into tears all the time. You steadied me. I hope you don't think I was using you because, seriously, you have helped me so much."

He lets go of my hand and puts his on the railing, leaning his head sideways so he faces me. "Naw. It was good for me, too. I think my crush on you, which I knew was cursed from the beginning, helped me shake free my crush on Cheyanne. We helped each other." He winks. "Besides, I passed my vocabulary quiz, thanks to you."

We sit in the comfortable silence I've come to expect from Levi until there's the slightest vibration in the bridge.

"Train," we say at the same time as we both start nervously laughing. "Come on." I stand up and wipe the gravel off my jeans. "Let's go to Stan's and get milkshakes.

My treat. Maybe we'll find a cute girl for you."

"Or you," he says as we turn in the direction of my house.

I take a deep breath. "Too soon," I say. "Way too soon."

40

Now: Five Weeks, Two Days After

Greer and I have found a steady rhythm in her studio. She does all the design and forging work, and I'm the welder, grinder, fetcher, toter. Her show is a holiday fair at a downtown arts center, so we're focusing more on the garden art and small things for tabletops, rather than larger sculpture. When we take a break, she hands me a bottle of water from the mini-fridge.

"Got a note from McGovern that your time at Cabinetworks is almost up."

Technically, this Thursday, two days from now, my four weeks of in-school suspension is up. But McGovern already told me I was with him through Friday because of a technicality and because main campus thought it better if I saw the week through to the end.

"I'm working on staying."

"Oh yeah?" Greer wipes sweat from her brow. The forge area is hot, even though the temps have dropped to a more seasonal mid-forties.

"Trying to convince my mom to let me do online classes next semester so I can stay with McGovern and keep coming out to do Cabinetworks stuff."

Greer chuckles. "You're an odd bird, Jess Perez. There are not many people who would choose to hang out with McGovern five days a week."

"He's all right. Once you figure him out. And I don't mind the guys in class either. They're not all as bad as their reputations."

She caps her water bottle and takes mine before chucking them into the recycling bin. "Well that's good, because I want you to keep working here with me."

"Would one hinge on the other?" I swallow down my rising panic, since me staying is nowhere close to a done deal.

"If you're not with me at work, how will you get here? I don't have time to come pick you up, drive back here, and still have the hours for getting my stuff done. It's crunch time for me."

This is not good. If I'm only working on the weekend,

I'll never save enough money to buy a car so that I can get to work all the days Greer offers me.

"Yeah, sure," I say. "I'll figure something out." I don't want to tell her there might be an issue because I don't want her hiring one of the other guys in my place.

Back at work, my brain stews as I grind welds and sand the edges of the plasma cut creatures. It figures the moment I let myself relax into the idea of blacksmithing, the whole opportunity might disappear.

Last night, when I was working on applications per Mom's ultimatum, including the school in Carbondale, I realized I'd really screwed myself by tossing my portfolio. Art *is* my hidden talent. Pretty sure Vivi wouldn't want me to throw it all away. Even if drawing and using my inks is still too painful, I'd begun to think about blacksmithing in a new way. Like that lady at the art center who made furniture, and Greer who made garden gates. What if there was a way to still use my hands, but stay a little clear of the pure emotion of drawing and painting? Greer's offer of letting me make a few personal pieces had planted a seed. I'd started to consider cobbling together a portfolio . . . to see what might happen.

When we're done for the day, I broach the subject, aware that it might be a moot point if I can't get here, but

I'm going to try to stay positive. "Remember when you said I could maybe try my hand at a few of my own pieces?"

Greer perks up. "Sure do."

"I, um, of course I'd do it after doing what you need, but I think I might be into it."

Greer beams. "I'm so glad you've had a change of heart. Any idea what you want to make?"

I shake my head.

"I find it helps to combine things you love."

"Example?"

"Sure. Take my work. It's Dr. Seuss meets the woodlands. Or garden surrealism. There's a cohesiveness to my pieces."

"Your style," I say.

Greer nods. "Yeah, my style, though I think it's easier to develop style as you go."

"Hmmm. I've got nothing." But as I say it, I'm staring at the same chandelier I noticed on the day Greer first gave me a tour. Now I see it. It's a nest. For a multitude of birds, and even though it still feels like a Vivi betrayal to have a moment of excitement, it's there all the same. "Could I use that old chandelier?" I ask.

Greer turns to her scrap pile. "Don't see why not. I kept thinking it was going to speak to me and tell me what it wanted to be but it never did. What's it saying to you?"

I shake my head because I'm not sure I can say it out loud.

"I won't laugh."

"No, it's not that." Then I figure what the hell, Greer doesn't know the connection. "A nest," I say. "It wants to be a nest."

Greer contemplates it again. "I see that. Can't wait to see what you do with it. Quick sketch some ideas and I'll help you figure out how to make it happen. Why don't you take a few pictures of it, then we'll get back to work for about another hour before I take you home."

"Sure thing." The light's not great, but I get a couple of clear shots from different angles and my mind buzzes with possibility. Vivi thoughts flood my brain, but this time the throat lump doesn't lodge, just moves up and away, until it settles into a smile. She would love this.

41

THEN: A Total Bluebird Enthusiast

My mouth settled into a smile as I wagged my finger at Vivi. "No hiking today. No way. Nohow." I wiped my brow and felt speckles of sawdust stick to my sweaty skin. It was late July and the heat was brutal and reminded me of that day we'd gone to look for eagles. Vivi would not have an asthma attack under my watch again.

"Got it, oh overprotective one."

"It's only because I love you."

She leaned over and kissed me. "I know."

We were under the lake house deck working on Vivi's latest project—bluebird houses. She marked lengths, while I used the Skilsaw to cut the boards. Then Vivi used a hole cutter bit to drill out a perfectly circular opening in one of the cut boards. We clamped the boards together to make nailing easier.

"Why are we doing this again?"

"You know why," Vivi said through a mouthful of nails.

"For nesting habitat, I got that." I pushed up my safety glasses and motioned to the twelve birdhouses we'd already built. "Why so many?"

Vivi sighed. "Because the ornithological club asked for members to help out, and because one of the summer lake house people is both a member of the club AND an ecology professor at State. I'm trying to kiss some apples."

I loved Vivi's cuss alternates. But I was also getting pretty tired of sawdust sticking to my skin. "Can this be the last one? Then you'll have a baker's dozen and no one can see you as anything but a total bluebird enthusiast."

"What else do we have to do?"

I looked toward the lake. "Swim?" I looked back at the rec room. "Air-conditioning? Let me draw you?"

Vivi laid down her hammer. "Draw me?"

Heat rose into my cheeks. I'd been secretly adding figure drawing into my sketchbooks when Vivi wasn't paying attention. Just studies, fast line sketches to capture movements and angles. But the art teacher at the high school told me most schools want to see a broader array of subject matter and that portraiture and figure drawing would be a good enhancement for any portfolio. "Yeah. Draw you."

"Hmmm. Can you draw on the dock? We can swim, then I can work on my tan while you sketch?"

"Deal." I made the last cut for the birdhouse.

Once we'd changed and put all our stuff onto the weathered picnic table, I ran to the edge of the dock and cannonballed into the water. "You coming?" I yelled back at Vivi.

She executed a perfect surface-cutting swan dive. I raced her out to the neighbor's floating platform. We climbed up the ladder and lay there, letting the sun soak us warm again. Vivi called out scientific names of birds as they flew overhead. "Do you ever think about your dad when you see birds?" she asked.

I watched the clouds drift in the sky. "I guess. Since you told me the story about your grandmother. But I figure maybe his energy's been reincarnated by now. I like to think of parts of him reborn in some way. Unless heaven is real, then he's definitely hanging out up there with kids who died too early. My dad would have been a good teacher if he wasn't in the service."

Vivi smiled. "That's sweet."

A boat full of guys cut across the cove and headed toward us. When they got close, they whistled and catcalled. "Hey, ladies, want to go tubing with us?"

"No, thanks. We're good." I lifted my thumb to prove it.

A different guy held up two beers. "We have cold beverages."

A third guy flexed, then patted his abdomen. "More than one kind of six-pack on this boat."

Vivi whispered, "Stay calm, okay?"

But I was already answering. "No, seriously, we're not interested. Y'all have fun. It's a beautiful day out there." I waved goodbye to them.

The boat's driver cut left from the platform and motored away. The two "six-pack" guys made tear fists, then waved, before the boat picked up speed again. Soon the platform was rocking with the rippling wake left behind.

"Wow," Vivi said.

"Wow, what?"

"You. When I first met you, you'd have been standing up screaming at them and shooting them double birds. I'd have been grabbing your arm and begging you to calm down. It's really cool to see how far you've come, that's all."

I shrugged, but pride rippled up through me. I felt different. Little things didn't bother me like they used to, and I knew that even though Vivi was part of it, she wasn't all of it. It was my own progress. My work in therapy, my wanting to be less angry, my recognizing my triggers, and diving into artwork had all added up to make me a person I liked. "Come on," I said. "Let's swim back before those idiots cut this way again and I disprove your point."

We swam back to the dock and climbed the metal ladder. Vivi laid out her beach towel in the sun and I dried off, then unfolded the lounge chair and grabbed my sketch pad and pens.

"Should I pose?" Vivi arched her back and extended a leg to the sky, rounding her lips in an exaggerated way.

"No, just lie however you're comfortable and let me work."

Vivi saluted me, then settled on the towel.

I put my pen to the pad and began by shading from the dock toward Vivi's body. I didn't want the hard, graphic lines of an outline, but something softer, and more organic. Not such a difficult task with a subject matter like Vivi. As I hatched and crosshatched my way across the page, I soaked in all of Vivi's details. The curve of her breasts and hips. The medium swell of stomach Vivi had a love-hate relationship with, but I found perfect. Every detail was utterly feminine and beautiful and even now, close to two years later, I marveled at having a girlfriend like Vivi. My pen became an extension of my feelings, the love for my subject matter pouring onto the page. As I worked, I paid attention to my mood, my heart, my psyche. Vivi was right, I had changed.

When I finished the drawing, I cleared my throat.

Vivi cracked her eyes open, then lifted her hand to shade them from the sun. "Can I see?"

I flipped the pad outward and Vivi was quiet long enough to worry me. "Is it that bad?" There was a glisten in Vivi's eyes. "Are you crying?"

Vivi nodded and wrapped her arms around herself. "You made me look so beautiful."

I slid off the chair and down onto the towel next to her. I wrapped my arms around Vivi and kissed her cheek. "I draw what I see."

Vivi nestled her head into the space between my cheek and shoulder. "You know, I'm going to marry you one day."

"Not if I marry you first." It was our running joke. But today, I really hoped it would turn out to be true.

42

Now: Five Weeks, Four Days After

McGovern has two boys blocked into a corner, his marine sergeant yell making the cords of his throat pop out. I've learned to block it out, to let my mind wander, even if it leads to dangerous thoughts—like Vivi and the future we'll never have. When Deuces raps on my desk and points to the door, I jump and quick wipe my eyes before anyone makes an asinine comment. Swaley stands outside, a folder in hand, her eyes bugging at the sight of McGovern's classroom management techniques.

I hop up, torn between interrupting him to tell him where I'm going, or taking my chances and leaving. When I see spittle form at the corner of his mouth, and Chuck Norris's stare glowering at me from the poster on the back wall, I figure begging forgiveness might be easier than asking permission.

I pull the door shut behind me and follow Swaley to the bench outside the classroom.

"Is he always like that?" The guidance counselor tries to peer back around me to peek through the door's window.

"Sort of. But it works, I guess. We all get our work done."

She half smiles. Not a good sign. "I understand that you'd like to enroll in computer courses for the spring."

I sit up straighter. "Yes."

She pulls my transcript out of the folder and with it, a list of required coursework and credit hours. "You're in good shape to do it. Really you only need two more courses to be able to graduate. One of those is a science elective, and there are plenty of opportunities online. Any thoughts about what else you'd like to take? There are more electives available than at the high school."

I was ready for this. "Yes, I'd like to take an art history course."

Swaley nods and jots down a note on her list. "That should work. Let me tell you how the online courses are handled. You'll be placed into the classroom of a teacher for their planning period, but it's very self-motivated type of work. Your teacher-of-record, the one who grades your work, is actually online as well. The teacher you sit with will do your attendance."

"So, I'll still be able to work at Cabinetworks?"

Swaley smiles, then her smile drops, as McGovern flings open the door and cranes his neck out. When he sees who I'm with, the fire in his eyes dims and he acknowledges me with a grunt before stepping back into the room and pulling the door shut.

She shakes her head. "Close call, huh?"

My laugh surprises me. "Yeah, you could say that."

She continues. "I've spoken to the management there and it seems that they are willing to take you on board as a work-study intern for next semester. This semester you will have to return to the classes you left at the time of your suspension."

"What?" A second ago I thought we were talking about me staying with McGovern, but I'm hearing her say something completely different.

"Was I unclear?" Swaley slides the paperwork back into her folder.

"I'm not clear about going back to main campus. I thought I would stay here. Finish out here."

She shakes her head. "Oh no. It's not necessary and we all think it's better if you return to Grady."

Frustration eats at me. "Did my mother talk to you?" I've done everything she's asked of me with applications. I'm not quite finished, but she knows I've made a ton of progress this week. "If I'm at main campus, I have no way to get to Cabinetworks."

Swaley frowns. "I haven't spoken to your mother, but I'd tell her the same thing. Transportation will be on you for work study. If you have no way to get to the internship, we'll have to get you into other classes. There's no bus to deliver work-study students. And we are certain you will be better off back on main campus."

A minute ago, I'd been so psyched thinking this would actually happen, but now the future looks as awful as when I got in-school suspension. Even more so, because I was finally starting to feel the tiniest bit of hope for happier days.

She stands. "We'll see you Monday. Same schedule as before. Your teachers have all said you've done a remarkable job of staying up with the curriculum, so you shouldn't have too much trouble easing back in. Stop by my office if you need anything, and do let me know as soon as possible about your transportation issue so we can fix next semester's schedule if this won't work."

When I slink back into the classroom, everything's calmed down and everyone is nose to their papers, at least pretending to get some kind of work done. I glance at McGovern to make sure we're cool. He points to my desk.

Deuces turns slightly when I sit down and whispers low, "You sprung?"

"Monday," I say. I hadn't mentioned my wanting to stay to anyone but Mom and Nina, because I know for some of these guys, being here is akin to prison and I don't want to make light of their situations.

"Damn," he says. "You're going to make me all teary. Hanging out with you again was cool."

"It will be like middle school all over, unless you text me sometime."

"Two-way street, lady lover. But yeah, I'll connect. It'd be cool for you to meet Tonya."

"That'd be awesome." I hope we both follow through and don't let our lack of daily proximity keep us from staying in touch.

McGovern taps his desk and we both shut up.

I can't believe it. Tomorrow's my last day at the forge.

That afternoon Nina picks me up to take me to the VA for my therapy with the littles. Good thing, because I'm too pissed at Mom to be civil. She could have at least called and talked to Mrs. Swaley. Pleaded my case in her gonna-be-a-lawyer way. She gave me hurdles to clear and I'm more than halfway there. Where's the good faith?

Mr. A has switched it up a little bit and now we all have beanbag chairs to chill in but a bigger part of the floor is left open. He's got cumbia playing on the tape player and I can't help myself when I start moving my hips and stepping my legs backward.

"Ah, a fan."

"Yeah. My grandfather and my cousins taught me when I was little. We always have these barbecues when I'm in Texas, different from here—down there it's just grilling out, no sauce. But the music is always playing and there's always dancing in the carport. My cousins complain that it's old people music, but secretly we all love it."

Darla comes to the door, holding her mom's hand. I motion for her to join me and I show her a simple four-beat rhythm that she picks up on superfast. As the rest of the kids file in and Mr. A greets the parents, more kids join in and follow me. The song switches and now we're all standing in a big circle, moving together. But I see what Mr. A is doing here. There's not a frown in the room. Everyone is smiling, myself included. It's hard to let grief weigh you down when you're wiggling your hips.

Later, when he pulls out the drawing boards and markers with the assignment to draw a musical memory, I circle the room, helping the kids. The markers feel almost foreign in my hands, I've refused them for so many weeks now. But as I show kids how to think about adjusting lines, or jump in to add something into their pictures at their request, there isn't the leak of anguish onto the page. It's just color and line and shape.

Maybe I'm wrong. Maybe the point is not to stop doing the things that remind me of Vivi, but to find a way to ensure she lives through me, even if the future we painted together has been permanently gessoed over.

43

Now: Five Weeks, Four Days After (Night)

Cheyanne has Emma Watson in her arms as she looks over my shoulder at the computer screen. I have successfully completed applications for three of the small private colleges she brought me the brochures for. Nina helped me research the GI Bill my dad transferred to me before he died, and it turns out it will cover about two-thirds of my tuition cost per year at these schools. Combined with the results of my FAFSA, money shouldn't be too big of an issue. Which is a huge relief.

None of them have great art departments though, so I've got two other schools I'm researching. The university in Asheville and the school in Illinois with the blacksmithing program.

"State is out?"

"Yeah," I say. "I ditched my artwork. I have no portfolio. And the deadline's next week."

"What if you had a portfolio?"

I shake my head. "No. State was Vivi's dream. Besides . . ." I pet the space between Emma Watson's ears and she turns her face up toward me with a closed-eye smile. "I can't even see myself on that campus without her."

Cheyanne considers this. "You're probably right. But what about that Carbondale school? Won't you need a portfolio to get in there?"

"I don't know. I need to call, couldn't find anything on the website for the undergrad degree. It doesn't look like it, but their deadline is over a month away. Now that I won't have a job, because I don't have a car, I will have more time to make art. But . . ." I sigh. "As much as I used to love to draw, Vivi's death did kind of snuff out that candle. I'm just not inspired to do it. Not yet anyway."

Cheyanne hands me Emma Watson and swivels around to the bag she brought over. "Well, in case you change your mind. I saved this."

She pulls out the red folder I'd thrown in the trash the day I got sent to alternative school.

"How did you . . . ?"

"You were right outside my classroom door. I watched

you, remember? The minute you left I pleaded a bathroom break and saved it. If not for you, for me. These are really good."

I've already got the folder open and am flipping through the work. When I get to the portrait of Vivi on the dock, I still. She was so beautiful. It doesn't seem possible that one minute she could be here, real, flesh and blood, and the next minute gone. Death is so weird. I look up with tear-glazed eyes. "Thanks, Chey. I'm happy you saved these. Saved me from my stupidity throwing them away."

"Any kind of happy is good, right?"

I manage a weak smile in between cautious strokes down Emma Watson's back, which she arches into with a manic twist of her tail before swatting my hand away. "Happy is good." I'm not sure I'm really there, but I'm better than I was and Cheyanne did save my artwork for me.

"Well, hopefully you'll be able to use them to get into one of these programs. I'm glad you're back to wanting to do something." Her voice is the gentlest I've ever heard it.

"It's weird she's gone isn't it?"

Chey nods. "Yep. That first couple of weeks afterward, I'd walk into the classes we had together expecting her to be in her seat. I even had moments just thinking she was out sick, then I'd remember."

"Me, too. I'd pick up my phone to call her or text and then I'd remember."

We both sit with shoulders slumped until Chey sits up. "You've got three out of five done, and the last two seventy-five percent done. Yes?"

"Yes," I say.

"Let's call Levi and meet at the tracks."

"You think?" Even though he and I left it on a good note, it still feels kind of awkward.

"Totally." Cheyanne's already got her phone out sending a text. It only takes a second before she gets an answer. I watch her brows furrow.

"Something wrong?"

She looks up. "He can't join us because he's out with Simone."

"Simone?"

"First violin."

"Cute?" I ask.

Cheyanne pecks at her phone's screen, then flashes me a pic of a short-haired blond girl.

It makes me laugh. "I guess he had his fill of brunette rejection." I open my phone and shoot him another text.

Tell her we will kick her ass if she's mean to you.

I get a smiley face in return.

"Stan's?" Cheyanne asks.

"Rain check?" I look back at my computer screen. "I need to finish everything I can, then figure out what to say to my mom about school."

Cheyanne hefts her bag. "She's only doing what she thinks is best."

I turn Chey's own resting bitch stare back on her.

"Sorry." She holds up her hands in surrender and backs toward my door. When she drops her hands, her voice gets quiet. "You're not going to bug out on me again, are you? Because even if I get into Berklee and I'm freezing my fingers off in Boston, I need to know you and I will reconnect every single school holiday so I'm not stuck with my parents and my brothers."

"We still have a whole semester and the entire summer."

"I need a blood contract."

"That sounds more like the Cheyanne I know." I dig the Case knife out from my jeans pocket. "Blood swear?"

"Ew. Tetanus does not make for lasting friendships."

"You're no fun."

She smirks. "That's my line." She winces. "Sorry, I know there's a reason you've been no fun."

"I can't promise fun yet."

"I know," she says as she walks a few steps to the door. "But you can promise we're good. From now on?"

"From now on," I say. "I am officially finished with being a dick to you. You're my best friend. I don't want that to ever change."

She steps back across the room and hugs me hard, then pulls away just as fast and makes for the door. I don't follow her. Cheyanne likes her tears in private.

Around ten thirty, I see my mom's headlights flicker across my window. I gather the printouts I'd made of my application confirmations and wait for her in the kitchen.

"You're awake," she says as she drops her keys, purse, and laptop bag on the table before pouring herself a glass of white wine.

I don't say a word, simply spread out the four completed applications and the one for Carbondale still in progress across her things.

She sips and looks, picking up the papers and placing them down again. "One more to finish," she says.

"I have to make a phone call to find out something first but then I'll be done. Five schools just like you asked." If she's not going to bring up State, I won't either. She must understand why I can't apply there.

Mom puts the last paper down. "Jess. I want you back at main campus."

"But you said if I did this you'd talk to them. You of

all people should know how hard it will be for me to go back there. I'm happy at the alternative school. I get to go to a job that I love and that I won't get to do if I go back to Grady, because I don't have a car and y'all are too busy to give me rides. Being the youngest sucks, I'm left with the scraps of your and Nina's lives."

Nina chooses that point to push in through the back door. She's got a Stan's to-go cup in her hand. "What about my life?"

"You're spoiled, that's all."

Nina arches her eyebrows and looks at Mom for backup.

"Jessica Viola Perez." Mom's tone means I have it coming. "Your sister started babysitting for you and the neighbors when she was thirteen. She saved every dime until she could buy her car. I matched her one thousand dollars, just as I've promised you, but until this year you've shown no interest in working. This is life. Not privilege. And I'm sorry that transportation is an issue. And I'm completely empathetic to the emotional difficulty of returning to main campus. But it's time for a reality check, Jess. You've got to figure out a way to live with your grief. Find times to put it on a shelf and times to take it off and when it sneaks up on you, as it's prone to do, recognize it, acknowledge it, even give it a little hug like an old friend, then take a big deep breath and keep walking. You can't avoid it." She pauses and takes a sip of her wine.

"Now, as for your transportation issue, we are both happy to help you, when we can, but perhaps you should look for a job in the strip mall behind us, or some place your bike will take you, and when you've saved enough for your own vehicle, insurance, and gas, then you can work wherever you want."

I grunt in frustration and Mom turns away from us, washing her glass, then with a goodnight kiss on each of our cheeks, leaves for her room at the end of the hall.

Nina hands me the rest of her milkshake. "She's right, you know. You were always hanging out with Vivi."

"You think I don't know? I wouldn't change that, not for a minute."

"But you need a car."

I slump into a chair and suck up creamy chocolate sweetness through the straw. "Yes. Greer can't pick me up for work because it will cut into her time, and even though I could do work study back at main campus, I have to have transportation to get there."

Nina thinks about my dilemma for a minute, then holds out empty palms. "I've got nothing." She drops one hand onto my shoulder. "But, I can promise to give you a ride over to Greer's on Sundays. We'll have to make it fit around my work schedule though."

I think about Greer's offer to work on my own pieces and I think about the chandelier waiting to be transformed into a nest. It's another peace offering from my sister, who's turning out to be much less of a pain in the rear than I like to pretend she is. It won't help me get a car, but it will help me as I try to figure out the post-Vivi Jess.

"You'd do that? Consistently?"

She pinches my shoulder. "Don't be a nudge. I said I would, and I will."

"Ouch." I brush her hand away. "Okay, okay." I pass back the last of her shake. "Thanks, Neens."

At least it's something.

44

Now: Six Weeks After

I talk Nina into swinging by the Bea's Donuts drive-through on my way to work. When I walk into Greer and Eliza's, I'm loaded down with hot, glistening donuts and three lattes.

"Oh, you little goddess." Eliza takes the drink tray from my hands and I slide the box onto their kitchen table.

Rufus sticks his nose under my hand and I oblige him, scratching the bony area at the top of his head. "I'm afraid it's a goodbye gift."

"A goodbye gift?" Eliza lifts an eyebrow, then glances at Greer.

"I didn't fire her. I swear." Greer grabs a donut from the box.

"What's the story then?"

I explain about the end of my suspension, the lack of a car or a ride, and no way to connect with Greer to ride here from Cabinetworks.

Eliza thinks for a minute. "What about one of those fund me campaigns?"

I shake my head. "My mom would kill me. She doesn't understand the whole crowd-sourcing thing and sees it as charity. Hard work is the only way. She reminded me about it a few nights ago—dangling the fact that my sister saved money to buy her own." I lift a shoulder. "She's got a point. I didn't work until now."

Eliza pouts. "Does this mean we won't see our baby homo at all anymore?"

This makes me laugh. "Sundays. Nina agreed to drive me over here on Sundays. But, I will have to get another job. For a car. I'll need it next year."

"Then it's settled," Greer says.

"Settled?" I ask.

"Sundays you will do a little quick work for me, then we dedicate some time for you to make your own projects. In the meantime, I'll keep an ear open for cheap cars. Sometimes the guys at the shop are selling them."

"Same," Eliza says. "We'll try to help you out if we can."

Out in the shop, I do welds on the lawn ornaments and

grind the joints. When I finish the stack Greer has for me, she motions toward the chandelier.

"Okay, here's your baby. Do you have sketches?"

I dig in my pocket and pull out the crumpled sheets of sketch pad paper. There'd been a moment of hesitation as I lifted my pencil. Fear that the sorrow would once again leak onto the page. But I'd thought about what Mom said, about greeting grief as an old friend, and it had worked. I'd drawn. It had been okay. Maybe even better than okay.

Greer studies the drawings and my notes. "I think this is doable. And you're on the right track. But you sure you want to cut off the hanger and make it a standing piece? Wouldn't it be interesting if it still hung, like a nest in a tree?"

I can't believe I didn't think of it that way, but I've been so busy helping her with her grounded pieces that my mind got stuck there. "Yes, you're right."

"Okay, so first step is the handheld grinder and safety glasses and a mask. Take it out back and grind the finish down till you've got raw metal. We can put some kind of lovely patina on it when it's all finished, but for now you don't want to be dealing with that flaking paint surface. I'll be thinking on how to approach the birds while you're working."

I nod and grab the equipment. My heart flutters in my

chest. It's the first thing that's felt right since Vivi died. Because it's about Vivi. Birds were her thing until they became our thing. It only seems natural that I would carry on her interest, just incorporated into my own interests. As I start grinding the ivory paint off the metal, I feel a few of my own layers shed away. Stepping forward doesn't mean I let her go. It means I take her with me. Every piece I create can contain some piece of the Vivi I knew and loved.

When I'm done, Greer explains her ideas to me about how I'll create the birds I want to put on the piece. It won't be done in a single Sunday, but if I don't screw up, I think I'll be able to have a photograph of the piece in time for the Carbondale deadline.

"You could also take photos of the work you did with me," she says.

"You don't think that's cheating?"

"Well, you'd have to attribute me as well. But there's nothing wrong in collaboration or helping a future lady blacksmith get into the college of her dreams."

"Okay," I say.

"And," Greer adds. "We can put the nest piece in the show. You might not want to sell it, but if it turns out as cool as I think it will, you should be able to charge a pretty penny for it. An amount that will go a good ways toward your mom's matching funds. And if you have a car, you've got work study at Cabinetworks and a standing job with me whenever I need some extra help."

I grin. "Which, after the world sees your art, you're going to need a ton of extra help to fill all the orders."

She high-fives me just as Nina honks her horn from the front of the house.

"See you Sunday," I say.

"See you then."

As I push through the gate, I feel the smile creasing my face. I feel a warmth inside of me that's been gone. The cavity and gravity are still there, but they're more compartmentalized. Sure, they break through when I least expect them to, and they never fully go away, but I'm learning to live with them. I'm figuring out how to fill the spaces around them. I know it's what Vivi would want.

45

THEN: The Hummingbird

It was a lazy Thursday evening. I'd picked my mom's backyard hammock because of the way my body filled the spaces around Vivi when we lay in it together. Vivi had her favorite book of Mary Oliver poems, *Owls and Other Fantasies*, open to shield her face from the sharp setting sun. She read aloud, pausing in all the right places, painting pictures with the words. Poems about catbirds, and herons, and small silvery hummingbirds. She took deeper breaths than usual though, slightly thick with the encroachment of a cold.

"Do you need your inhaler?" I asked, winding my fingers through hers, taking the pad of each finger and rolling it between my own as I explored the world of Vivi's hand.

"I'm okay. Just getting a cold or something."

"Read me another one."

Vivi read a poem titled "September" about walking in pinewoods and encountering a nighthawk lying along a branch. Then finding it again the next year in the same place.

"Can we make a date for a year from now to lie in a hammock and you read poetry to me? Just like the poet and her bird friend?" My other arm was wrapped around the top of Vivi's head and I gently lifted strands of her hair. Languorous calm coated my bones. Love was way better than anger.

Vivi snuggled closer in answer. "Poetry September. I like it."

After Vivi left for home, I opened my sketchbook. I remembered the lines from the poem about the hummingbirds. The poet climbing the tree, disturbing the small nest, hummingbird faces blinking in surprise. I loved the imagery of the silvery bursts and the pale-green dresses, so I drew Vivi there among branches, using the tiniest tipped pens. When the outline was to my satisfaction, I opened my inks to mix the perfect shades for the leaves. Inside my heart hummed with the love coursing through my veins. Things kept getting better and better with Vivi. I finished the touches on a pale-green dress, blending into the leaves, and snapped a picture of the impromptu drawing to check the composition. Satisfied for the moment, I put it to the side and sent Vivi a quick I love you before drifting into sleep.

The next morning, Friday, I saw her response. I love you, too.

I hunted for Vivi at our morning break meeting spot at school, but she didn't show; instead she sent me another text saying she wasn't feeling well and was leaving school early.

On Saturday, Vivi wasn't answering her texts. I tried to call at noon and two, and then at four, Abigail answered Vivi's phone. She was whispering. "Vivi's sleeping, Jess. The doctor says she's got the flu."

"Is she all right?" Something about Abigail's voice was tighter than normal.

"Don't you worry. We've got a close eye on her. Sleep is the best thing though so I'm going to be turning off her phone for a bit."

"Thanks for letting me know."

"I'll be sure and tell her you've been trying to reach her when she wakes up. Okay?"

"Yeah, okay."

Abigail hung up.

I decided to work on the sketch to quell my worry.

Besides it would make Vivi smile when I showed it to her once she was feeling better.

I went in with the finest pen yet and added delicate strokes to the hummingbirds' feathers. I darkened the background of trees so the birds and Vivi popped in the foreground. When I'd reached the point that I feared overworking the scene, I put in the finishing touches, a mixture of silver-and-green-colored ink on Vivi's wings. By then it was late and I crawled into bed. I picked up my phone one last time, checking to see if maybe I'd heard from Vivi and missed it, but there was nothing. I sent off a quick kiss emoji and an "I'm thinking of you." Even if her phone was still off, she'd see it when she turned it on.

I dreamt we were in the hammock again, nested in each other's arms. Vivi's hair was a wild cloud around her head and she squeezed me tight, her eyes focused intently on mine. Vivi opened her mouth to speak and instead of words, birdsong came out, the pretty trill of a wren. As she sang, she transformed.

She began to rise, her arms turning to a blur of wings, her body taking on a shimmering green plumage, her hair turning from its dark hues to a softer green. She continued to sing and trill as she darted around the hammock. I tried to reach for her, but my arms were heavy, unable to move, and all I could do was watch.

"Vivi," I said. "Why are you flying?" A low-level panic vibrated under my skin.

Dream Vivi darted about in her hummingbird wings and disappeared into the sky, then darted back, lingering just out of my reach before laughing and saying, "Oh, Jess, you wouldn't believe it. It's magnificent. I can go anywhere I want in the blink of an eye."

As she zipped away, her bright wings growing smaller and smaller against a cerulean blue sky, I cried out.

The hammock grew cold, its webbing cutting into my skin.

I stared at the spot, waiting, waiting for Vivi's return.

"Vivi," I cried, trying to summon the hummingbird back. "Vivi."

"Jess." The voice sounded so far away.

I looked to the sky and saw nothing.

But then I felt myself being shaken. My mother at the edge of my bed, a warm hand on my temple stroking me awake. "Jess, hon, I need you to wake up."

"Mom? I had the weirdest dream." Then I saw the tears streaking down Mom's face and Nina lingering in the doorway and in that moment, I knew.

"What?" Then as I looked at their stricken faces I shook my head. "No, no." I hugged my comforter to me and stared at my mom, willing her tears to be something else. But my heart knew. It was the hummingbird, just like in Vivi's story. Just like in the poem. Just like in my dream.

"Oh, sweetheart," Mom said and came to me, cradling me in her arms as she whispered into my ear. "They rushed Vivi to the hospital late last night. She's gone."

Vivi.

Gone.

In the blink of an eye.

Like a hummingbird.

I grabbed my pillows, my blankets, and balled them all around me, and screamed. I screamed until my voice was gone and then I screamed in silence. Mom and Nina didn't leave my side, but it didn't matter. I was gone, too.

46

Now: Eleven Weeks After

Gone.

Five weeks I've been gone from McGovern's.

Five weeks of no Cabinetworks and life on the main campus.

Lucky for me, some sophomore boy got caught up in a viral meme scandal online and I'm old news. No one looks at me anymore. I've become invisible and it's fine with me. Swaley, in a fit of feeling sorry for me, somehow managed to convince the art teacher to let me take double classes with her in combination with my one science and an online art history course for next semester, but it still doesn't fully mitigate the sting of not getting to go to Cabinetworks.

But, as luck, or unluck would have it, I haven't been able to find a job close enough to walk or ride my bike to. I even begged Nina to see if I could work at the chicken shack with her, but they weren't hiring.

When I get home that afternoon I'm surprised to see Mom's car in the driveway. Over the sound of the "Jingle Bells" of our motion-activated Dancing Santa, I yell, "Mom? Is everything okay?"

She comes out front with a stupid grin on her face.

"What? Did you win the lottery?"

"Something like that." She grabs my hand. "Come on, I'm buying you a milkshake at Stan's."

Suspicion takes over. "Ooookay." But I follow her out the back door, past the hammock, between the cut-through at the back of the strip mall and around front to Stan's. Parked in front of it is a familiar rusty-orange-colored Honda Element. "That's Vivi's car," I say.

Mom nods. "The Bouchards are waiting inside. Go on." She pushes me along as I dawdle, unsure of what's happening.

"Jess." Abigail and Henri stand and kiss me on either cheek, then do the same to my mother. I'm surprised at the flood of emotions racing through me, though by now I know I shouldn't be. "We're sorry to do this in such a public place, but we wanted to surprise you."

I look to Mom to see if she knows what's happening, but she only grins bigger.

Henri takes my hand and Abigail fishes a cream-colored envelope out of her bag. "Vivi's letter came from NC State, and even though your mother has told us your plans have changed, we thought you might like to open this with us."

I take the creamy paper from Abigail's hand and use my pocketknife to make a clean cut in the envelope. I reach inside. It's thick, always a good sign. I pull out the top sheet.

Dear Vivi Bouchard,

We are pleased to inform you . . .

I stop reading and look up. "She got in," I say. Abigail's eyes well with tears and she and Henri squeeze each other's hands.

"Of course she did," my mom adds.

"Thank you for this." I hand the envelope back to the Bouchards. "She would be so excited." Then, "It's really good to see you."

"It's good to see you, too, Jess, but this isn't the main reason we're here."

"It's not?"

Henri smiles. "No. We've spoken to your mother about a holiday gift we'd like to give you and much to her credit, she feels it's too much. Because we want to respect her wishes as much as our own, we have a proposal."

I glance again at Mom and she's still grinning.

"We'd like you to have Vivi's car," Abigail says.

"What?" My mouth drops open.

"This is where I come in," Mom says. "You know how I feel about your having a car."

"I have to earn it."

"Correct. However, I do realize this is an unusual circumstance, so what I've proposed is you pay the Bouchards a certain amount each month that they will put toward a scholarship fund they're creating in Vivi's name."

Even though a part of me is wincing—whose mom turns away a free car?—another part of me is totally on board. I love the idea of contributing to something that memorializes Vivi.

"Are you all sure?"

Henri clasps my hand and hands over the keys, still on the Eiffel Tower key chain Vivi loved. "We are sure."

"And I've made the first payment with your matching funds. You and the Bouchards can work out the payment schedule for the rest."

Later, sitting behind the wheel, I fight the urge for tears. The Bouchards cleaned it—looking for scraps of their daughter, no doubt—but there are still telltale signs of Vivi. The Candle Company air freshener in Sunny Citrus that she bought from one of the fund-raisers at school, a hair tie they missed, looped around the turn signal bar, one strand of Vivi's hair still trapped. I lean over and flip open the glove box and pull out the manual. Cradled in its pages is a note I wrote to Vivi.

Love you most. Love you always. xxxxxxxxxxxxx and okay, ooo ~ J

Shit. Weight and gravity press against my buoyancy.

I shake it off and turn the key. The engine purrs right to life. I glance up at the sky. "Thanks, Viv. This is awesome."

Then I put the car in drive and head over to Greer's.

47

Now: Twelve Weeks After

The hall smells like evergreen and cider. Christmas music is pumping over the speakers set up in every corner of the cavernous space. Greer and I are rolling in her pieces on a metal furniture dolly while Eliza and Deuces, minus his ankle bracelet, work to hang drapery on the pipes that create the walls for our corner display space. Greer had done so well at the first show that she hustled to find a second one for us to enter and even hired Deuces to help with random muscle work. I'm psyched it's going to be so easy for us to keep hanging out.

"I'm not as sure about this," Greer says.

Looking around, the other artisans are setting up crafty, kitschy kind of booths with holiday themes. The work is more hobby store than Greer's fine art. But there are a few other true artisans sprinkled in among the hobby crafters.

"The people who like real art will find you," I say.

"I hope you're right. All I can say is thank goodness you got that car so I got to keep my studio assistant slash cheerleader."

What Greer doesn't know is I've got something else to cheer her up with if the sales are super slow. My Carbondale acceptance letter arrived yesterday and I've got it tucked in my back pocket to share at the perfect moment. She's going to be so psyched for me. We roll the cart to a stop and I jump in to help Deuces secure the burlap backdrops. Greer rolls out a carpet and soon the illusion of a store is created and we start setting up the artwork. The final piece is my nest, which we have hanging from a hook I forged out of rebar. I haven't decided if I'm ready to sell it, but it looks good on display.

Deuces rotates the piece so he can see the welded pieces of twig and leaves I crafted around the chandelier's frame. On top are seven birds. Seven birds to remember. There's a sparrow, to commemorate that first lunch Vivi and I shared. A dove—the soundtrack to the amazing hug by the teeter-totter. Two robins, springtime and friendship and traveling in flocks, they represent Cheyanne and Levi.

A great horned owl signifies the moment I laid my truth bare to Vivi and she still wanted me, plus its size adds a nice balance to the piece. A bluebird because of all those damn boxes we built and because Vivi loved them and I think they're pretty. Finally, a hummingbird, to represent her. It's my favorite, welded at the top of the chandelier, its buzzing wings frozen in time. The piece isn't perfect. But for the first in a series I envision building upon, it's not bad.

Deuces studies each one closely, then asks, "You going to teach me how to make something like that?"

"Only if you're not scared to get those shoes dirty."

"Ha" is his only response.

It takes about another hour for us to get everything perfect, but then it's showtime. Eliza takes off with Deuces, and Greer and I ready ourselves for sales.

Sadly, it seems she was right about the crowd at this show. They're milling about without bags in their hands or they're lined up ten deep for the homemade scented candles at the corner or the kettle corn booth at the end of the hall.

"This sucks," Greer says.

"Why don't you take a mental health stroll? I'll watch the booth for you."

"Thanks. I'm going to take you up on that. Bring you

back a coffee, black with sugar?"

"Perfect." I lift my hand as she wanders away.

I'm perched on my metal stool when I spot the family headed down the hall. They're dressed interesting, kind of hipsterish, and I notice they don't really linger at the craft booths, but stop instead at the booths where an artist's hand has mingled in the making. I decide I'm going to make a sale for Greer while she's gone.

My eye for the right kind of client is spot-on as they veer hard into Greer's booth. The dad looks at me. "Is this your work?" His voice sounds surprised.

I shake my head. "No, my boss's. She stepped away for a moment."

His partner is holding up various garden animals, assessing them. The little boy, about ten, is giving thumbs-up for the giant rabbits. They make me smile.

From behind me, I hear a female voice. "Dad, Papa, you have got to see . . . whoa, this is seriously cool."

I turn, and a girl—short fuchsia hair, huge brown eyes, black bowler hat—has her hand on my nest. She looks at me. "Is this yours?"

"That one is."

Her smile is shy and there's something about her that feels familiar.

"Imani." The dad standing with the boy holds up the largest hare and a frog for her approval.

She nods. "Yes, awesome." Then she points to my piece. "And this one."

"Oh," I say. "It's not really for sale. It's just for display. It's the first one."

She rotates it and I see her take in all the details. "Too bad. It would look amazing at our house."

The other dad is listening in. "Get her card." Then to me, "You do take commissions?"

I sit up straighter. "Um, yes, totally." And thanks to Greer I even have a card. I fish it out and hand it toward the dad, but it's the girl, Imani, who takes it. She reads it. "Jess Perez. Blacksmith." She looks at the nest again. "You know a lot about birds?" Her smile is genuine and maybe, just the tiniest bit, flirtatious?

"I do," I say.

"Cool." She pockets the card and looks up at me from beneath thick lashes. "We'll call you."

Greer returns at that moment and jumps in to finish the sale. When she's finished writing it up and running their credit card, the dads and the boy walk away with their yard art pieces, but the girl lingers. She lifts her hand in a slight wave and smiles, then holds up my card before sliding it back into the pocket of her miniskirt.

When she's halfway down the hall, Greer pokes my side. "What was that about?"

I shrug. "Nothing."

"Nothing, huh?" Greer winks and hands me the coffee she'd set down.

"Yep, nada."

"Too bad, she was cute and from a sweet family." Greer flicks my forearm. "And potentially interested judging by that little show at the end."

I feel my blush, but the reality is, I'm not ready.

I'm still learning this grief. How to live with it, how to embrace it as a friend. My grief is part of me. I see now how grief can trick you and push you into dark places if you don't acknowledge it. But when you respect it, greet it, welcome it, grief can transform. It spotlights your capacity for love. It micro-focuses the things that matter. Love is made sharper and keener by it and no matter how hard it hurts, or how deep it cuts, its presence is going to help me grab up the good things. I won't let my father's or Vivi's losses be in vain. I'm going to live full and love hard.

And if I'm extra lucky, maybe one day, I'll meet someone who will let me teach them about birds.

Author's Note

This novel was born from loss. In the words of Lin-Manuel Miranda, I tried to write my way out, but like his protagonist, Alexander Hamilton, I learned there is no out, only through, again and again and again. Jess and Vivi gave me words I thought might never come again. Their story is not my personal story, but in the writing of it, Jess's journey often mirrored my own. Grief is universal. We have all experienced it. Some of us have had greater losses than others, but grief, like love, is something that shapes every human on the planet and is one of our primary emotional colors.

In early grief we make mistakes, we try new things, we cling to the old. We cry, we gnash our teeth, we push the good people away, we might pull the wrong ones close. There are people who show up for you when you most need them, then as the pain becomes manageable, they drift back to the shadows of your life. Grief weaves its threads through every corner of your being. It affects each forward step you take. The trick is to keep taking the forward steps.

If you are hurt and scared and grieving, surround yourself with love. It's hard to do. But it's those moments with friends and family—when you laugh, and remember, and smile—that teach you how to walk your new path. Take your palette of emotions, blend grief with love, and find your rainbow. They don't come after sunny days. They only come after rain.

Acknowledgments

This is the happy part of my sad book—gratitude for the multitudes who help a book come to fruition.

First, to my readers, thank you so much for taking the time to read my words. What an honor to write for a population of young people so empowered and alive and willing to stand up for what they know and feel is right. You are beautiful. You inspire me every day. Thank you for reaching out and letting me know how much Jo and Mary Carlson in *Georgia Peaches and Other Forbidden Fruit* meant to you. I hope you will find similar joy, even through the sadness, with Vivi and Jess. Love is love.

As always, thank you to my powerhouse of an agent, Alexandra Machinist. I'm not sorry if I made you cry.

To my wonderful editor, Chris Hernandez, thank you for keeping me on track in all the right ways. I appreciate your insight, guidance, and wisdom. All authors should be so lucky. I'm thrilled you loved Jess and Vivi like I do.

To the team at Harper Teen, including production editor Jessica Berg, designer Jessie Gang, and everyone else who worked to bring this book to life. Thank you! And to my talented cover illustrator, Elliana Esquivel, I love, love, love what you do! Yay art, and thank you for the beauty.

To early readers of all and parts of this novel, Pat Esden, Nina Moreno, Kip Wilson Rechea, Kristi Helvig, Erica Cameron, and Noah Valentine Styles, big hugs and kisses. Thank you for being gentle with my girls and me during a time when writing felt so fragile. And if I've left anyone out, forgive me?

To the tremendous writing posses out there, most especially, The YA Valentines, the Nebo Crew, the gang at Kindling Words West, and the Fall Fourteeners. Lifelines in this business are so, so good. Speaking of lifelines, Robin Constantine, you're a boss bitch! And Lisa Maxwell, want to go listen to some tinka tinka music?

To my Boston Public Library gang—thank you Jenn Mann, Adrienne Kisner, and Rachel Simon for writing dates, scintillating conversation, and lunch in one of the most beautiful spaces in the world. You made my

Northern transition so very easy and helped me get this book written.

To the Webster family for opening up your arms wide and bringing me in. I'm lucky to know you.

And finally, for Ann. You arrived at exactly the right moment in rainbow brilliance. Here's to our two sweet hummingbirds and all the days they will bring us. Love is love.